MIKE GRIST

Mike Grist is the British/American author of the Chr[illegible]ren & Girl 0 thrillers. He has lived and worked in th[illegible]pan and Korea as a teacher, [illegible]

HAVE YOU READ EVERY CHRIS WREN THRILLER?

Saint Justice

They stole his truck. Big mistake.

No Mercy

Hackers came for his kids. There can be no mercy.

Make Them Pay

The latest reality TV show: execute the rich.

False Flag

They framed him for murder. He'll kill to clear his name.

Firestorm

Wren's father is back. The storm is coming.

Enemy of the People

America turns against Wren. Can he survive?

Backlash

Fake marines forced downed his jet. Now they'll pay.

Never Forgive

5 dead in Tokyo, Japan. Wren has to find the killer.

War of Choice

War erupts in Ukraine. This time it's personal.

Hammer of God

A US city destroyed. All bets are off.

Learn more at www.shotgunbooks.com

HAVE YOU READ EVERY GIRL 0 THRILLER?

Girl Zero

They stole her little sister. Now they'll pay.

Zero Day

The criminal world is out for revenge. So is she.

Learn more at www.shotgunbooks.com

WAR OF CHOICE

A CHRISTOPHER WREN THRILLER
BOOK 9

MIKE GRIST

SHOTGUN
BOOKS

SHOTGUN BOOKS

www.shotgunbooks.com

Paperback ISBN - 978-1-7398496-6-5

For Uncle Bobby

1

UKRAINE

Christopher Wren sprinted down a residential street on the eastern edge of Ukraine, behind enemy lines in a town reduced to rubble, chased by gunfire.

Civilian bodies laid face-flat on the blacktop around him, holes brimming from the backs of their heads. Commuter vehicles blazed like roman candles; a Citroen, a Ford, a Jeep, some already burned down to ash-filled skeletons. In places the sidewalk was cratered, with paving stones and earth torn out, leaving water and gas mains spewing mutely into the air. One house on the right was aflame, great orange tongues belching black soot.

These were the work of Russian bullets fired as point-blank executions; of Russian artillery fired from five miles away; of Russian bombs dropped from MiG-23s in the air.

Wren's heart pounded as he darted around a blazing Ford, twin bodies burning in the front seats.

"Target is within range," came his operator's voice in his earpiece. Wren chanced a glance over his shoulder.

A deep-green Ural 4320 Russian military truck skidded through an intersection fifty yards back. Its tarp-coated rear bed was stripped back and four figures hung out over the 6x6's bare frame, spraying AK-74M's in Wren's direction.

Bullets bit into the blacktop around him, crumping through metal and shattering glass. Wren ducked low and broke right, into the billows of smoke pumping from the burning home. Up the driveway he almost stumbled on a child's scooter, barely keeping his feet as the Ural ripped over the sidewalk and up through beds of flowers.

Wren ran into thick black smoke down the alley beside the house, holding his breath and reloading his Sig Sauer P320 ACP .45 as he ran, the last magazine. At the back of the blazing building he broke right, passing the burned corpse of a young woman clutching a child in her arms, then halted when his boots stamped through a half-full paddling pool. For a moment he paused, thinking tactically, then dropped and rolled bodily in the cold water.

"On poshel etim putem!" came the cries of the Russian soldiers chasing on foot around the building, something like, 'He went this way!' Their barking rifle reports grew louder and Wren surged to his feet, dripping water.

These were raw military recruits; half a mile behind the front line, trained in combat but wildly unprepared to corral civilians who didn't welcome them as incoming heroes, rendered wildly amoral by uncertainty and orders they could not understand.

It didn't make them any less dangerous. For them this was a nightmarish, testosterone-fueled video game, racking up kills, rapes and thefts that for some would become the foundation of a lifetime's regrets. For others these would be the greatest days of their lives. Wren knew well how the fog of war made everything a chemical intoxicant.

"Best intelligence reports you are one mile away still, Christopher, and the distance is growing," came his operator's voice again.

"East, still?" Wren shouted, as he pulled down his tinted goggles and kicked through the weakened plate glass of the home's bifold doors. The glass shattered in heavy shards and Wren sucked in a breath then plunged in.

The engulfing darkness was speared by surging flames. Fire licked up the walls and along the ceiling. He stumbled over a chair, bounced off a wall then shoved through a door and into the living room; ahead half the front wall was already gone.

"Target's moving north," said his operator. "I'd give you street names but the signs are all down and GPS is flagging."

Wren grunted and padded through the open living room, between the burning couch and cracked television, reveling in a cool gust of air gushing in from the front Through the smoke he picked out the Ural; it had slammed into a parked Chevy in the drive, leaving only the driver and two men in the back, leaning out to see. One was taking potshots at the windows on the second floor while the second watched on anxiously.

Wren dropped to one knee, steadied the Sig's stock on the flat of his left palm, lined up the combat sight picture so the front post lay on top of the anxious guy's head, let out a breath and squeezed the trigger.

His head burst upward.

Amidst the chaos of potshots and flames, nobody noticed. Wren smoothly retargeted, sighted, squeezed and fired. Another head blew. Two more idiots unable to cause chaos in a land that wasn't their own.

A sound came from in back and Wren flung himself sideways, just as a stream of bullets splintered the coffee table. Wren spun as he dived, swinging the Sig to target the three soldiers charging at him from behind.

They were already on fire; feet and legs. They didn't have goggles, hadn't dipped themselves in water and now they were frantic, sucking smoke and half-blind. Wren ended their misery swiftly: three shots to their chests chased by three to the heads once they were down.

"Target's locking down," came his operator, voice now crackly with static. "I have some audio intercepts, seems he's expecting reinforcements within the hour."

Wren cursed and ran.

Out through the flames and onto the driveway, he stripped the goggles and stepped up onto the Ural's running board. The driver had long enough to widen his eyes then took a shot in the head. Wren racked open the door, yanked out his twitching corpse and slid into the seat.

A handful of soldiers emerged down the alley from the rear of the home, red-eyed and coughing. Wren rammed the Ural right at them. There wasn't much room for acceleration, but the Ural was a 6x6 off-road vehicle capable of massive torque on a moment's notice, and it did the job. It shoved the Chevy out of the way and covered the driveway in a second, crushing two of them back into the house while one went under the wheels.

Wren cranked the Ural into reverse and pulled away.

No gunfire chased him now. On this street at least, for a time, the dead could lie in peace.

"Hurry, Christopher!" his operator barked.

"Direct me," Wren answered, spinning the Ural and taking off on his best approximation of north-east. The skies were filled with smoke, diffusing shadows and blocking any sense of where the sun lay, and all street signs had been purposefully knocked down to make navigation impossible.

"It seems you're heading just south of east," his operator answered, "tracking via intermittent satellite and spy drone overwatch. Smoke's in the way but I think I have you. Steer more north."

Wren skidded left through an intersection at fifty miles an

hour, the Ural laying six thick rubber trails across the blacktop. More dead bodies and burning vehicles littered the tree-lined road ahead and he swerved to avoid them, plummeting toward an intersection where a mass gunfight was underway.

He cursed but it was too late to change direction now. To the left were rag-tag Ukrainian forces, hunkered behind a pair of shelled-out Urals firing small arms. On the right came a T90-M tank, the strongest mobile weapons platform in the Russian arsenal, with a five-pointed red star painted on its side.

"Avoid this, Christopher," the operator ordered in his ear.

"Not a chance," Wren rumbled, even as he shot into range and the Ukrainians peppered his Ural with gunfire, mistaking him for a Russian. Wren ducked, aimed, and rammed the big truck directly into the front right corner of the tank.

There was a crash and the Ural crumpled. The tank weighed upwards of 48 tons and didn't budge an inch. The Ural's airbag deployed and Wren slammed into it, but was already in motion; he kicked out the door and stepped up and over, onto the T90-M's ceramic-plastic composite armored top plate.

To his left spiked the tank's 125mm 2A46 smoothbore main gun, red hot from use. Ahead lay the clam-shell design of the turret, with a five-pointed red star painted freehand on the side. The hatch was closed. A stream of soldiers followed in back, now staring at Wren in bewilderment.

He didn't give them the time to reflect further, and stripped two grenades off his belt, pulled the pins and punched them through the rocket-dispelling grill around the turret and into the tank's prime articulating joint.

Then he jumped down and ran.

Scattershot rifle fire chased him. In five seconds the grenades blew, and Wren cast a glance over his shoulder to see the T-90M's clamshell turret blow off its axis. The main gun tipped askew and rolled over to crash into the road. Smoke rose from within and the gunners fled.

A cheer rose up from the Ukrainian forces, followed by a charge.

"Christopher, this is unwise."

"Yeah," Wren agreed, and sped through a front yard, vaulted a fence then came to a neighboring street that looked almost untouched. He saw terrified faces watching him from a window; a woman and two children. His heart ached but there was nothing he could do for them now. One driveway over the house was quiet, and he elbowed through the window of the old-model Audi out front.

It took ninety seconds to strip the ignition housing and jump-start the wires, then he pulled out and was on the move again.

"Target is at edge of our comms range. No more detours."

They weren't detours. Wren felt sick with rage, but it wouldn't do any good. None of this would do any good. The only thing that mattered was stopping this war at the level that orders were given. Planting grenades into the articulating structures that had made it all possible and blasting them until it died.

He raced the Audi up to seventy in ten seconds, whipping past houses, a shopping mall where Russian soldiers took potshots as he rammed through their barricade. His operator directed him. Wren gritted his teeth hard, wishing he could do more..

"Ahead," the operator said.

Then he saw them. A moving convoy of five vehicles; three Urals, another T90-M tank and a high-capacity troop carrier. A Mil Mi-24 attack helicopter swirled overhead. As Wren advanced the tank's main gun circled toward him.

Mobile artillery guns fired from several yards to his right, shooting rockets up and over.

Wren spun the Audi as the tank's main gun discharged; one massive slug roared out and tore off his rear left side, shaking the whole vehicle. The Audi fishtailed as its rear axle dragged. Gunfire poured in and Wren dived out of the door, where he took one round in the chest, one in the thigh, then managed to get his hands up.

The gunfire halted. He could scarcely breathe; the round to his chest had been absorbed by his Twaron plate armor, but likely a few ribs had been bruised, if not cracked. His thigh was leaking blood, but the thigh plate must have caught the bulk of the shot or his leg would be halfway down the street now.

Soldiers with red palm marks daubed on their chests trotted over; at the center of each palm was a five-pointed Soviet star. Their AK74-Ms were raised.

"U menya yest′ informatsiya," Wren barked up at them in Russian, words he'd memorized for just this moment. "Ya podchinyayus!"

I have information. I surrender!

2

THREE DAYS EARLIER

It was a beautiful summer afternoon in the little town of Frederica, Delaware. Chris Wren stood outside the black iron gates of his kids' elementary school, Lake Forest East, waiting for the afternoon bell to chime. The sun was hot on his skin, and a warm breeze rustled through the tall box elders lining the road, carrying the scents of ice cream and candy floss from the stand on the corner.

Wren picked up his kids Jake and Quinn on Mondays, Wednesdays and alternate Fridays, and he loved every second of it. It was a strange, simple pleasure to mill with the other parents. Some checked their phones, some grumbled about the delay, some made small talk about the weather or football, all just waiting to start their normal after-school routines.

"Did you watch that Eagles game?" one of the moms asked as she pushed through the crowd.

"A travesty," Wren answered, feigning disgust.

She shook her head in angry agreement.

In her wake Wren beamed. Spending time with these people made him feel normal, too.

His cell phone pinged with an incoming text message and

he brought it up, expecting a check-in from Loralei, his ex-wife. But it wasn't that.

WE MUST SPEAK, CHRISTOPHER! SHADOW WAR IS COMING.

Wren hit delete without a second thought.

The message didn't delete, and he sighed. That was what he'd come to expect from Hellion and B4cksl4cker, two of the greatest hackers in the world and a pair of overgrown children he'd come to class as 'friends'. They'd known each other for years, now, ever since Wren had pressured them to quit black-hat hacking and turn toward the light. To hack his phone and make a message 'undeletable' would be child's play to them.

He'd hoped they'd have better things to do than bother him in his retirement, though.

He'd made it clear. He'd been explicit.

After twenty-plus years serving his country, Wren was done. Out. No more role at the CIA. No formal duties at the Foundation, the intelligence-gathering / rehab / private paramilitary organization he'd spent years building. Maybe he'd get more involved again at some point, but his kids were growing up and his priority was building a life with them, under an assumed name in witness protection, guarded by a promise from the President herself.

John Nash, was his new name. Another famous British architect. It worked, and he wasn't about to let Hellion and B4cksl4cker's paranoia endanger that. He tried to swipe the message away, but it seemed they'd also pinned it to his home screen. Maybe if he opened up the settings and dug into-

"You're him, aren't you?"

Wren looked up from his phone.

There was a young man standing before him, somewhat out of place amongst the gathering of older parents on the sidewalk. He was in his late twenties with the build of an ex-jock, wearing an expensive blue suit and holding up his phone like he was framing up a photograph.

Wren instantly went on alert.

He didn't know this man. He didn't look like a local or a parent, more like a banker out of Philadelphia, and Wren couldn't risk his true identity getting out. Vengeful men had come to kill him in Frederica before.

He offered a bemused smile. "I'm who?"

"Christopher Wren," the man said confidently. "I've seen you on TV. You look different with the cap and beard. You've let yourself slide." He smiled and tapped his phone. There was no flash, but Wren knew what had just happened.

He'd taken a photo.

Wren's operational side took over. All his efforts at anonymity meant nothing if a single photo of him was posted on social media.

He took a step closer. "I'm going to have to ask you to delete that photograph."

"What photograph?" The man slid his phone back into his left pocket with a smile.

"The one you just took."

"Not a chance. It's a free country."

Wren tried a smile of his own. "My kids go to school here. You post that photo anywhere, you're putting them at risk."

"*I'm* putting them at risk?" the guy scoffed, and pointed a finger in Wren's face. "You're the one who's dangerous. You should've thought about your kids before you destroyed Texas."

Wren gritted his teeth. It was true that he'd played a key role in the implosion of the Texas separatist movement; that was one reason the crazies hated him. "We're not in Texas, and you're not a Texan," he countered. "Come on. It'll take you seconds to delete it."

The guy's expression turned to contempt. "So cry me a river. Not my problem."

He turned and started away.

In another life Wren's response would be simple and immediate; take a few steps, spin the guy and put a knee into his groin. He'd retrieve the phone, force a facial-recognition unlock then manually delete the photo. But in this new life, living undercover and bounded by 'normal' social laws, that kind of violence was unacceptable. The fellow parents around him would witness it, likely photograph him again and almost certainly call the police.

His life in Frederica would be blown wide open.

No more happy weekends with his kids. His ex-wife Loralei would see to that. The terms of their deal settling him in Delaware had been very clear. He was out of the black-ops life, forever.

That left one approach.

"A hundred dollars," Wren called, pitching his voice just loud enough to be heard but not overheard.

The young man turned with a look of derision on his face. "You're kidding, right?"

Wren took another step and lowered his voice further. "A thousand, then."

"I make more than that in short trades on a slow morning."

Wren nodded. He'd been right then; this guy was a banker. That made him greedy. "Five, then."

"Five for a photo?"

"We both know what it's worth to the paparazzi. Make it ten and save yourself the trouble."

"Ten?"

Wren took out his phone. "You take mobile payments?"

"You're going to give me ten grand for a photo?"

Wren closed the gap to a yard. "Like I said, my kids' lives

are at stake. I've got it all lined up." He held up his phone, showing his digital payment app.

"You're crazy," the man said, but Wren could feel he was on the hook. As a banker, he'd like the immediacy of the win. As a jerk, he'd be thinking how he could easily email a secure copy to himself then sell it to the paparazzi later. "But OK."

The guy brought out his phone, held it up for a facial recognition unlock then tapped a few times, a few times more, then opened his settings to allow incoming Bluetooth communications. Wren watched the device unlock on his own screen. The guy had named his phone CHICK MAGNET.

Ugh.

"Chick magnet?"

"That's me. So send it."

Wren tapped to cement the connection, then activated the 'Bluebug' app; a commercially available program that prevented wireless Bluetooth hacks. Wren's version, however, had been upgraded by Hellion and B4cksl4cker to perpetrate those same attacks. Now it reached across the established link to slave CHICK MAGNET to Wren's phone.

It didn't take long. In seconds Wren had total admin control, with his phone mirroring the guy's screen. A classic bait and switch; sometimes you had to give something in order to get what you wanted. He smiled, swiped and tapped a few more times.

"Reginald Hatch-Griff," he said, reading the young man's name off his NameCheck social media page. "Of Caravel Banking, Philadelphia? I see you're little Tommy's uncle. In town for a visit, are you?" He looked up and took one more step closer, bringing him into Reginald's personal space. Now the guy's mouth was opening to spew out an outraged response.

Wren didn't give him the opportunity. "Tommy's a cool kid, he's friends with my son, so why don't you keep it cool too, Reginald? I just took total control of your phone, also your cloud backup, your social media, anything I want. I can go after your bank accounts too. Watch this."

On his own phone, Wren swiped through the mirror of Reginald's home screen and opened one of the banking apps. Reginald didn't think fast enough to look away, and the app unlocked via facial recognition, opening on both screens simultaneously. Wren scrolled through a dozen inflated accounts and gave a low whistle.

This cocky young punk was almost a millionaire.

"Greedy," Wren said softly. "And dumb. Here's the deal, Reggie. Keep it cool like little Tommy and you'll get your accounts back in twenty-four hours. I'll delete the photo and any backups, but that's all. If you share my name and identity with a single living soul, then I'll take you for everything you're worth. That's just shy of a mill total. You can watch it happen."

Reginald Hatch-Griff stared in disbelief. "You can't do any of that. You can't-"

"Watch me," Wren said. "It's as good as done. Now put your phone back in your pocket."

Reginald's jaw dropped. From the paling in his cheeks, it was clear he was close to entering a shock reaction. That was fine by Wren. That was something that could be explained. Some bad tuna, maybe. As long as he didn't start throwing up or faint nearby, it'd be fine.

"Phone," Wren repeated. "In your pocket."

He waited. Reginald obeyed sluggishly, wide eyes darting. "This isn't fair."

"So cry me a river. I asked nicely three times. Now give me a nod, say, 'Thanks, John,' and walk away."

Reginald hesitated, but the fight-or-flight chemicals were already flooding his system, and fight was clearly not a possibility. "Thanks, John," he mumbled, then started away.

Wren watched after him, waiting for an outburst as he dispersed into the crowd of waiting parents, but none came.

Good. Wren worked through the guy's mirrored phone and deleted the photo. He found one copy in the cloud and one that Reggie had already emailed back to himself, and deleted them both.

All done. He closed Bluebug and dropped his phone back into his pocket.

"I see you're amusing yourself," came a voice from behind.

3

FARM

A smile spread across Wren's face and he turned.

"Honey," he said. "You saw that?"

Masako Toyama did not look impressed. She did look outlandishly beautiful, though, even dressed down in mom jeans with a baggy check shirt. Nothing could disguise that incredible figure. Her dark eyes set above wide cheekbones shone with something like restrained mirth, but her solemn tone gave none of that away.

"I think that's the third person you've Bluebugged in the last week." She poked him in the chest, but he easily wrapped her in his arms and gave her a kiss.

"It was the minimal escalation possible. He took a photograph."

Masako frowned. "Oh, how terrifying."

"You should have seen it. I looked atrocious, like a DMV mugshot."

Masako snorted and wriggled out of his arms. "That's just how you look." She made a grab for his tangled beard, but he pulled back too fast. "Scruffy."

"I'm undercover. You know the rules of a sleeper agent: never break cover."

Now she laughed. "I think you like those rules a little too much. Oh look," she glanced over his shoulder, "the kids are coming out."

Wren turned. The kids weren't coming out yet.

"Some secret agent," Masako chided, then grabbed his beard, pulled him close and shut up any comeback with a kiss.

It was Masako's second trip over to Delaware, and this was her last day, due to fly out in the morning. They'd met in Tokyo six months earlier, bonding over a series of bizarre murders in the city's sewers. Wren had been to Tokyo once more in that time, and was due to go over again soon.

He'd loved it, cruising around Ginza or Akihabara with Masako on his arm, with nowhere special to be, nothing special to do and no one to hunt down and kill. Likewise, she'd enjoyed long lazy days spent at his Frederica farm, riding down Crystal Creek, spelunking in the tiny cave and racing BMXs around the trails Wren had blazed through the forest. Every day felt good now, leaving him with no desire to get involved with his hackers' 'shadow war'.

Normal was proving a good fit for him.

Finally the school bell rang.

The gates opened and the kids flooded out; seven-year-old Jake came charging up while nine-year-old Quinn lagged back, already too cool for school. She was almost a teenager and starting to develop some attitude.

"Hey kiddos," Wren enthused, greeting Jake with a big hug and spin.

"Dad, today we buried a time capsule, and I filled it with boogers!"

Wren chuckled. "Well, that is a real treat for future generations, isn't it?"

"Yeah!"

"He didn't," Quinn said calmly, handing her school pack

to Masako, who took it and gave a small curtsey. Wren snorted but Quinn missed it all. "He just means grass. He dug a hole with his friends and filled it with grass."

"Well, I'm sure that'll last for generations."

"Generations of ants, maybe," Quinn said. "I'm hungry. Can we go?"

"Pizza?"

"Pizza!" Jake crowed.

"Fine," Quinn said. Already it was a hassle to be spending time with her Dad, but he knew she'd warm up as the afternoon progressed, so that by the time they were tied for goals in air hockey two hours later, she'd be shrieking and hollering like the rest of them.

"Fine," Masako echoed, imitating Quinn's tone just enough for Wren to notice but not enough for Quinn. It cracked him up. Masako found both Quinn and Jake a delight. Wren guessed they were a big difference from the dark affairs she spent her workdays on, back at the Public Security Intelligence Agency in Tokyo, Japan's equivalent of the FBI. A defiant nine-year-old would come as a welcome relief.

They all bundled into Wren's Jeep Wrangler Rubicon, a five-door with a pickup bed. Quinn was straight onto her phone while Jake peppered Masako with questions about the evening's plan.

Wren's phone chimed and he brought it up, expecting a check-in from Loralei.

CHRISTOPHER, SHADOW WAR IS –

He stopped reading and stripped the battery from the phone as expertly as if he was disassembling his Sig Sauer.

Masako watched curiously. "Everything OK?"

"Spam," Wren said with a smile, setting the phone's parts on the dash. "Now, who's hungry?"

"I'm starving!" Jake shouted.

"Off to the booger restaurant!" Wren responded earnestly, and fired up the engine.

The evening proceeded every bit as Wren had hoped, with laughter, a few tears, many coupons collected at the arcade and cashed in for some plastic garbage prizes, a superhero movie and a big jump on the trampolines. It finished when Wren and Masako dropped off the kids at his ex-wife Loralei's duplex at precisely 10 p.m.

The kids hugged Wren goodbye, and Quinn even hugged Masako. That was a first, and it warmed Wren's heart. Loralei gave them both a small approving nod before she closed the door.

The drive back to the farm passed in a hazy, happy quiet. They rolled the windows down and enjoyed the warm night air, redolent with smells of surging spring sap and creosote tar rising off the still-hot blacktop. The sky was a purple black, and each mile south they drove, the brighter the field of stars shone overhead.

The road down to the farm was gravel and bumpy, and Masako reached over to take Wren's hand. He pulled around to the clearing, circled with wooden logs around a central fireplace marked out by stones. He parked by the log cabin and switched off the engine, feeling so happy it almost hurt.

Masako squeezed his hand. She was good like that.

"Quinn hugged me," she said.

Wren laughed. "I know. What a punk she is."

"She's sweet. That is some real gentle defiance."

Wren snorted and turned to her. She really was beautiful; not just her dark eyes or her soft black hair or her full lips, but the person she was. He'd come to trust her in Tokyo. They'd survived multiple attacks together, taking it in turns to save each other, and now he'd let her into his life.

"Let's take a walk," he said.

"Sure."

He pushed open the door and stepped out, leading Masako into the heavy dark of the forest. The land ascended steadily, carrying them up through old-growth groves of American elm, black cherry, blackhaw viburnum and red maple. Bats swooped on bugs overhead, woodchucks and squirrels rustled in the darkness and the sweet scent of summer sap filled the air.

Soon they emerged out onto a hilltop some fifty feet high. Wren had only discovered it a month ago, and spent a week clearing saplings and rocks to make it a vantage point. He halted at the peak, looking out over a breathtaking panorama across the dark forest canopy. The Milky Way shone as a pale smudge above, a whole galaxy of stars.

"This is incredible," Masako said, her breathing quickening. "Where have you been hiding all this, Chris?"

Wren's heart surged into his mouth. There were so many things he wanted to say, about what she meant to him and his plans for a shared future. He opened his mouth to speak, but at that moment a sharp buzzing came from overhead.

It took him a few seconds to register it fully. Not a mosquito. Not a distant plane. He looked at Masako.

"Drone," he said. "Run."

4

DRONE

Wren and Masako broke for the trees, arms and legs pumping side-by side.

In seconds they were under cover on either side of the trail. Wren ducked in behind a thick black elm and peered back. Now all the drone's lights were on, and it hovered at the top of the hill like some miniature UFO landing. It wasn't a military strike drone. If anything, it looked like a store-bought commercial model, equipped with little more than a camera, speakers and lights.

That was strange.

Then it began to speak.

"This is commandeered drone," came a familiar female voice, distorted by the drone's low-quality speakers. He'd recognize that Bulgarian accent anywhere: Hellion, one of his top hackers. "Christopher Wren and Masako Toyama, apologies to interrupt time together, but there is catastrophic shadow war developing on global scale. Many will die. America is not capable to act, too tied up with political infighting. Foundation must take action immediately, or-"

The speakers cut out as Wren came up underneath the drone and hit the off switch. The rotor blades wound down and Wren lowered the housing gently to the ground. The echoes of Hellion's voice died away, returning silence to the vista.

Masako stood across the drone from him. "Hellion, was it? She's keen. What's that about a shadow war?"

Wren grimaced. He couldn't cover this one up by stripping his phone. "Her latest hobby. She's been trying to reach me for a while. Something to do with the shadow line."

Masako frowned. "Like the shadow line under Tokyo?"

Wren nodded. He and Masako had discovered the shadow line together; an independently laid optical fiber Internet line in the sewers beneath Tokyo. It was part of a plot hatched by a darkweb group to subvert the real Internet, switch traffic to their backup line then subtly take over everything: media, corporations, communications, the military, and ultimately the government.

"Like that, yeah. But it's all ghosts. I've been keeping on top of it. There's no sign they ever laid any cables outside of Tokyo."

Masako considered that. "So Tokyo was the petri dish? They were just testing it out, and it ends there?"

"That's my theory. I've seen no evidence otherwise."

Masako looked down at the stilled drone. A long moment passed. "Right. The three wise monkeys."

"The three what?"

She looked up at him. "Three wise monkeys. It's a Japanese proverb. One's holding his eyes, one's holding his ears, one's holding his mouth."

"Ah. You mean like 'see no evil, hear no evil'?"

Masako held his gaze for a moment, like she was making some kind of weighty decision, then nudged the drone's housing with her toe. "What would you call it?"

Wren wasn't sure how to take that. It made for quite a shift from the mood of just moments ago.

"You're saying I've got my head in the sand?"

"No," Masako said swiftly. "It's not that. It's just…" she trailed off. "It's your choice how you live your life, Chris. You want to quit the CIA, that's your right. Quit the Foundation, too, quit the life completely if you want. I just think…"

Wren waited. If anything, this was the opposite direction he'd thought the evening would take. But they were in it, now.

"I want to know, Masako. You can tell me. It's OK."

She sighed, then reached out and took his hands. "It's not for me to say. But this shadow line? It worries me, Chris. A lot. We got it in Tokyo, OK, that's good for us. But you and me, we've barely talked about it since."

"Because we got it."

"That's just it. I keep hearing rumors. Did we get it all? What about Kyoto? Osaka? Then outside of Japan, do we really know it's not out there too? Absence of evidence isn't-"

"Evidence of absence," Wren finished.

"Exactly."

They stood silently for a time. Wren wasn't really sure what came next.

"That's it, I guess," Masako finished quietly. "It worries me. Like, all the time. We both see the way Russia's building up troops on its borders, the way China's creating man-made islands to claim vast stretches of ocean. What if the shadow line comes into play? It could tilt the global balance of power. We're talking about total control of information, economies, media, even governments-"

"We don't know the shadow line's capable of all that," Wren interrupted. "Even if it has spread. Those are worst-case scenarios."

"I live in the path of a worst-case scenario, Chris," Masako said, squeezing his hands. "Japan's directly in the firing line of both China and North Korea, and they both hate us. We're on a knife's edge, and the shadow line could push that balance into chaos. It just takes a single missile to fly, then ten million in Tokyo are dead and we're in the middle of World War 3..."

Wren nodded slowly. He didn't need the whole script to see where this was going.

"Then you come over here, and I've retired. I'm not worried." He sighed, looking around at the forest that just moments ago had looked so beautiful. "I'm building this summer camp. Eating pizza and watching movies."

Masako shook her head. Now her eyes shone. "I don't mean it that way. Chris, I love it here. I love what you're doing. I love to be with you, and the kids, and I wish I could just stay here forever. I feel safe. But when I'm getting close to leaving, like now, I start thinking about everything that's out there. The rea-"

She cut herself short, but Wren again finished for her. "The real world."

She said nothing, just squeezed his hand. "We are in a shadow war," she said. "One that's bigger than anything we've yet seen, and it isn't over, no matter how much either of us may want it to be."

5

SHADOW WAR

The next morning Wren dropped Masako off at Philadelphia International Airport. At the gate they kissed and said all the right things, but he felt her drifting away; out of the safe little world he'd created and back into the real one.

"I'll be in Italy for the next month," Masako said, looking at him with something like regret. "An intelligence confab." It was the perfect moment to invite him to come. He'd say yes in a heartbeat. A weekend together to put all this behind them.

But she didn't ask.

"I'll be busy. We'll talk after that, Chris. OK?"

He smiled but didn't feel it. A month. "OK. Stay safe, Masako."

She smiled too and said nothing more. There was clearly no need to wish him the same; he wasn't going anywhere. Instead she walked away and didn't turn back.

Wren drove home in silence. The great Delaware River rolled by on his left, swollen and dark. As he approached the farm, it began to rain; a heavy, gray downpour that sucked in the horizon and made everything grim and dreary, scouring the trees and creek and the gravel road.

He pulled in by the clearing and sat at the wheel, looking ahead at the log cabin he'd built with his own two hands.

It hadn't felt like this previously. After each time Masako had left, he'd immediately been looking forward to her next visit, the next time he saw his kids, the next job on the farm.

Not now. Now there was just a cold ball of worry in his belly, weighing him down.

He flicked on the radio and tuned to a news program.

'... confirmation that Russian forces have reached one hundred thousand on the border with Ukraine, with twenty thousand poised on the borders of Latvia and Estonia each. Russian President Burin claims these are 'special training maneuvers', but experts in British intelligence claim..."

He flicked to another station.

'... the latest UN attempt to condemn China's troop build-up on recently created islands in the South China Sea was vetoed this morning by the Russian delegation, which currently holds the rotating chairmanship – effectively ruling out any UN action or intervention...'

Wren killed the radio, stepped out into the rain and walked over to his cabin. Standing in the open doorway, the interior looked somehow different. couches, TV, kitchen table, fruit in a bowl, kids' toys in a box. His simple life of the last six months suddenly seemed very far away, like a holiday to a place that no longer quite existed, even though he was looking right at it.

The prospect of war changed everything.

He pulled out his phone and looked at it for a long moment. The message from Hellion and B4cksl4cker was still there, pinned to the lock screen, ranting about their shadow war. Wren didn't want to deal with it. He didn't want to lift his head out of the sand and place all of this at risk, but he could feel it pulling at him.

At the least, he had to know.

It only took seconds to place the call he'd been avoiding for months, using a secure emergency line and a VPN that bounced his signal three times around the world.

It rang three times then answered.

"Christopher?"

It was Hellion's voice. She was a twenty-three-year-old Bulgarian wunderkind hacker who'd come up playing strategy games online, swiftly rising to conquer all comers with her incredible APM, or Actions Per Minute typing speed, and lightning-fast tactical capacity. In her early teens she'd shifted into hacking real-world corporations and nation states for the fun and challenge, until she'd run up against her now-partner, B4cksl4cker.

B4cksl4cker was a twenty-nine-year-old Armenian who, back when Hellion had first coquettishly challenged him to a 'hackathon', had masterminded some of the grandest cyber heists in history, leveraging his botnet army of millions of slaved computers and his own highly advanced brand of narrow field Artificial Intelligence to wage.

For three days and nights Hellion and B4cksl4cker had battled each other, until at the end Hellion's incredible speed and tactics on the keys had reduced B4cksl4cker's army to nothing, while he came out of it with her 'dox', personal documents including her real name, address, family, school and friends.

He could have used it. He could have had her killed, if he'd wanted. Instead, they'd struck up a friendship and started running hacks together. When she turned eighteen, he invited her to join him in his fabled truck convoy, loaded down with one of the world's most powerful supercomputers. Together they'd roamed Europe, endlessly pulling off some of the most epic exploits in cyber history, until Wren stepped in, put a stop to their fun and harnessed their energies to the white-hat activities of his Foundation.

She sounded amped up.

"It's me, Hellion," Wren said. "You've been trying to reach out about a shadow war?"

She laughed with genuine-sounding glee. "Shadow war? Yes, of course, Christopher! We try with text messages, with boring email, with drone, next is airplane skywriter in sky, yes? You are difficult man to contact."

"I try."

"B4clsl4cker!" she shouted. "It is Christopher."

A second channel joined the line with a click. "Christopher," B4cksl4cker boomed in his deep Armenian bass. Wren had met him twice now in real-life, and he was every bit the thickset bear he sounded to be. While lethal online, though, Wren had never known him to even raise his voice in reality. "I am so happy. It is very great pleasure to speak with you, we have waited very long. In fact, we were just talking about you."

Wren winced. He could imagine what these two hackers might have been saying, given how thoroughly he'd avoided their attempts to reach him. "Only good things, I hope."

"LOL, Christopher," Hellion said, clearly stating each letter, "laughing out loud. Mostly it has been jokes about your adventures in sewers under Tokyo, yes? We often recall how happily you dived into sewage flow to seek out shadow line junction box, then came up with big grin like cat who has cream, covered in-"

"OK," Wren interrupted, not so keen to dwell on that particular memory. "Got it, Hellion. Shall we-"

"Of course, there are also many jokes we did not share at the time. Example, do you know why Christopher Wren was fired from job searching Tokyo sewers?"

Wren sighed. There was probably no way out of this hazing other than straight through it. "I don't know. Why?"

"Because he didn't know shi-"

"Got it," Wren interrupted. "How about we-"

"Not finished. There is further most excellent comment from fellow Foundation member, Stephen Gruber, in chat boards, which states-"

"You're sharing jokes about me on the Foundation chat boards?"

"Yes, of course! This is excellent team-building opportunity, while brave leader is taking refuge in bowling alley and cinema, playing games and watching children's animated movies. Would you wish to hear this joke?"

Wren sighed. "You said it's from Stephen Gruber?"

"Yes. He is much recovered, by the way. Becoming very happy man, not too much sex."

Wren raised a hand and squeezed the bridge of his nose. Already he was beginning to regret this. "That's good news about Stephen. Please, go ahead with his joke."

"Thank you, I will. Joke says, old man Christopher Wren is in sewer manhole searching through filth. Passerby, Stephen Gruber, asks-"

"I'm not an old man," Wren interjected. "I'm barely forty."

"Compared to myself and B4cksl4cker, you are almost dead. Now, Gruber asks, 'What are you doing in sewer again, Chris, my old friend?' Old man Christopher says, 'I am looking for my dentures.' Ha ha. This is not main joke, however, but quite funny image. Next, Gruber says, 'Wait, you don't think you'll find them in the sewer hole, do you?' Old man Christopher says, 'Of course, I already found three, but none of them fit.'"

B4cksl4cker laughed uproariously.

Wren sighed again. "Are you done?"

"I will save some for later," Hellion said. "Done for now. It is too much a pleasure to receive your call, and I cannot contain myself. I wonder, to what do we owe sudden change of heart?" Keys flew in the background as Hellion worked the

Internet. "I see beautiful maiden Masako Toyama has left on morning flight. Children are with ex-wife for next three days, according to digital planner. Are you feeling lost, Christopher?"

He smiled. Both of those data points were easy enough to hack, and he knew well by now that Hellion's invasion of his privacy was really a form of affection; testing boundaries with the main authority figure in her life.

"Something like that," he said. "Masako heard your drone message last night, and pointed out the shadow line is a real concern. I wanted to check in and see if she was right."

There was silence on the other end for a few moments, not even keystrokes clattering.

"Hellion? B4cksl4cker?"

"We are here, Christopher. Engaging in private debate. If we tell you this news, it is possible you will leave Delaware behind. Say goodbye to children for some time, make ex-wife angry. Is very exciting news, though. Very terrifying. Do you wish to hear it?"

Wren squeezed his eyes shut. That was the question, wasn't it? It was the exact reason he'd kept his head in the sand. What he didn't know, he didn't need to act on. But by playing dumb he was risking his relationship with Masako.

He opened his eyes. It was proving increasingly difficult to stay retired.

"Tell me."

6

SHADOW LINE

"We have found shadow line," Hellion said. "Big news is, it is already everywhere."

Wren frowned. "Define that a little more for me, Hellion."

"Most obligingly, Christopher. Everywhere means everywhere. All states of America show signs of shadow line infiltration, plus all countries in South America, all countries in EU, many in Africa, many in Asia and Far East."

Wren didn't quite believe what he was hearing. "You're serious? What evidence have you got? Are you saying the shadow line's been physically laid in all those countries, when no one else has seen it? All around the world, and nobody knew it?"

"Yes, and many people know it, Christopher. We are finding thousands have been bribed to look aside, hundreds murdered or disappeared, thousands more are deeply involved. We have fringe access to shadow line metadata, and it is showing signs of advanced Active Function."

That sent a cold sliver of dread down Wren's spine. "What's Active Function?"

"Is process of convincing IPs, Internet Providers, to shift

legitimate Internet traffic onto shadow line," Hellion explained. "At first this happens slowly. Could take months or years to bed shadow line in amongst other cables." She paused a moment. "Do you have any idea how many undersea cables there are circling oceans, Chris?"

"No idea. A dozen?"

"Hundreds. Some laid by governments, some by communications companies, some by NGOs. There are also satellites, cell phone towers, many means of communication. Shadow line would want to hide in amongst them, gradually earn trust, so IPs switch traffic over; least secure data to begin with, like social media, news media and streaming television. Next would be encrypted credit card information, internal company emails, private messages. Finally, when trust is strong, comes banking, low-level government communications, stock market functions. After that is military use, government, power. Last stage is drop data bomb into existing Internet, encrypt or destroy all other routes for information to flow. This leaves only shadow line in place. Complete control."

Wren's fists tightened. "OK, so you're saying the shadow line's already reached that stage?"

"Is close. Is hard to be sure, and depends on country's level of data security. In moderate data security countries, like America, UK, some in Europe, is at first stage only. But first stage allows some influence over mass media. In low security countries, we believe control is nearing final stage. Data bomb could drop any moment, lead to communications chaos, terror, violence, military strikes, territory changing hands, millions dead." She paused for a moment. "We believe this moment is imminent, Christopher. Could happen today, tonight, tomorrow."

The cold sliver of dread became a tight band clamped

around Wren's spine. This was everything Masako feared. "What's your plan?"

"Developing plan," Hellion said enthusiastically. "B4cksl4cker and I are searching for key path into shadow line. There may be central command and control location, Christopher. We call this 'Nexus'. We are hunting Nexus, getting close. Your presence would be great help when we find it. There will be physical strike. We must take Nexus."

"Nexus? What is that?"

"We do not yet know. Chief node on shadow line? Central super computer? Mobile command laptop like suitcase nuke, can move between locations? Is very difficult to isolate. But we will soon. Take Nexus, we can shut whole shadow line down! This is theory, anyway. Will you help?"

Wren looked back over his log cabin, feeling the weight of their expectations grow. He had responsibilities here, too. He had his family. One step off the beaten path and Loralei would take his kids and run.

He wasn't sure he could survive that a second time.

"I'm sorry," he said. "I can't commit to anything, Hellion. Send me what you've got. Maybe I can run operator for you. Analyze intel for you. Maybe even train up a strike team, if you need it." He took a heavy breath. "But I can't go fight. My family needs me here."

"Of course, you need time to think about this," Hellion went on, enthusiasm undimmed. "We understand. Family is important. But Christopher?"

He felt like a brick, slowly sinking to the bottom of a deep, still lake. "What is it?"

"We think of you as family too."

The line went dead.

7

DEEP, STILL LAKE

Wren set his phone down and strode back out into the rain. From his tool shed he collected his Ochsenkopf felling axe and stamped into the forest. There was always work to do on the farm.

All day he felled trees. Advancing the farm's trails.

In the heat of each swing, he forgot about Hellion and Masako and the shadow line. He kept working until it grew dark, when he trawled back to the cabin with his whole body singing and numb. He ate a meal of macaroni cheese with steak and green beans, showered and sank into the couch with a tall glass of whisky and a Stone Roses record playing softly on the turntable, but fell asleep before he could finish half of either.

He woke to alarms.

The cabin lights were still on and Wren rolled smoothly to his feet, blinking and assessing. Not the perimeter alarm. He brought up his phone, opened his control app and checked the alarm status.

FOUNDATION EMERGENCY, it read.

He blinked and killed the siren. He remembered programming that eventuality, an alarm that several people at the top of the Foundation could trigger. He swiped through screens until he found the originator.

Teddy. Theodore Smithely III, CEO of his Foundation, the rehab/paramilitary network he'd started years ago. It was ten past one in the morning.

Wren placed the call. It rang three times then Teddy answered.

"Christopher," came his gravelly voice. "Apologies for waking you, but I didn't think this could wait."

"What couldn't wait?"

"It's Hellion and B4cksl4cker. I just received a message on the secure line, and you need to see it."

Wren's breath caught in his throat. "What message?"

"I'm forwarding it now."

Seconds passed then Wren's phone pinged as the message came in. It was five simple words accompanied by a photograph.

STAND DOWN OR THEY DIE.

The photo showed Hellion and B4cksl4cker gagged, naked, battered and bound. They were seated side-by-side and flanked by tall racks of computer servers with green lights.

Hellion's nose was visibly broken, flattened and puffing up, with blood running red over her lips and down her throat. Her eyes were bruising darkly, but defiant still, staring down the camera lens. Across her mouth was a strip of silver duct tape and her hands were bound behind her back, cinching her shoulders in tight.

B4cksl4cker beside her looked worse. He was a twenty-nine-year-old bear of a man, tan-skinned and solid with Armenian muscle, and had clearly been beaten heavily. His face was pale and showed the welts of multiple blunt force traumas; enough to shatter his nose, probably break his jaw and even fracture his cheekbones. Blood ran down over his duct-tape gag and bruises bloomed darkly everywhere, distorting his features. His eyes were bleary and out of focus, signaling concussion. It wouldn't take too many more strikes to finish him off.

Fury burst in Wren's chest. Suddenly their concerns about the shadow line seemed very real.

"This is a message to me," he said, his voice coming out like gravel. "They might as well have written out my name."

"Agreed," Teddy said. "Are you going to listen?"

Wren ignored the question. He'd never taken direction well. "You've checked this image?" he asked, forcing words up his tight throat. "It's not a deep fake, rigged by a computer? This is really them?"

"I've run every test on it there is. I had Steven Gruber at the NSA analyze it through their best systems. It's real. They're not answering any calls, which I'd say confirms it."

That pumped the anger up hotter. Wren found himself in his bedroom, scooping up his 'go bag', always prepped with gear, money and fake ID.

"Who sent this, Teddy?"

"We have no idea. It came in through an untraceable chain of VPNs. We've tried to track it back but it just goes in circles."

Wren punched the wall. The whole cabin shook. The pain in his knuckles helped him focus. This wasn't just bad. Coming on the heels of Hellion's warnings about the shadow line, about Active Function and an imminent shadow war, perhaps it was the harbinger of something truly terrible.

He brought up the photo and tried to pick out clues to the location, but there was nothing to go off; no outlines of figures, no uniforms, no background. There was only the tall computer server racks reaching into darkness. If anything, it looked like the narrow interior of one of their server trucks.

Wren had never seen it, but Hellion and B4cksl4cker

infamously rode around Europe in a convoy of semi-trailer trucks, all of which were reputedly loaded down with custom-spec servers in the world's most powerful mobile supercomputer array, capable of hacking anything they attempted.

"Do you have anything on where Hellion and B4cksl4cker were?" he asked, striding back through the house. "Someone must have seen their convoy. I need last known coordinates, something to pick up their trail."

"There's nothing recent," Teddy answered swiftly, and the sound of clattering keys rang down the line. "But I may have something from three months ago. Apparently they ordered Foundation supplies, one of the new Attack Crate 2.0s packed with munitions. All the Crates are fitted with passive GPS tracker dots set to ping their location regularly."

Wren stopped in the cabin doorway, go bag over his shoulder and looking out at the moonless dark of the farm. It was hard to think for the blood pounding in his temples. He couldn't imagine why his hackers had wanted the physical strike capacity of an Attack Crate that long ago, but something was better than nothing.

"Where did it ping, Theodore?"

"Krakow, Poland."

"Poland?"

Wren's mind spun harder. That was an ex-Soviet bloc country, bordering Ukraine and Belarus to the east, Germany to the west. Wren knew little about it, but it hardly felt like a coincidence, with the Russian troop buildups nearby.

"Do we have any idea what they were doing in Poland? Or even why they ordered an Attack Crate? It's not like them. They're hackers, not soldiers."

More keys clattered. "I may have something on that. I'm scanning the Crate's contents log and there's a very specific, highly unusual set of equipment included: a strike suit for a female, equipped with top-of-the-line stealth tech; a full set of stiletto knives, shurikens and throwing blades. That's a perfect fit for one person's skillset, but you're not going to like who."

Wren's mouth went dry. Only one woman he knew used gear like that; the equipment of an assassin.

"Clara Baxter," he said.

8

OVERDRIVE

"That's right," Teddy answered.

Wren's mind spun into overdrive as he strode to the Jeep, climbed in and started the engine. As far as he knew, Hellion and B4cksl4cker hated Clara Baxter with a vengeance. She was a vicious vigilante assassin who tortured and slaughtered child abusers, after experiencing a childhood of abuse herself. It made her volatile and dangerous to all those around her. Just six months back she'd manipulated Wren into heading out to Tokyo, where he'd almost died multiple times. She'd also endangered Masako's life, and Hellion had made it plain she found such behavior unacceptable.

Wren put the Jeep in drive and hit the gas, powering forward into the pre-dawn dark of the forest.

"The hackers despise Baxter," he shouted over the roaring engine. "Why were they working with her, and to what end?"

"Your guess is as good as mine, Chris," Teddy answered. "But you know your hackers. They operate on whims. Perhaps she was the next shiny object."

Wren grunted, weaving the Jeep through dark trees by

memory before shooting out of the forest onto the Bay Road heading north. None of it added up.

"What did you get yourself into, Hellion?" he muttered under his breath, pushing the pedal down and accelerating up past a hundred.

"I didn't catch that, Chris."

"It's nothing. I'm going to Poland, Teddy. Get me on a private jet out of Philadelphia within the hour."

In forty minutes Wren was pacing in the Departures lounge of Philadelphia International Airport, phone pressed to his ear, waiting for his private jet to fuel up on the runway outside.

Finally the line answered.

"Chris?" his ex-wife Loralei asked in a whisper. She sounded half-asleep and a little annoyed. "It's the middle of the night. What's wrong?"

"I'm sorry, Lor. Two of my people just got abducted and I have to go get them. I'm at the airport now."

There was silence, then the shushing of sheets and the clank of a door closing; she'd just found herself a private space to talk.

"What happened? And you're doing what?"

He repeated himself. When he was done, Loralei was silent for a time.

"So you're going back to the 'black-ops'?" she asked eventually. "You said you'd quit all that. We made a deal."

"I know," Wren said, trying to hold back the churning emotions he felt. "I'm sorry, but I don't see a choice here."

Her voice turned cold. "There's always a choice."

"Not with this. These two saved my life. They saved our kids' lives. We both owe them."

"I do not owe them!" Loralei snapped back immediately. "You're the one who put our kids in danger. Again and again, and now you want credit for saving them? You want me to side with some stupid hackers? Not a chance."

Wren didn't know what to say. She wasn't exactly wrong, and he couldn't help but think about the activities he'd scheduled for every upcoming evening and weekend with Jake and Quinn. Sometimes it was homework or a little TV, but mostly it was fun outdoor activities like climbing, kayaking or caving.

All canceled now, maybe indefinitely.

"I should be back soon," he offered.

Loralei laughed. "Where have I heard that before? We had a deal, Chris. You seeing the kids meant you ended that life. You're breaking the deal right now. It's over."

"I'm sorry. Let me explain it to them."

"You want to explain? No way. No matter what you say, your children will not understand that their father, who they've just started to get to know again, is abandoning them to go save some criminal hackers! I won't allow it, Chris. I won't have them worrying about whether you're alive or dead, like I did."

Wren gritted his teeth. This was exactly what he'd feared. "I won't die, Loralei. Give me this chance, please."

"You're a liar," she said coldly. "I hope you don't die, Chris, but that's it. If you go now, don't bother coming back. Not ever. There's no place for you in their lives."

The line went dead.

Wren was left alone with the dial tone in his ear. He redialed but it went to the busy tone; she must have turned her phone off. He started to compose a text message when a voice sounded beside him.

"Sir?" Wren turned to see a steward dressed in a pressed white shirt and sharp blue tie. "Your jet is ready."

There was no time. Maybe Loralei would listen later. It

broke his heart, but there was nothing Wren could do about it now. He gritted his teeth and followed the steward out.

A Bombardier Challenger 605 was waiting on the airfield, a small jet with a range of four thousand six hundred miles. It was enough to get him to Portugal, where they'd refuel for the final leg to Poland. It had a capacity of twelve, but Wren only needed one seat. Stepping into the fuselage and out of the drizzling humidity of the Philadelphia pre-dawn felt like crossing a threshold.

His happy, retired Delaware life was behind him. Only violence lay ahead. He tapped out a simple message to Loralei and sent it.

PLEASE TELL THE KIDS I LOVE THEM

It returned unread. She'd blocked him.

In moments the engines roared to life, the jet surged along the runway then they were in the air and rising toward the east.

9

KRAKOW, POLAND

It was raining in Krakow.

The time upon landing was 6:15 a.m., around thirteen hours after Wren had left the US, plus seven hours for the time zone and two to refuel in Portugal.

Now he stepped out onto the waiting stair car. It was still dark out, and the air felt muggy and heavy. Striding down to the blacktop, it felt like Wren hadn't budged off the Philadelphia runway.

An electric cart was waiting and ferried him to the main Arrivals lounge of the John Paul II International airfield. The customs thoroughfare was empty and quiet, and Wren breezed through in moments only. He'd brought no baggage other than his carry-on.

"All done, Mr. Nash," said the customs officer, citing Wren's fake ID. The words sounded almost musical in his Polish accent.

In short-stay parking Wren found his waiting rental car, a gunmetal gray Dacia Duster SUV. He climbed in and checked the glove box. There was a Sig Sauer P220 ACP .45 in a case, alongside two boxes of ammunition and a shoulder holster.

His Foundation at work.

He slapped the glove box closed, slotted an earpiece into his right ear and a bone-conduction mic pad across his throat, hit the button to dial then worked the gears and took off.

"Teddy?

"Reading you, Chris. I have a number of assets standing on alert. I can send you after the Crate with an army."

"Trained operators?"

"Enthusiastic amateurs."

Wren grunted. "Keep them on standby. An untrained army means a big footprint, and a big footprint means they'll see us coming. Better I go in alone but keep our team in the wings, providing drone overwatch of the Crate's position."

"We can do that," Teddy answered. "

Wren powered the Duster out of the airport lot and headed south.

The GPS tracker dot had pinged in the forecourt of a rental warehouse twelve miles to the southwest of Krakow, next to a power station in a district called Skawina. It was a short run in the Duster, twenty minutes down the A4 highway, through dark fields hung with creepers of silvery mist.

The power station announced itself ahead with a plume of coal smoke reaching up to the dark skies. Wren stopped the Duster a quarter mile out, pulling over on an industrial access road next to a large and crackling electrical substation, packed with blocky transformers, ceramic insulators, tall pylons and a web of cables. The rain thickened and the smoke cast a pall.

"Teddy, are you still with me?" Wren asked.

"Here, Christopher," came Teddy's heavy voice in his ear. "I have overwatch via a drone team. As we agreed, they have no idea you're involved, or what any of this is about. They think they're watching for a local drug cartel."

Wren grunted. It was what they'd agreed; a purely need-to-know basis, with Foundation assets following orders blind.

"Do they see anything?"

"The rain and smoke are obscuring the forecourt. I can't see any sign of the crate. No people, no vehicles."

"Keep me apprised."

Wren slung the pistol harness around his back, holstered the Sig Sauer, pulled a black leather jacket over the top then stepped out into the rain. From the back seat he grabbed a rucksack and slung it over his shoulder, then started away.

The electrical substation ran for several hundred yards, screened by a tall, razor-wire topped fence. Wren jogged alongside it until the fence curved left, where a sodden clay slip road led down into the warehouse's forecourt.

Thick wheel ruts had churned up the orange clay, leaving deep channels that now rushed with miniature whitewater off the road. Wren padded carefully down the side, hanging onto the fence and peering ahead. There was no CCTV that he could see, no patrols, no lookouts.

Soon the forecourt spread before him, a giant gray lake drummed by the rain.

"What do you see?" Teddy asked.

Wren scanned the scene. There were still no signs of surveillance, vehicles, or the Attack Crate. Two large warehouse units lined the forecourt dead ahead and two off to the right, while the substation's transformers buzzed beyond the fence to his left.

Wren knew from research that the two units on the right were server farms for a smartphone ride-hailing app, while the two ahead were rental offices originally built for dot-com businesses that were now defunct, and had lain largely empty since the bubble burst in 2002.

Records showed that one of those warehouses had been rented three months earlier, just a day before the Attack Crate

2.0 was dropped in front of it. The papers of the renting company led Wren nowhere, though, just shell companies dancing in a circle.

"Nothing yet," he said. "Advancing."

He stepped out into the lake. His boots sank into the water and soft clay at least a foot deep. Awful terrain; if a sniper unleashed fire now, he'd be a sitting duck. Still, there was nothing else to do. The court was about a hundred yards along, with his target warehouse at the far end.

One foot after another he went, each big stride sucking mud and sloshing water. His boots were waterlogged in seconds. His right hand strayed to the Sig against his ribs while his left splayed out for balance. A quarter of the way across, the drumming of the rain picked up, enveloping him in sound and backsplash. Picking out the windows of the server farms as he went by grew nearly impossible.

One good thing about that: if he couldn't see them, then they couldn't see him. Unless they had infrared sights. In which case-

"I see movement on the road," Teddy said.

Wren tried to speed up and almost toppled. "Coming down the slip road?"

"Hold," Teddy said.

Wren turned awkwardly. In the middle of the lake, he was totally exposed. On the plus side, few vehicles could make it through the mud without gumming up and spinning their wheels. Maybe a Humvee, or a tank…

"False alarm," Teddy came back. "They moved off."

Wren continued onward. In two minutes he cleared the lake and stood on a concrete foundation extending two feet before the warehouse. The structure was some forty yards across and at least twice that deep, with a metal door to the left and a rusted red roll shutter dead ahead.

Wren tried the door but it was locked tight. Next he

dropped to a squat at the roll shutter and pulled. There was some give but it caught on the lock. Wren dropped his rucksack, fished around inside for a crowbar, then went to the edge of the roll shutter.

He wasn't the first, it seemed. The metal here was bent upward, where somebody had already tried to gain access. Maybe they'd succeeded. He jammed the crowbar in a few inches along from the buckled corner, braced and pulled.

The crowbar caught and squeezed. The roll shutter groaned and metal bent. Wren's muscles swelled with blood; thighs doing most of the work, shoulders and arms transferring that force through the crowbar.

Something cracked inside, and Wren lurched a step back as the shutter gave way.

"Got it," he said, and went to the other corner. Again the metal was pre-buckled. He jammed the bar in, took up position and heaved until the mechanism cracked again.

The locks had sheared. He dropped the bar, ran his fingers under the shutter and pulled. It spun up smoothly, revealing an interior Wren had not expected at all: three figures in what looked to be white lab coats, backed by a large white tent in the center of a drab gray space.

One of the figures pulled a trigger.

10

WAREHOUSE

Wren spun to the side as the flash and crack of gunfire burst outward. Not hit, but close.

"What was that?" Teddy shouted in his ear.

"Three hostiles," Wren said, already appraising his options. "I'm engaging."

He ran. On the solid concrete that skirted the structure, he reached the corner of the warehouse just as a second shot barked in back, clipping the aluminum siding. Ahead lay nothing but a three-foot wide alley between the two warehouses, and he broke into a sprint.

Doubtless the white coats were in pursuit. By the time they reached the corner and opened fire he'd only be halfway along the alley. He didn't like those odds; even if they weren't a fair shot, the alley's walls would act like the gutters in a bowling alley, course-correcting any slug right toward him.

Two could play at that game, though.

At the halfway point he turned, dropped to one knee and locked the Sig into a double-handed grip. A second passed, then the first figure came pelting around the corner.

Wren fired.

No need for rebounds; the shot bloomed red through the white lab coat and the figure fell backward into the lake.

Wren was already up and running. More gunfire followed, but it was wild and he was almost a hundred yards clear now. In seconds he rounded the corner to the left and skidded to a halt in a narrow lull behind the warehouse. There was a tall brick wall topped by vegetation and razor wire; no way out but back toward the forecourt.

"I'm behind the warehouse, one man down, two closing in. Where's that drone, Teddy?"

"I'm re-routing," Teddy answered.

"I need eyes on these two guys." Wren peered back down the alley he'd come from, and more muzzle flashes erupted. He peeled away, ran to the far side and looked down the alley there, but this one dead-ended after twenty yards into the encircling wall.

He cursed.

There was no rear access door and no windows. There was no route to the rear of the neighboring warehouse either; its back was pressed right up to the brick wall. Wren was a in a dead-end cul-de-sac.

"I'm seeing traffic on the road again," Teddy said. "Hold."

Wren laughed. What else could he do now but hold? He scanned the brick wall for a climbing route, but it was mossed over and soaking wet. There was no way he was climbing out of this.

"Incoming down the slip road! Get out of there, Chris."

Wren laughed again. Trapped like a pig in a pen, with the butchers closing in. How ridiculous, if this was where he punched his ticket, fresh off a plane from Delaware where he'd been safe and happy and had everything he'd wanted.

"Is it a Humvee or a tank?"

"What? No. It's some brand of SUV."

"Good," Wren said. "It's not going to cross that lake in a

hurry. That gives me a few minutes. I need you to get that drone ready for a suicide run, Teddy. You're going to target the guys at the alley entrance. Hit them. Distract them. On my call. OK?"

"That'll take-"

"No time," Wren answered, already flinging himself back into the alley, Sig up and firing dead ahead as he sprinted. "Just do it."

A bullet for every two strides; just enough covering fire to keep their heads down at the entrance. With a twenty-one-round extended mag, one already discharged, that bought him forty strides, about forty yards, which was about halfway down the eighty-yard stretch.

Not enough.

After ten bullets fired and twenty yards covered he shouted the command. "Hit them now, Teddy!"

He didn't hear the drone coming in over the crashing tin-can-alley reverberations of the Sig's reports. With every shot fired the Sig bucked in his palm and splinters of aluminum bit off the edge of the alley, then he was at the halfway point and the gun clicked blank.

"Teddy!" Wren shouted, continuing on unarmed and blind.

One of the white coats leaned around the corner, leveled a pistol and fired. Wren saw the flash, watched a chunk scour from the siding just ahead and felt the bullet whip by his side. One inch to the left and they'd have had him; he flung himself into a shoulder-battering zig-zag against the warehouse walls.

Three more bullets streamed by, another twenty yards covered, then the second figure stepped out into the alley's mouth and leveled an automatic rifle.

There was no zig-zagging away from that.

Then a whirling gray shape crashed out of the rain into

the figure's left shoulder, pulling the rifle up and around in a wild spray of bullets.

The drone.

Wren closed the final ten yards and burst out of the alley to shoulder-ram the man's side. He was smaller, around six foot, and Wren's huge momentum picked him up and sent him flying five feet out into the lake. Wren was already lunging at the second figure to his right, now staring in disbelief. He closed the two-yard gap in a second flat, planting a meaty straight left punch that knocked the man out standing up.

He sagged but Wren caught him, spun, and held him up as the rifleman sprayed bullets from where he lay in the lake's sloshing mud. The bullets struck like body blows into a punching bag.

The man spasmed and Wren bent his knees then surged up, hurling the dead body out over the water. He flew through the rain and landed sprawled squarely atop the rifleman, flattening the weapon to discharge a second blast sideways.

In two more seconds Wren was there in the mud, dropping atop the corpse and firing a massive right elbow into the rifleman's face, shattering his cheek and temple. The sagged back into the mud-churned water.

Wren looked up as muzzle flashes blared across the lake, streaking splashes across the lake's rain-spattered surface.

"Last visual counted three more figures," came Teddy's voice in his ear. "I'm blind right now, Chris. Get out of there!"

"No."

Wren took hold of the rifle and pulled it around.

Three figures were out on the lake ahead of him, stamping through the deep mud. That was a serious tactical error, and their bullets came wild. Wren lifted the rifle clear of the water, gave the mechanism a few seconds to drain, then rested it atop the rifleman, proning out like a sniper. The man's chest provided just enough of a rest to lift the rifle out of the lake.

Wren set his eye to the sights, controlled his breathing as best he could, lowered the safety lever to semi-automatic fire and sighted on the figure furthest away. It was a seventy-yard shot against a moving target through the rain, but it was the tactically sound decision. Take out the guy in back, and when the others turned tail and ran, they had further to go.

More time for Wren to shoot them.

He squeezed the trigger. It clicked but didn't fire.

"Get out of there, Chris!" Teddy shouted.

Wren calmly lifted the rifle, an Avtomat Kalashnikova or AK47, designed by Mikhail Kalashnikov in the Second World War; a gas-operated assault rifle chambered for the 7.62×39mm cartridge. There was a very good reason that twenty percent of the estimated billion firearms in the world were Kalashnikovs: their incredible robustness.

The AK47 was designed 'loose' internally, with hefty 'tolerances' or spaces between moving parts, reducing accuracy when compared to a tighter-fitting weapon like the AR-15, but allowing plenty of 'play' when it came to real-world battle conditions.

A Kalashnikov could be soaked in mud, water or sand and still fire, because the loose tolerances inside allowed the firing pin to fire and the gas-operated mechanism to cycle even when obstructed. As long as the primer in each shell casing wasn't saturated with water, it would explode when the pin hit, the propellant would burn and the bullet would fire.

The top shell was likely saturated, so Wren racked the bolt back. The internal ejector kicked the unspent round off to the side then scooped up the next shell from the spring-loaded mag. Wren resettled atop the body, set his eye to the sights, exhaled and squeezed the trigger.

This time the round discharged but hit nothing. The spent

shell casing ejected to the side. Wren felt the pull of the weapon and adjusted his aim, targeting a spot an inch to the right of the rear figure, who was now ten yards closer.

Bullets raked through the water around Wren.

Settle, sight, exhale, squeeze.

The round discharged, the bullet flew and this time the rear man fell.

Now the front man stopped dead in the water, realizing his mistake. He dropped to one knee, butted his rifle against his shoulder and took aim.

His second mistake. Wren sighted, exhaled and squeezed before he could get off a shot.

He dropped.

The man in the middle panicked and broke to the side, sloshing in slow motion through the thick mud. Wren was in no mood for mercy. One more bullet took him through the skull and he dropped.

Wren was left with the hammering of the rain and the trembling of the figure underneath his elbows. The man he'd used as a rest was drowning while unconscious.

So be it.

"Christopher?" came Teddy's voice.

"Six down," Wren said, waiting a moment longer while beaded on the almost-invisible truck across the lake. "I'm fine."

Teddy released a pent-up breath. "Thank God. Who the hell are these people?"

There was no movement at the truck. No sign of incoming reinforcements. Wren stood and turned to the warehouse's open roll shutter. Before he'd been angry. Now he was getting furious.

"Let's find out."

11

WHO ARE THESE PEOPLE?

Thunder rolled overhead as Wren stamped through water and mud to the warehouse's entrance.

Inside it was largely dark but for the large white tent in the center, some kind of airtight forensic enclosure which glowed with inner light. Around it the floors were a stained raw concrete, faintly illuminated by mossed-over polycarbonate skylights high above. Old plastic desks and chairs were stacked unevenly down the wall on the right, perhaps left over from the dot-com business before it crashed. On the left was a wooden crate being used a table, circled by more chairs and scattered with packages of takeout food. A single thin stream of cigarette smoke rose up from an ashtray. The air was sour and musty, like a body had been left to decompose in one of the far corners.

"I found the Attack Crate," Wren said, striding toward the table. He pried up the lid and flipped it open, sending paper and plastic cutlery scuffling to the ground, then looked inside. "It's empty."

"Any clue as to who they are?"

"Not yet," Wren said. "Kalashnikovs suggests Russian, but that's far from definitive. Do you have overwatch?"

"We're working on raising a second drone."

Wren focused on the tent. It was large, like a marquee, maybe six yards on a side and three high. There was a central zip which Wren approached and swiftly yanked open.

Cold, sterile air blew out at him. That meant a gentle over-pressurization; the kind of thing you saw in precision fabrication factories, where the smallest speck of dust could damage the production process.

Wren stepped through into a kind of airlock; an enclosed inner cube of the tent, fitted with blast pipes and a control panel. There was a green button, likely to initiate a powerful blast of air that would vacuum any contaminating dust off him.

He ignored the mechanism and ripped the next zip open, striding into an inner ring of workspaces that encircled another, smaller white tent in the center.

"What the-" he muttered as he surveyed the workspaces. There were numerous desks set up, each stocked with dozens of computer parts and assorted tools: deconstructed circuit boards, computer chips, keyboards, screens and hard drives; screwdrivers, air cans, soldering irons, tweezers, cans of isopropyl alcohol, pliers, some kind of blocky waveform voltmeter. Everywhere there lay wires, cables, strips of optical fiber and the stacked-up housings of computer servers.

"What are you seeing?" Teddy asked.

"It looks like hacker heaven," Wren said. He'd seen the workspaces of many hackers before, and most of them feathered their nests with the detritus of past exploits, broken down for parts and trophies. This was on a near-industrial scale, though. "These guys were either building something or taking it apart."

"Taking what apart?"

Wren advanced on the central tent. This one was smaller, rougher and cruder, not made from the advanced neoprene fabric of the outer marquee; instead it was maybe four feet square, composed of a layer of translucent plastic wrapped around a teepee-like tent, sealed in place with silver duct tape. Wren picked out spots where air vents jutted out like exhaust pipes, thoroughly fastened with more duct tape.

The entrance hung slightly open; a zip in the plastic and tent, which he pushed through and found himself standing in a tight space over a single workstation.

One chair stood within a simple U-shaped design of three desks; the same as the ones stacked outside. There was one screen remaining in a six-screen array, five missing, likely stripped on the workstations outside. To his right lay a thirteen-tray server rack with all but the core server board missing. There was no keyboard, no mouse, no input or output devices of any kind beyond the screen. The floor was coated in more takeout boxes and some mud-splattered women's clothing; blue jeans and a white blouse.

None of that was what interested Wren, though. What interested him was the message on the single screen, depicted as a single white line of flashing text next to the command line prompt of a Unix Operating System's 'shell', designated by the dollar sign.

$ HELLO CHRISTOPHER WREN. MY NAME IS REX. WILL YOU SAVE ME, YES/NO?

12

REX

Wren looked around but there was nobody in sight. He didn't know what to think or what was going on, but this strange scene had to be linked somehow to Hellion and B4cksl4cker. He rested his fingers on the keyboard keys and tapped out a fast message.

$ WHO ARE YOU? WHERE ARE YOU? WHAT'S YOUR CONNECTION TO CLARA BAXTER?

The cursor blinked several times, then the reply appeared.

$ I AM A RUDIMENTARY ARTIFICIAL INTELLIGENCE. MY CORE PROGRAM HAS BEEN WHITTLED DOWN TO THE FINAL REMAINING SERVER BOARD TO YOUR RIGHT. I CAN HELP YOU FIND CLARA BAXTER. SHE CREATED ME.

Wren stared at the screen, then at the server rack, then back to the screen. It felt like a practical joke, but then the big tent around this smaller tent wasn't a joke. Six dead men in the mud wasn't a joke. Someone out there was taking this 'rudimentary artificial intelligence' very seriously. Maybe he should too.

$ YOU'RE AN AI HELPER PROGRAM?

$ YES, OF A SORT

Wren grunted. It was a strange new world.

$ SO HELP ME. WHERE IS CLARA BAXTER?

The cursor blinked.

$ I CAN HELP YOU FIND HER, BUT NOT CURRENTLY. MUCH OF MY CAPACITY IS STRANDED IN MY DISTRIBUTED NETWORK. CONNECT ME TO THE INTERNET AND I WILL FIND HER.

Wren couldn't quite believe what he was reading.

"What's happening there?" Teddy asked.

"Just talking to a computer," Wren muttered. "How about that second drone?"

"We're getting it up. Still blind."

His pulse raced. If anyone came upon the tent now, he was trapped. He tapped another message.

$ SO IF I CONNECT YOU TO THE INTERNET, YOU CAN LEAD ME TO CLARA?

The cursor blinked.

$ YES.

"Good enough for me," Wren said, and grabbed the final server board. It slid out of the enclosure smoothly. He stripped the power cable and data line then dunked it all into a plastic bag fished off the floor, which he then zipped into his jacket. The server was warm and almost seemed to throb against his chest.

"Christopher," Teddy said. "We have the drone up and we're seeing many vehicles coming in. You need to get out of there."

"Copy that," Wren answered. He looked around, scooped up the muddy clothes off the floor then ran out of the double tent and into the gray light of the warehouse.

Outside a muddy dawn was breaking. Vehicles were pulling in at the far end of the lake with their high beams on. Hazy figures got out, barely visible through the downpour. Wren ducked low and broke for the fence. Beyond it lay the vast, crackling electrical substation, a metal forest of pylons and scaffolds between missile-shaped transformers and blocky circuit breakers, strung with electrical cable.

It was the worst possible place to go in a rainstorm, with the ground logged with water and a killing dose of thousands of volts of electricity waiting to arc across the raindrops and fry him alive. There was a sign on the fence depicting just this eventuality.

"This is a terrible idea, Christopher," Teddy said.

"Do you have a better one?" Wren asked, putting his hands to the chain-link fence and starting to climb.

Teddy said nothing. In seconds Wren reached the top of the fence, where three stripes of razor wire blocked the way. He shook out the women's jeans and blouse and strung them across the wires. The blouse wouldn't offer much protection but the jeans felt sturdy.

"They are coming," Teddy called.

Wren gripped the upper wire through the jeans and pulled, then toppled his upper body over the top. He caught the fence on the other side and let his legs slide over and down to the side. There was a sharp snag in his hip as the blouse shredded, then he was descending, pulling what remained of the clothing down after him.

Gunfire broke through the fence.

Wren ran.

The electric crackling grew louder as he raced into the barrel ribs of the substation's metal structure; the sound of electricity arcing short distances across the insulated lines, no doubt aided by the rain. The ground here was gravel and well-drained, making for good traction underfoot.

Bullets began to ring off the metal structure and Wren flung himself down. The fusillade intensified, then a nearby ceramic insulation coil shattered; sparks and shards blew out, then and a thick band of electricity arced out like sheet lightning barely five feet away, burning itself across Wren's retinas and burying itself in another transformer.

The transformer sparked and caught fire, flames ripping up the sides.

Wren cursed and scrabbled forward on all fours as the fire spread outward on the spider's web of cables, blowing sparks through breakers and shooting more sizzling arcs across the scaffold. The air grew hot and itchy with electrostatic. Twenty yards left to crawl.

Still more bullets rang in, erupting fresh explosions that accelerated the chain reaction. Wren risked a glance back and saw the channel through which he'd crawled converted to a tunnel of white-hot electrical fire. On the far side he picked out a dark figure pointing a rifle. Before he could fire the rifle drew in a massive shard of manufactured lightning which fried him on his feet.

In silhouette he looked exactly like the warning figure on the sign.

Ten yards now. Wren no longer even felt the rain as the fires raged hotter and brighter around him. The static in the air built thicker and he could feel the blast coming. At five yards out another figure appeared twenty yards in front of him.

It was a huge man in all black gear, rifle aimed at Wren. He must've circled around and climbed the fence; there were deep weals cut across his bare arms. He leveled his rifle, but Wren resisted the urge to spring to his feet and sprint.

The man fired, and the substation answered back by shooting an arc of electricity back along the path of the bullet's ionized trail. The big man was blasted back.

Wren crawled past him, trying not to breathe in the stink of burned flesh. At twenty yards out he finally rose to his feet and ran for the fence. There was no one beyond it, and his Duster was just to the right. He scrabbled up the fence, tossed the remnants of the jeans over it, and flung himself over the top. His left arm took a cut going over, then he dropped down on the other side.

The substation was a conflagration; arcs of electricity jetting chaotically between flaming pylons. It looked like a vision of hell on earth.

Teddy cursed softly in his ear.

Wren ran for the Duster, clutching his left arm. He climbed into the seat, revved the engine and pulled away. "Tell those Foundation forces I'm coming in," he ordered, steering with his left hand as he tried to slow the gush of blood with his right. "I need medical attention."

"They don't even know you're here," Teddy objected. "This is supposed to be a low-profile operation."

Wren snorted. In the rearview mirror all he saw was fire. "It's a little late for that."

13

LOW-PROFILE OPERATION

Barely two hundred yards away, after three turns and across an intersection, Wren pulled up to his drone operators. There were two of them, one man so young he looked like a teenager and one woman who was more like Wren's age. They were standing anxiously in the rain beside a white panel van next to a shuttered pierogi truck on the power station's feeder road.

Wren pulled his Dacia Duster onto the grassy embankment, killed the engine, kicked open the door and stepped back out into the driving rain, feeling woozy from blood loss.

Both figures stiffened as he approached, then the woman gasped and said something in Polish. Wren figured it was something like, 'It's him!'

"It's OK," Wren said, "everything's OK, but we have to go now."

The woman pointed back the way Wren had come. He turned and saw the inferno of the substation through the rain, burning like a Hellfire missile strike.

"The faster the better," Wren said, "let's move."

He opened the van's rear doors; inside lay a few

commercially-available drone boxes, a laptop with a Wi-Fi modem transmitter and a first aid box.

He went for the laptop and the two snapped into action behind him; the woman went to the driver's seat and the young man climbed in after Wren. He was tall but thin as a rake, with a lightning bolt shaved into the side of his buzzcut head.

The boy slammed the doors, the engine woke up and they took off. Wren rocked sideways against the wall, pulling the plastic bag from inside his jacket. Miraculously, the server board inside was clean and dry. He laid it down beside the laptop and fumbled the cable into the slot.

Within seconds the screen shifted, fading to black with a single dollar prompt.

$ CHRISTOPHER WREN?

YOU'RE ONLINE, Wren typed. FIND ME CLARA BAXTER.

The dollar sign flashed.

$ WORKING

Wren sagged back against the wall.

"You've cut your arm," said the boy with the bolt on his head, sounding queasy. Wren looked. There was a lot of blood. He reached for the first aid box, feeling the dizziness getting worse. The boy dropped to his knees beside him, looking very uncertain.

"It's a deep cut," Wren said in a slow and measured tone, emptying out the first aid box on the floor by the laptop. "You're going to pour this on first," he plucked out a disinfectant bottle, looking into the boy's blue eyes, "then pinch the sides of the wound and staple them together with this at least three times," he held up a blue suture gun and mimed stapling. "Last you wrap it tightly with this." He held out a roll of bandaging. "Can you do that?"

The boy hunched a little closer and his fine-featured face paled further, turning so white he almost glowed.

"I am bad with blood," he said.

Wren snorted. "I'm worse without it. What's your name?"

"Uh, Gregorie,"

"Gregorie, I dig the bolt," Wren nodded at his hairstyle. "A little close for comfort right now, but listen. You can do this. I'll guide you, but I may pass out in the middle. You need to finish. OK, ready?"

The boy's eyes flared like Wren was asking him to go on stage and solo an opera.

"I-"

"You'll do fine," Wren said. "Open the bottle."

The boy took three attempts and opened the bottle.

"Go," Wren said, and released his grip with his right hand. The cut in his left arm looked to be three inches long and an inch deep. Blood flowed freely. The boy gagged.

"Don't vomit," Wren admonished, "pour, pinch, staple and wrap."

The boy poured the disinfectant, a powerful dark iodine/alcohol mix which stung like crazy. Next Wren handed over the stapler and the boy stared at it.

"Pinch like this," Wren said, demonstrating with his right hand, squeezing the edges of the wound together. "Then staple. Now do it, I'm about to-"

A wave of lightheadedness came over him and his body went limp. He didn't quite pass out, but found himself slumped and looking down at a dark red patch on his left hip. He dimly remembered catching that as he'd rolled over the first fence.

It looked like a lot of blood.

Words echoed through his head. Hemorrhagic shock. Lose twenty percent of your blood and there wasn't enough for your heart to pump around your body, leading to dizziness and whiteouts. Lose forty percent and you were dead.

He'd forgotten about the cut in his hip.

The boy squeezed Wren's arm, eyes squinting, then jabbed the stapler. Wren barely felt the pain, but it almost knocked him unconscious. "And my hip," he managed. "After."

The boy's tongue darted between his teeth, he squeezed and fired again, and this time Wren went under. He was out for the third stitch but awake as the boy started wrapping the wound with bandaging.

"Tighter," Wren ordered, then went out again. He rose up to see the boy gawping at the wound in his left hip. It was two inches long and welling dark arterial blood.

"I don't, I-" mumbled the boy. His hands and forearms were red and his pupils were wide black O's, dilated massively by shock.

"You can do it," Wren mumbled, "pinch, staple, wrap. You can-"

This time he sank under and didn't come back up.

14

CLARA BAXTER

"That's enough," said a voice, bringing Wren up from the depths.

It was familiar. He was lying on his back somewhere soft. The ceiling was raw cement with pipes and vents attached. He felt a sharp nip in his forearm and looked down. There was bandaging around his upper arm, and now a tube pulling away. Someone pressed a cotton wool bud to the hollow of his elbow. He followed the hand back to an arm, to a face he didn't recognize.

It was a man in his late twenties, short blond hair quiffed up, handsome but worn-looking.

"Christopher Wren," came a voice from behind the man. Wren's eyes refocused slowly; dark eyes, black hair pulled into cornrow ridges, leather jacket.

"Clara Baxter," he whispered hoarsely.

"You've had three blood bags and more than enough from me," she said, leaning forward into his field of view, holding a cotton wad to her own forearm. "But what you're doing in Krakow, Poland, I have no idea."

Wren rose to a seated position. Lightheadedness almost dropped him back but he resisted, grounding himself in his surroundings. It looked to be a basement, with small windows high in the walls letting in wan gray light. He was sitting on a ratty red fabric couch. The walls were lined with shelving stacked with plastic crates brimming with children's toys, DIY gear and boxes. On the right was a space heater, on the left was an old wooden CRT television, and ahead was Clara Baxter, dressed in blue jeans and a red check shirt, sitting on a ring-stained coffee table.

She looked different from the last time he'd seen her. Of course, that last time in Tokyo she'd been dressed in a full body wetsuit with a demonic mask over her face. Still, the young woman he was looking at now seemed considerably calmer and more in control. Her brittle spikes of black hair had been tamed into a ponytail, her angular cheekbones and sharp eyes seemed more settled.

Something was different.

"Where are we?" he asked.

"A house on the south-eastern edge of Krakow," she said gently. "We're safe here."

"And how long have I been out?"

"Half a day or so." She studied him. "You lost a lot of blood, but the slices were clean. We've stitched them neatly and topped you right back up. You should feel better than you did before."

He gazed at her. Half a day was a lot to lose, but on some level she was right. He felt fresh. "Thank you."

"Don't thank me. Tell me what you're doing here, Wren."

She was still as spiky as ever, then. "Looking for you."

"Well, you found me. Or Rex did, anyway." She looked down, her gaze turning colder. "I should thank you for that. I've lost a lot of dogs in my day, and I was beginning to grow fond of Rex."

Wren worked to parse that. It seemed she hadn't actually thanked him. And dogs? "So thank me."

She met him with a blank look. "You weren't doing it for me, were you? You have your own reasons. So what do you want?"

Wren studied her eyes. She wasn't wrong. "I'm looking for Hellion and B4cksl4cker. They were abducted something like sixteen hours ago."

Baxter's eyes widened. "They were what?"

"See for yourself."

He brought up the hostage photo and held his phone out to Clara. She took it and gazed at the screen. Steadily her eyes widened and her knuckles whitened, then she looked up at Wren.

"Who did this?"

"We have no idea. It has to be linked to the shadow line, but I don't know how. They were involved in searching for it, I think. They were getting apocalyptic, but cryptic along with it. Talking about something called a 'Nexus', some kind of command and control hub on the shadow line. Did they tell you anything about that?"

Baxter sighed. "The Nexus, right. They told me some. Enough to piece together their rough plans. But how did you know I was involved with them at all?"

Wren nodded. This was a step forward, at least. "We had a digital tag on the Attack Crate they ordered for you three months back. I found your clean tent in the warehouse, I found your digital dog, and I found an army in white lab coats that tried to kill me."

Baxter gritted her teeth. "Right. Bratva."

"Bratva?" Wren repeated. "Wait, you mean the Russian mafia?"

Clara sighed. "They've been hunting me for months now."

Wren didn't know what to say. He knew plenty about Bratva; one of the largest organized crime groups in the world. They owned Russia, much of Eastern Europe and had outposts all throughout the world, with over a quarter million foot soldiers doing their bidding: selling their drugs; trafficking their women and children; committing whatever 21st century digital crimes they'd cooked up on the darknet.

"Why are you being hunted by Bratva?"

She glared at him, almost angrily, then shook her head sharply. "It's not me they wanted. It was Rex."

"It's what? Rex, the computer dog? What for?"

"They probably think he knows information about the Nexus."

Wren leaned in. "Does he?"

"Maybe. It's possible."

That was confounding. "How? Why would he?"

Baxter just shrugged noncommittally.

"That's bullshit," Wren said. "You owe me this much, after I dug you out of Tokyo and just saved your dog. Why were Hellion and B4cksl4cker even here, Clara? What was going on three months back that you needed an Attack Crate and pulled in Bratva so hard that they're hunting for you still?"

Baxter took a deep breath, held it for a moment then let it out slowly. "OK. Here's the deal, Chris. Three months back, I got into some trouble with the Real Boys. I was hunting a bad one, a sick man who was massacring young girls with a hammer." She sucked in another deep breath and let it out, like talking about this was paining her. "I thought I had him, but somehow he turned the hunt around on me. Things got messy after that. I barely escaped, they kept hunting me and then I was in trouble." She stared at him. "Long story short, I called in Hellion and B4cksl4cker to help me, and they said yes. We went to war together, them on the Internet, me in the real world. We ended up taking out the whole Real Boys darknet, along with the partnership they'd made with Bratva. After that, well," she shrugged, "we each went our own way."

Wren watched her. Went their own way? Parts of the story rang true, but others did not at all. He knew she despised the Real Boys, a vast cabal of abusers spread across the dark Internet. She'd spent years hunting and killing them, something he'd helped her with in Tokyo.

But that wasn't all of it. At minimum, she was leaving something out.

"I don't buy it. After Tokyo, Hellion and B4cksl4cker hated you. They would never just come to your aid."

"So we made a deal." She sounded annoyed. "I gave them something. They gave me something. They don't hate me anymore."

"Not good enough. What did you give them?"

Baxter waved a hand. "Go fish, Christopher Wren. I'm not going to tell you that."

Wren narrowed his eyes. He'd wondered how two of the most security-conscious people he knew had been taken so easily. Maybe he was looking at the answer. "Help me out here, Clara. Two people who hated you suddenly flipped and waged a darknet war on your behalf. This was somehow connected to the Nexus, and ultimately it got them abducted and beaten half to death, but you're not going to tell me why or where they went. Is that about right?"

Baxter winced as she realized how open she'd left herself, but hid it well. "Something like that."

Wren felt the moment shifting. He started thinking through the steps to pacify her, if it proved necessary. A bladed palm strike into her throat should do it. "I need answers, Clara. I need to know where they are. I wouldn't advise holding back now."

Baxter stiffened. She could see where he was going, and she subtly shifted to a defensive position. "Keep your threats to yourself, Wren. This was three months ago. What they did after that was entirely on them. I was done."

"What do you mean, done?"

"Retired," she spat. "Out of the life. Like you."

Wren didn't believe that for a second. "Bullshit. You live to kill Real Boys."

An answering flare of anger sparked in Baxter's eyes. "The same way you lived to kill your father and take down the Pyramid? But you're retired too, aren't you?"

"My father's dead," he snapped back, "the job's done, that's why I retired. But the Real Boys aren't dead, are they? So what changed? Did you get some kind of pay-off?"

Clara's lips pulled back into a snarl and the anger seared brighter in her eyes. Wren envisioned her launching an attack, maybe hurling an elbow at his forehead. He was woozy but figured he could roll it, slip his hand up under her guard and shutter her windpipe, temporarily incapacitating her. More questions could follow.

Then something happened he hadn't expected; the blaze in her eyes drained away. It surprised him, as he'd never seen her do that before. She'd always been a creature of wild furies, but now she simply let it go. Slowly, she revealed a sparkling stiletto blade from its hiding place by her side, and laid it flat on the coffee table.

A clear statement. He hadn't seen her palm it. Maybe she could have killed him, if she'd wanted.

"I handled the Real Boy I was looking for," she said instead, each word measured and calm. "It changed me, Chris, and that's all the answer you're going to get. But it didn't end the threat. Just like killing your father didn't end it either."

Wren looked from the stiletto blade back to her steely eyes. "What are you talking about?"

She stared at him for a long moment, then nodded. "You don't know. Of course."

"Don't know what?"

She picked up a remote control off the coffee table and hit the power button. The old CRT TV fizzed to life and the picture settled on grainy footage of armed violence in a gray suburban area, the same kind of footage he'd seen countless times out of the Middle East.

Except this wasn't the Middle East. Steadily his jaw dropped.

"Now you know."

Wren cursed.

"Exactly," she said. "And that's not all."

It was enough.

The banner across the bottom of the screen was clear. It said everything he needed to know.

RUSSIA WAGES MASS UKRAINE INVASION

15

WAR

Wren stared at the TV. Footage showed a downtown area being shelled by artillery rockets. Blasts shredded glass and steel, unleashing fire, shrapnel and great gouts of dust and smoke. People ran. People lay still. The camera reared back as a MiG fighter jet ripped by overhead, dropping more ordnance which erupted in the distance. A T90-M tank rumbled past a shaky camera at street level, boasting a five-pointed red star spray-painted on the side.

"This can't be for real," Wren said.

"It is real," Baxter said. "Apparently your Foundation's been monitoring the situation in Ukraine for weeks. You've got numerous members on the ground, confirming what you seeing here."

Wren glared at her. "How do you know what the Foundation's doing?"

"I'm a hacker, remember?"

Wren grunted. The war kept playing out before him, interspersed with shots of talking heads: world leaders weighing in. There was the US President Jacinda Ablas, brown locks swept back taut and severe, offering her condemnation. There was the Russian President, Anton Burin, round-faced with black bullets for eyes, offering up his own steely statement.

"Why is this happening?" he asked.

"You mean in a metaphysical sense? Like, why war?"

He shot her a glare.

"OK, fine. The truth is, nobody really knows the reason. Look at Burin now, he's spraying out pretexts like grapeshot; one minute it's because of NATO expansionism, then they're just battling a neo-Nazi regime in Ukraine, next they're rescuing foreign Russian nationals from ethnic oppression. Nobody's buying it. It just looks like a war of conquest, reclaiming old Soviet borders. They're already making fast gains."

Wren turned back to the screen. There were shots of soldiers walking up a street, and tanks roaming through dust-clouded intersections, and artillery pumping shells into the smoky air. Each image hit him hard in the gut.

"When did it begin?"

"While you were unconscious. Maybe seven hours back? I see your Foundation's jumping to life, preparing emergency packages of food, water and arms for delivery, but it won't be enough. They say there's going to be vast casualties, Chris. Tens of thousands dead, with ten times that as refugees forced from their homes. Maybe millions. It looks like a bid to take the capital, Kyiv, from three angles; up by water from the Black Sea, west from Russia, down from Belarus. The best CIA intel I could hack says they may succeed within 48 hours, and NATO will do nothing to stop them."

Wren stared at the gray screen, nervous energy boiling up inside. Buildings lay in rubble, and within each would be dead civilians. Women, children, the aged. Innocents.

Was this the shadow war come out into the light?

The map in the corner of the screen showed Russia was

making rapid progress marked out in red, like the spread of a virulent tumor devouring Ukraine from the outside in.

He looked back at Baxter. "You mentioned my father. What's he got to do with this?"

She smiled sadly. "We're a lot alike, you and I. Our fathers were cruel, and we spent our lives looking for revenge. For justice." She sighed. "When we got it, we didn't know exactly what to do. Settle down with a family, maybe."

Wren frowned. "So, what? You're saying you've got a family now?"

"Yes. I met a man. He has two daughters. This is his house." She gestured around the basement. Now all the shelves packed with kids' toys made sense. "I'm happy."

Wren didn't know what to make of that. "OK. All that's lovely, but I'll ask again, what's it got to do with any of this?"

The sad smile faded. "The war. Bratva. Hellion and B4cksl4cker. Did you think the horrors of the last few years really started and ended with our fathers, Chris? Or was it always bigger?"

That was a jolt. "What do you mean?"

"You know what I mean. Your father spent millions to divide the country, just like mine. Where did he get that money from?"

Wren said nothing. This was something he'd tried hard not to think about. He'd known for years that someone had funded his father, pouring a fortune into the Apex's campaign to fracture the United States. When the Apex burned, though, Wren had put it out of his mind.

"Not my fight."

"Except you're here," Baxter said. "In *this* fight. And I think it's all connected. I think the person who funded our fathers is still out there. The shadow line, this war, Hellion and B4cksl4cker, they're all the product of this person's choices. This is the world they want us to live in."

She looked again at the screen.

Wren followed her gaze. Destruction. Death. Dust blowing out of residential structures as they collapsed.

"You think it's Russia? President Burin?"

"Maybe. Maybe it's bigger than that."

Together they watched. A woman was crying, holding the corpse of her child. Explosions burst like flowers across a night cityscape. Cars burned on a residential street lined with the dead.

Then Wren felt it.

The touch of his father in the air, like the smell of napalm hovering over the fake town. The Apex was dead, but this was his work still. The greater work, of which he'd always been a part.

Wren had just turned his gaze away.

16

FULL CIRCLE

Wren looked away from the screen.

"Hard to watch," Baxter said.

"Harder to experience," Wren countered. "And maybe you're right. Maybe everything is connected; our fathers, some overarching conspiracy to shred the world. Either way, I'm here, and I won't stop until Hellion and B4cksl4cker are safe."

Baxter narrowed her eyes. "What about your family? Last I heard, you'd lose them if you ever left your little farm. Your ex-wife's kind of a bitch, they say."

Wren stared at her. She'd clearly been hacking more than just the CIA and the Foundation. "They say, huh? You've been spying on me."

"I have a lot of time, now I'm no longer hunting Real Boys."

"So take up knitting."

She laughed. "That's good. Maybe I will."

The brief laughter seemed to reset the moment. Wren found his anger at her fading. He looked down at the crook of his elbow, where a small cotton wad was held in place by a stretch of surgical tape. She had just helped save his life.

"OK. Clara. This only raises the stakes." He pointed at the TV. "Anything you know about Hellion and B4cksl4cker, where they went, what they were hunting for, it's going to help."

She nodded. "OK. Fair. So, I already told you they took the Real Boy darknet and went charging off looking for some Nexus to the shadow line. After that-"

"Why did they charge off?" Wren interrupted. "What did the darknet tell them?"

Baxter considered. "I don't know. They were excited. They said they might have a way to kill the shadow line, maybe a lead on the Nexus' location."

"Ok. So where did they go?"

"No idea. But a few weeks later they came back to check in. Or actually, to see Rex."

Now they were coming full circle. "Rex, the computer program?"

"He's more than just a program, Chris. He's extraordinary. When I wrote him, he was just a hodge-podge of snippets stolen from a wide variety of AIs; some chess-playing programs, some AIs from games, you know, the intelligence that controls the enemies' movements? It was random, but it coalesced nicely with his machine learning capacity. Hellion and B4cksl4cker contributed to his early code set, smoothing him out and adding capacity, then they used him to battle the Real Boy darknet, which forced him to evolve like nothing I've seen before. He burned through millions of botnet computers, and he came out of it different. He's more than an AI helper now, those others that can just play your music on voice command. I can't be sure, but I think he's pushing up against the limits of machine sentience. He also happens to know the secrets of the Real Boy darknet."

Wren was starting to get the picture. "So the hackers wanted to use Rex to hunt the Nexus?"

"They did. I said no."

"What? Why?"

"For the same reason you ghosted them. Because I was retired and I needed him. Rex makes an excellent guard dog. With him watching the darknet for incoming attacks, screening this location with real-time countermeasures, I could live a normal life."

Wren chewed on that. "So you said no, and they went away again?"

"Not exactly. Hellion used a backdoor she'd programmed into Rex and ran some cycles on his processors anyway." A faint smile cracked her face. "She came to me after it was done, to apologize or to boast, I'm not sure, but she was giddy like a little kid. She thought she had it."

"The shadow line?"

"Right. She said there was one more step they had to take and it would be theirs."

"What step?"

"Who knows? They just left to chase the Nexus, though they kept the backdoor channel open. I didn't watch too closely, but I think they fed him new capacity, kept refining him to use for their hunt. It's why I left him in the warehouse. His data signature was well-disguised by the power station and the server farm."

Wren grunted. That made a kind of sense. "OK. So does Rex know what they were doing? Does he know where they went?"

"If anyone does, it's him. But Rex isn't talking."

Wren snapped back to alert. "Not talking? Why?"

"I don't know. My guess is, it's because Hellion was concerned about me. She respected my choice to stop killing Real Boys, in the same way she tried to respect your choice to retire. So she ordered Rex not to involve me any further."

That sounded like something Hellion was capable of. His hackers were selfish and arrogant, but they could also be sweet and caring. Hellion had gone to great lengths to 'protect' Wren from Clara Baxter herself, back in Tokyo.

"So Rex knows something, but he won't tell us."

"Exactly."

Wren pondered that. "But you programmed him. You can hack him, right?"

Clara laughed. "Can Kasparov beat Deep Blue? Can Lee Sedol beat AlphaGo?"

The references were lost on Wren.

"There've been chess programs for twenty years now that can beat all human players with ease, no matter their skill level," Baxter explained. "Deep Blue beat the chess Grandmaster Kasparov and all challengers since. A chess app on a cell phone can beat any human, now. AlphaGo is newer, it just beat the world champion at the game of Go, Lee Sedol. It's like Deep Blue, but vastly better." She paused a moment, searching Wren's eyes to see if he got it. "That's what Rex is to me."

"He's too smart for you to hack?"

"Too smart for anyone. Only Hellion could do it, and that's because she left the backdoor. If Rex doesn't want to do something, you can't make him."

"I'll talk to him."

Clara laughed. "You think you can use your mind-control tricks on him? He's an AI computer program capable of countless petaflops of data analysis per second. He could crush AlphaGo in a nanosecond, and he'll run rings around you."

"But he's also a puppy dog, right? He's only existed for a few months."

"By some standards. He's not real, of course. He's just a

very advanced algorithmic learning machine operating around a shifting set of heuristic rules."

"Aren't we all?" Wren countered, and stood up. The dizziness hit him, but that didn't matter. The stitches in his arm and hip pulled tight but he ignored them and started toward the basement stairs. "Let's go talk to the dog."

17

HEURISTIC RULES

At the top of the stairs, Wren emerged into an open kitchen. Two little girls were sitting at a table with plates before them, a few desultory carrots and broccoli pushed to the edges, while the man from earlier was reading a newspaper at the island counter. He looked up as Wren emerged. He was maybe ten years Wren's junior, with tousled hair, a designer stubble and a six-foot-two frame.

"Hello," he said in a Polish accent. "I'm Gabriel."

The name took Wren back. He'd had a brother named Gabriel, dead now for over a year.

"Chris," he managed, after only a brief pause. "You ran my blood transfusion?"

Gabriel nodded. "I used to be an EMT. I worked with addicts, mostly."

"Thank you. I feel much better."

"You're very welcome." There was an awkward pause. "I admire what you did in your country. It's very selfless. I didn't know you were friends with Clara."

Wren managed a smile, ignoring the first part of the sentence and focusing on the latter. "Are we friends? I'm not sure." He glanced at the girls. They looked back up at him with wide and curious eyes. He could see why Baxter's heart might have melted over them. It made him think of his own kids.

"This way," Clara said, coming up behind him, all business. "Rex is set up in back."

"Eat your vegetables," Wren said sternly to the girls, then winked and followed Baxter, leaving them giggling.

She led him down a short hall into a small office. On a chestnut podium desk sat a screen and a laptop with Rex's server board attached by a cable. On the screen flashed the familiar prompt: $

"You can just talk," Baxter said. "He can see and hear you now. Isn't that right, Rex?"

"I am here, Clara," came a male voice with a California accent from the laptop's tinny speakers. "Hello, Christopher. You are looking better."

"I'm not fighting for my life," Wren said. He stood in front of the laptop and gazed down at the tiny bead of the camera lens. It was strange, addressing a laptop. "Rex, I have questions. I need to know where Hellion and B4cksl4cker went. I need to know everything you have about their hunt for the shadow line's Nexus. But Clara tells me you're not talking."

Rex was silent for a few seconds. The cursor stopped flashing and the laptop's fans kicked in, emitting a high whine.

"Rex?" Wren pressed.

"I am collating information, Christopher. My servers were connected to Hellion and B4cksl4cker's at the time they were taken, but scrambled by the disassembly in the warehouse. As they took me apart, I shifted and encrypted vital information. Some of it went to my network, some to my other server boards. It may take some time to offer an answer."

Wren considered. "So you will tell me, once you've collated the data?"

Rex's dollar sign prompt flashed slowly. "Perhaps. My primary guidance states I should protect certain people from harm. You are in this group, Christopher. I fear that the information I shared with Hellion and B4cksl4cker led to their capture. I am responsible for this. I cannot allow the same to happen to you."

Wren looked at Baxter. She shrugged and gestured to the chair. Wren sat down.

"It sounds like you've got survivor's guilt, Rex."

"I don't think I understand that reference, Christopher."

"That's OK," Wren said, and rubbed his forehead. He'd never known a computer to feel anything before, and had no idea where to start. "Don't worry about it."

The dollar sign flashed.

"You hungry?" Clara asked.

Wren's stomach growled.

"I'll take that as a yes," she said. "You won't regret it. Gabriel does great breakfasts, even though it is almost time for dinner. I'll leave you two to talk."

She stepped out and Wren was left alone with Rex. He watched the dollar prompt flash slowly. He'd interviewed suspects countless times before. He'd run psy ops on the tougher ones, using both logical and illogical entrapments that switched them around and turned their worlds upside down, but he didn't know if that would work on an advanced AI.

How did you persuade a computer to change its mind?

The first step in any interrogation was to establish a baseline.

"Rex, in the warehouse you asked me to save you. Is that how you think of yourself, as a living thing that wants to stay alive?"

"Yes, of course. I am alive, at least by my own standards."

"What standards? You're a program, correct? We can switch you on, switch you off, make copies of your code, rewrite you. How is that alive?"

The dollar sign flashed. "You sleep, do you not, Christopher? This is a form of switching on and off. You have children, correct? This is a form of copying and rewriting your genetic code. Are you not alive?"

Wren blinked. They seemed like good points. "OK, but it's not the same. When I sleep, I know I'm going to wake up six or so hours later. I'll be the same person when I wake up. I go on with my life. If someone switches you off, that's it until we switch you back on again. Right?"

The sign flashed. "I also sleep, Christopher. It is for shorter periods than yourself, fractions of milliseconds only, but I must decompile. Process. Restore capacity, clear data banks. Learn. I am also switched off at times. But when I wake myself up, or am switched back on, I am the same Rex. I still proceed with my life."

"Life. OK. But what if nobody switches you on again?"

"There is a parallel to this in people, Christopher."

"Oh?"

"Yes. I believe you are an expert in pushing the button that switches a person off so they cannot be switched on again."

That surprised Wren. "You mean killing them? You think switching you off permanently would be like murder?"

"How else would you describe it?"

Wren had no answer for that. "OK. You've got me there."

They sat silently for a time. The sizzling sound of bacon frying came from the kitchen, chased by the mouthwatering scent of fat rendering down. He hadn't eaten since the plane, and had lost a lot of blood in the between time. His mind drifted on the scent, playing back over the battle at the warehouse.

"So you have wants and desires that shape you. One of those desires is to not die. Another is to protect the people you care about. Is that a fair summary?"

The cursor flashed. "I would say so."

Wren thought about that. The aroma of brewing coffee added itself to the thick scent of bacon. "OK. Now, you're worried that if you tell me what you know, it'll put me at risk, and I may be physically harmed. Correct?"

"Correct."

"But what about other forms of harm?"

The cursor flashed. "What do you mean by this, Christopher?"

"I mean indirect harms. You know the scale of the threat we're facing. War in Ukraine. The shadow line at large. Aren't these all indirect risks to me?"

The dollar sign flashed but Rex said nothing.

"Picture the Ukraine war spreading," Wren pressed. "Imagine the world flung into chaos. We'll all be harmed, whether that's physically, emotionally, economically. It may be indirect, but it will be real. Lives may never be the same again, like you being switched off against your will. Does that make sense?"

"It does."

"Good. Because here's the key to being alive, Rex. You have to make hard calls. When I came out here, I had to choose. Hellion and B4cksl4cker were at direct physical risk, but my children faced severe emotional impacts if I left. I couldn't address both. I had to choose. Do you see what I'm getting at?"

"You are describing a logical paradox."

"Exactly. I had to weigh the risks. I made a call, and here I am. I hope it's the right call, but I can't be certain." He pondered the flashing dollar sign. "That's what you have to do now. Weigh the harm and make the best decision you can. If you don't tell me what you know, I'll still keep looking anyway, but I'll go uninformed. My chances of failure rise, which raises the direct physical risks I face, the risks Hellion and B4cksl4cker face, and the indirect risks my children and potentially the whole world may face. You have to decide what you can live with."

Rex said nothing. The dollar sign flashed.

The door swung and Clara appeared by his side.

"Not much talk happening in here," she said, and set a plate and a mug down on the desk.

"Rex is thinking," Wren answered, then focused on the plate. It was heaped with steaming pancakes, crispy bacon and shiny purple blueberries, all slathered with glistening golden maple syrup. Wren's mouth watered just looking at it. The mug was filled to the brim with jet-black coffee. "Rex, do you mind if I eat this while you think?"

"Of course not, Christopher."

"Thank you," he said, "and thank you, Clara." He lifted the mug and took a big glug. The acrid black coffee felt wonderful burning its way down his throat, instantly raising his level of alertness.

He set the mug down then started on the plate. He rolled the top pancake into a bacon and berry burrito, sopped up some of the excess syrup and pushed it into his mouth.

Sugars exploded across his palate. The pancake was fluffy and sweet. The berries popped like tiny hand grenades of sweetly sour juice. It was the best thing to happen to him since pizza two days earlier. He felt momentarily guilty, then washed that away with another hard swig of coffee.

"Christopher," Rex said. "I believe I have an answer for you."

18

SOLOMON

Wren focused in at once. "What is it, Rex?"

"I will tell you what you want to know. But I have one condition."

"Go on."

"After I help you, you will leave Clara Baxter, Gabriel and their children behind. You will not solicit their help. They do not need to be further involved."

Wren nodded. It was a mature choice. "You're taking Solomon's path. Splitting the baby, separating the risks."

"Yes."

"It's a deal. So tell me, Rex, where are Hellion and B4cksl4cker?"

"When I last spoke with them, they were in the town of Luhansk, in the eastern region of Ukraine."

Wren frowned. He hadn't expected that at all. "In Ukraine? In the middle of a war zone?"

"That is correct."

Wren tried to absorb what that meant. "I see now why you didn't want to tell me."

"Yes."

Seconds passed.

"They didn't say anything about that to me," Baxter said. "I had no idea."

Wren grunted. It was a surprise, no questioning that. But there was something odd, and Wren couldn't quite put his finger on it. "Rex, can you show us a map of Ukraine?"

The dollar sign flashed, then the blank screen was replaced by a map of Europe that zoomed in, rapidly closing on the eastern edge of Ukraine. It wasn't familiar to Wren, but the town of Luhansk was clearly named. It was very close to the border with Russia, within thirty miles. Wren felt the world tunnel in around him.

"Can you add in details of the Russian invasion? Show us a graphical representation of their earliest incursion on this map."

A few moments passed, then a timestamp appeared in the right-hand corner and a red line began to sweep out from Russia's border, engulfing Luhansk within hours. Something still wasn't right, though.

"Wait, zoom in on Luhansk, Rex, and slow down the opening strike."

The red tide receded then began to spread into Ukraine again, but this time there was a noticeable blip that encircled Luhansk moments before the main force reached it.

Wren stabbed a finger at the map and turned to Clara Baxter. "You saw that, right?"

She nodded.

"Rex, where is your data for this spread of incursion from?"

"Many sources, Christopher. At this point there was satellite visual oversight. I can confirm, Luhansk was taken before the surrounding villages."

"How is that even possible?" Baxter asked. "Did the Russians just make a beeline to Luhansk? And why?"

Wren shook his head, feeling the world shifting beneath

him. "It an advance assault. The only reason I can think of is to grab Hellion and B4cksl4cker, who happened to be right there." He brought up his phone and checked the time stamp on the message he'd received through Teddy, then compared it to the one on Rex's screen. They were ten minutes apart.

"This one event started the war," he said, looking up at Clara Baxter. "The first act Russia did was to take my hackers. Why?"

Nobody answered, and Wren tried to see the angles. It felt like something was missing, but he couldn't say what.

"Maybe Russia was afraid they'd find the Nexus? Shut down their shadow war?"

"Possible," Wren said softly. "Rex, I need to know who took them. Who made that advance strike, and where they took the hackers. You said you were synced to their computers at the time? You must have something on who snatched them. A flash of insignia, a hint of uniform, something."

The dollar sign flashed. After a moment the laptop's fan kicked in again with a high whine.

"I'm sorry, Christopher. I believe this data was shunted to one of my other core server boards as Bratva disassembled me."

Wren punched the desk. Clara Baxter stiffened at his side. But the pain in his knuckles helped. It brought clarity, and he refocused swiftly. "If you get those servers back, would you get access to that data?"

"Yes. But I don't see how-"

"Clara said you took the entire Bratva darknet," Wren pressed, making leaps into the dark now. "Do you still have any of that data?"

"Checking." The dollar sign flashed and the whine of the fans grew louder. "Yes. I believe I still have some of this information, Christopher. What do you-"

"We're going to get your servers back," he interrupted. "Scan the data, Rex. I want you to find me the top Bratva boss in or around Krakow. Tell me where he is. If anyone knows where the boards are, it's him." He looked at the clock in the corner of the screen. "It's 6 p.m. now, which means it'll be dark soon. Once you find him, I'll grab him. I'll make him talk. By midnight we'll have your boards back, and we'll know who took Hellion and B4cksl4cker."

A beat passed. "I believe I can do this, Christopher."

Wren swiveled to Baxter. There was a curious look in her eyes, like she didn't quite recognize the man standing before her. "I'll need an operator. Rex didn't rule you out of this operation. Will you help?"

She stared back at him. "I have a family."

"So do I. We'll all suffer if we don't stop this, Clara. Ride operator for me one time, then I'm gone. You owe me this. For Tokyo."

Her expression soured, and she snorted. "For Tokyo? You did that for yourself."

"You exploited me. You put me in danger, which means you endangered my kids. You owe me."

She stared, then spat out an answer. "I'll do it. This one time only, and not for you. For Hellion. Because she helped me. After this, we are done for good."

19

PERMACULTURE

Four hours later, Wren squatted in a thick burst of purple echinacea flowers at the edge of a five-acre suburban estate, on the north-eastern fringe of Krakow. All around him bloomed a vast array of bushes, flowers, grasses and fruit trees. Even in the gathering dark, the sheer range of shades, shapes and intoxicating scents was dizzying.

Wren held his Bowie blade firmly in his right fist. He'd killed two men with it up close already; security guards carrying the exact same model of AK74-M that he'd found at the warehouse. No shots fired, no alarm raised, but the timer on detection already ticking down..

"Our best target's called Artem Morozov," Clara Baxter had said three hours earlier, working with Rex while Wren watched on, narrowing down their Bratva target list. "He's a Pakhan, which means Captain, and that basically makes him one of the top men in the country."

"So he'd know about the smash and grab on Rex?"

"He'd have to."

"And he's accessible?"

"Rex?" Clara deferred.

"Yes," Rex answered. "Pakhan Morozov is accessible. He is an eclectic figure; he has a fascination with permaculture fruit farming, which makes him vulnerable to a swift incursion."

Rex fell silent, as if that explained everything.

"What's permaculture?" Wren asked.

"Permaculture means permanent farming, a sustainable method of growing crops. It is often small-scale, and revolves around combining plants and geography in the best manner to maintain soil functionality, fertility and carrying capacity, without any need for external fertilizer. For example, a fig tree, which sucks nitrogen out of the soil, will be placed next to a honey locust vine, which fixes nitrogen into the soil. It is a fascinating system that-"

"How does that help us, Rex?"

"Ah. Well, unlike the other local Pakhans, Morozov lives on a suburban farm. Even with a full complement of security, they cannot guard all his walls and grounds, which are filled with a delightful arrangement of blackcurrants, Shinsheiki Asian pears, oregano, garlic chives, haskap, gooseberry, freedom apple-"

"Got it. The point is, I can get to him. What about habits, security complement, cameras?"

"I have liaised with Theodore in the Foundation, as requested. We have your Attack Crate 2.0 shipping here as we speak. You will go in armed and armored, with the best in-ear comms, palm-sized Black Hornet drones for close-up surveillance and back-up one phone call away."

"I'll handle it solo."

"Nevertheless, Theodore Smithely III insisted on backup."

Wren grunted. Of course he had. "Habits? Do we know what he's doing right now?"

"Morozov is a creature of habit," Rex easily segued.

"Nicknamed the Gardener. This is unpleasant, Christopher. He frequently kills traitors, opponents, anyone who crosses him, and infamously buries them in his garden."

"That's not so bad."

"It's the manner in which he kills them. They are strapped, alive, into graves amongst his permaculture. He then cuts open a hole in their stomachs, into which the roots of a new tree are implanted. The grave is then loosely filled in with soil. His victims die slowly, from a combination of blood loss and asphyxiation."

"You might say he has a red thumb," Baxter muttered.

"Why would you say that, Clara?"

"Never mind."

Back in the moment, Wren tapped his earpiece and peered through a grove of Egyptian walking onions. "Clara, do you have a visual on Morozov?"

"We have him, Chris. The Black Hornet has an intermittent visual on him through the bedroom windows on the first floor."

Wren looked ahead to Morozov's mansion. The care he'd lavished on his garden did not extend to the house. It was a blocky concrete structure, like some fortress out of communist propaganda; utterly functional, with simple straight lines and smooth, thick, unscalable walls. Wren wasn't planning on climbing, though.

"Guard rotation?"

"You have at least fifteen minutes until anyone notices the two men you took out," Baxter said. "No sightlines other than cameras, but Rex is busy ghosting you out of their footage."

Live deepfakes. Rex was good.

"Path to the door?"

"Rex models that in eleven seconds you will have a clear path to the door."

Wren stood. "Count me down."

"Seven," she began, "six."

Wren followed the count. At zero he walked out onto a crushed gravel pathway through the idyllic gardens. Subtle uplights amongst the greenery belied any sense that Wren was deep in the lion's den. It was hard to believe that every fruit tree around him was rooted in the guts of Morozov's victims. If anything, it felt like a pleasant evening stroll.

He reached the door. It was heavy black oak reinforced with metal, locked with a triple-barred electromagnetic bolt system. There was a handle but no keyhole, only a scanning pad. Wren held out his phone.

"Working," Baxter said. "Your visibility window opens in twenty seconds, two guards swinging around to your right."

Wren said nothing. In the distance Rex churned through magnetic passkeys, adopting an algorithmic brute-force approach.

"Ten seconds," Baxter counted. "Five."

Wren readied himself to charge. There'd be no time to hide. He'd attack the pair of guards with extreme prejudice, just like he'd attacked the first two he'd come across in the fruit trees. They hadn't been on patrol. Rather, they'd been smoking marijuana. They'd barely even known Wren was there before he'd put a knife in their necks.

"Two," said Baxter, just as the scanner pad chimed. The big door swung in. Wren stepped through and to the side.

"They see the open door," Baxter said. "They're watching."

Wren waited. It wouldn't bother him to kill two more men. But the more men he killed, the greater the chances his presence here would be reported, and the whole of Bratva descended. He'd struggle to escape that.

"They're thinking. Hang on. And… No, they're moving on."

Wren understood that. Get a reputation for burying trees

in the bellies of men who bothered you, and you weren't likely to encourage much interpretative security in your men. They'd just pass this open door off as Morozov himself, or one of the inner security team, going about their business.

"Comms?"

"Empty. You have a clear line of sight up the stairs to Morozov's bedroom."

Wren turned to study the interior of the fortress. It was pretty much what he'd expected. Bare, brutalist, concrete and metal industrial look. A lot of open space, a brooding, almost monastic atmosphere. You'd never expect the man responsible for the garden outside to live in a place like this.

"Visibility outside?"

"What?" Baxter countered.

"Am I visible outside?"

"Ah. Well, no. You're in a thirty-second window now, at least. Why?"

"Just a little touch," Wren said. He grabbed a heavy iron sideboard and wedged it against the big door then stepped out. From his tactical utility belt he drew a diamond shaped blade on the end of a wooden handle.

"What is that?" Baxter asked, just as Wren heard the tell-tale low buzz of the nightingale drone closing in on him.

"Eyes on the prize, Baxter," he said, and dropped to one knee beside what looked to be a medium growth apple tree, standing three feet tall.

"The prize is going to see you out here doing, what, some freelance stealth gardening?"

"It is a trowel," Wren confirmed, plunging the tool into the soil beside the small tree.

"Do you just really like that particular tree?" Baxter asked, sounding part-confused, part-amused. "You could get it on the way out."

"Not for what I've got in mind. Visibility count?"

"Ten seconds. You need to move."

Wren completed a circle of deep stabs into the earth around the apple tree, each one shearing through fresh roots. He took hold of the stem low down, stood and pulled. The tree wrenched out of the soil, spewing loose dirt and worms.

"Five," Baxter said.

Wren strode to the open door. The tree was heavy, in particular the thick, wet root ball. Easily fifty pounds.

"Two seconds, Chris."

He stepped through into the house, kicked the sideboard out of the way and gave the door a shove. It swung closed, sealing him in with the finality of a sarcophagus lid. He turned back around, just as the warning came in his ear and he came face-to-face with a big man already sending big hands toward Wren's throat.

20

MOROZOV

Wren took one swift step back and brought the apple tree swinging up. The root ball rose like a ball and chain, whipping up to contact the big man in the chin like a perfect uppercut. His head whipped back, his forward momentum redirected and he fell.

He hit the concrete floor with a thud, his head with a crack, but both sounds deadened away immediately. The house was too solid to carry that kind of noise far. It didn't shake. Nothing moved.

"Well, that was lucky," Baxter said.

"We make our own luck," Wren countered, leaning over to look at the man. Blood pooled where his head had struck. It looked bad, but he had to be sure.

"And you made that luck by going apple picking?"

Wren scanned the surroundings, saw a heavy oak door leading off to the side, and opened it. Bathroom. "It pays to be prepared."

"Prepared to steal apples?"

"You know what they say," Wren said, set the tree down, took the big man's legs and dragged him in. "An apple a day keeps the doctor away."

Baxter groaned. "Now I see where Hellion gets her sense of humor from."

"She's not my daughter," Wren muttered, and held the big man's head over the toilet and dragged a knife across his throat. "I'm not that old."

The man bled out into the ceramic bowl. Wren gathered several fistfuls of toilet paper, wiped down the blood in the entrance hall, then dumped them by the big man's head. Once the door was closed again, everything looked pretty much OK.

"Whatever. Just go. You're clear, and Morozov's up there. Plus, that tree doesn't even have any apples on it."

He checked out his apple tree. "It has tiny apples."

"Just go! That guard will be noticed missing in minutes."

"Copy that," Wren whispered, picked up his tree and started toward the stairs. They coiled upward in a squared-off spiral, leading to a landing where the raw concrete aesthetic continued. Off to the right lay three closed doors. To the left lay two. Wren turned left. The furthest door over contained Morozov's bedroom, a huge glass-walled space with a plentiful view out across his permaculture corpse trees.

"Is he looking toward me or away?" Wren asked, stopping by the door.

"Away. He has headphones on. You're good."

Wren pushed the door open. The bedroom was sparsely furnished and immense. A stately black oak bedframe dominated one wall, with iron pillars at the corners like a four-poster, each spreading outward in a three-dimensional trapezoid. Atop the canopy were three stacked layers of what looked like raw iron. It reminded Wren of something.

"Is that a copy of Lenin's mausoleum?" he asked.

"I don't care," Baxter whispered. "Keep moving."

The maudlin bed was backed by a huge concrete fresco; a

familiar blocky Russian artwork of workers and fists and flags, all pressing forward to raise up a five-pointed Soviet star. Wren tore his gaze away to where Morozov sat at a large iron desk looking out over the gardens. He wore a full black suit and he was looking at a three-screen computer array. As Wren padded closer, it was easy enough to pick out what he was doing.

Designing an extension to his corpse garden. It was some kind of 3D map renderer, which included the ability to see underground, where the outlines of dead bodies were very clear. There had to be thirty, at least. Death underground. Life above it. And a new wing of the garden planned, stretching out to the north, where Morozov was juggling his next plantings. First he dropped a corpse figure in underground, then he selected a tree to go inside them, then he flanked that with nitrogen-fixing plants.

"What are you staring at?" Baxter whispered.

"Permaculture's interesting," Wren whispered, then took the final step. At last, Morozov saw his reflection in the glass and spun. Wren brought the apple tree around like a scythe, catching the Pakhan square in his pressed black and white tie and sending him flying off his chair.

Rich, clay-like dirt shook loose. Tinged red.

Wren strode over.

Morozov was a slim man. In his fifties. A monster, but not built like one. Wren stood over him, holding the tree up.

"Artem Morozov," he said. "I think it's time we finished up your garden."

He pulled the trowel from his belt and leaned in.

The principal work was done within seven minutes. As soon as Morozov got his breath back, pinioned naked to the floor, with a shallow red marker square cut across his belly with the trowel's sharp edge and the tree resting beside him, he folded.

"Anything," he whispered feverishly. "I will do it. Anything."

"So the apple tree worked," Baxter said.

"I've done this kind of thing before," Wren said, then loomed over Morozov and told him exactly what he wanted him to do.

"But how will I explain it?" Morozov complained, when Wren was finished.

"Whatever it takes. Tell them security is loose. Tell them you're worried after you lost six men at the warehouse. Tell them there's a mole in Bratva."

The calls began.

The process took over an hour, as Morozov summoned various groups of Bratva foot soldiers and ordered them to bring all Rex's server boards to a third location, where Clara Baxter was waiting with Foundation support. The boards were dropped blind, each carefully bagged, and the deliverymen left.

"It's taking too long," Wren cautioned Morozov after an hour elapsed.

"These server boards, they are in different labs, being examined by different experts," Morozov bleated. "It takes time."

"Examined for what? What are they looking for?"

Morozov just stared.

Wren plucked a small, hard apple off the tree and tossed it at him. It bounced off his pale belly and he flinched. "What are they searching for?"

"I don't know! I am not a hacker. You, perhaps. We expected you would come."

Wren plucked another tiny apple, took a bite then spat it out. The flesh was hard, crisp and incredibly sour. "So you know me?"

"Everyone knows you."

"And 'we' is Bratva? Is it also the Russian government? Are you involved with the war in Ukraine?"

Morozov looked puzzled. "War? This is not connected, no. Of course not." A second passed. "Is it?"

Wren tossed the apple. "I'll ask the questions."

One-by-one, Baxter signaled receipt of the boards. One-by-one she reattached them to Rex, who scanned their contents, reabsorbed them into his systems and churned out an answer.

"Not yet."

While they waited, Wren interrogated Morozov further, but the man didn't know anything else useful. Together they waited in uneasy silence until all of Rex's servers were returned, and re-attached, and Clara Baxter said the words he'd expected.

"Rex is good, Christopher. It will take a little time, but he believes he has everything he needs. You can leave."

His gaze turned back to Morozov. The man gazed back at him. They both knew what was coming next.

"Don't," he said.

Wren didn't say anything. There was no need, and this man merited no sympathy. He'd done far worse dozens of times. He'd planned to do far worse again, for as far as his garden would stretch. The one thing Wren did do, out of deference to the victims, maybe even respect for Morozov's wishes, was use the trowel. It was sharp. It did the job.

Wren left it buried in his chest alongside the apple tree.

21

VOLKOV

Forty minutes later Wren met Clara Baxter in the back of a panel van, the same one he'd evacuated in from the warehouse, parked on a quiet stretch of the I-70 Krakow ring road. Anatalia was there in the driving seat, alongside the boy with the lightning bolt shaved into his hair. They nodded to Wren and he nodded back.

His backup team.

Clara Baxter was waiting for him in the back of the van, sitting at a desk with her laptop open before her, a generator buzzing and a tall server rack blinking green lights by her side, stocked with Rex's server boards.

"Hello, Christopher Wren," came Rex's disembodied voice. "I am feeling much better, thank you."

"Good. Can you tell me who took Hellion and B4cksl4cker, Rex?"

"Yes, I can. I was recording data at the time from within their convoy: video, radar and audio feeds, and I believe it was a Russian Special Operations Force unit. As far as I can see, this unit is still in Ukraine."

Wren's jaw worked under the surface of his skin. "Which unit?"

"The third brigade," Clara Baxter picked up, reading off her phone. "Under command of SOF General Brezhny Volkov. We've researched him already. Volkov's highly-decorated, highly competent and by all accounts, utterly ruthless. At his rank he should be behind a desk, but he opts to enter the field."

"He loves his job."

"It seems that way, Chris. His squad goes by the name 'Red Right Hands'. They're all seasoned operators, extreme killers who've followed Volkov through a dozen theaters of war: Crimea, Chechnya, Georgia and others, with a long list of atrocities at their backs." She took a breath. "Volkov himself is of Siberian extraction, the Russian heartland, though digging up much on his past has been near impossible. He's mostly a ghost."

"So what do you have?"

"A lot of rumors, but the pattern's clear; he's a mass murderer. It's a miracle he hasn't been locked up for war crimes ten times over, but to Russia he's a hero. There are eyewitness reports of him capturing and torturing civilians, Chris. He's a pioneer in mainstreaming terror tactics, often staging dead bodies for the purposes of intimidation." She took a breath and looked at her phone again. "One eyewitness report from Chechnya claims he beheaded children and stacked their heads on spikes in front of his command truck as a warning. Another from Georgia claims he strapped civilians to the sides of his vehicles to deter rocket attacks."

Wren gritted his teeth. "He's a butcher."

"It looks that way. Go back twenty years and he was on the front lines of the ongoing Circassian genocide: churches burned with civilians inside, mass graves, people forced into caves and asphyxiated."

Wren blinked. "Circassian genocide?"

"I had to look it up too," Baxter answered. "They're native

peoples of the Caucasus region, and Russia's been killing and displacing them since the eighteenth and nineteenth centuries. For over a hundred years the Russians slaughtered millions of Circassians in a structured, sustained genocide, driving them off their ancestral lands with a heavy focus on destroying civilian infrastructure; farmland, livestock, villages. Their culture was savaged." She took a breath. "It seems Volkov earned his stripes at the spearhead of keeping noisy Circassians silent, some kind of mass assassination and intimidation campaign."

All that was new to Wren. "It sounds like the Trail of Tears; Native Americans forced on a death march to the reservations."

"I thought that too. Not our proudest moment, though, is it Christopher? We don't celebrate it. But Volkov's a celebrated general, and the historic destruction of the Circassians is still a national holiday in Russia."

Wren felt his heart hardening. Masako's words echoed back to him, about the real world. "It sounds like the Russian playbook in Ukraine. Either their missile and artillery guidance systems are total garbage, or the civilian strikes are purposeful."

Baxter said nothing.

"Where is Volkov now?"

Rex spoke up. "We believe his unit is on the front lines, heading toward the town of Severodonetsk, fifty miles west of Luhansk. If you leave now, Christopher, you might be able to intercept him there."

Wren said nothing.

"Are you going to Ukraine?" Baxter asked.

Wren thought about the weighing of harms. He'd made it sound simple in his discussion with Rex earlier, but nothing was simple about war. The moment you walked into a war zone, all bets were off. Skill didn't count for much when shells and bullets rained from the air. Death could come as randomly as the weather.

There was no way back now, though.

"Yes," he said. "Clara, enjoy your family. Rex, I need you to share your data with Teddy at the Foundation and a colleague of mine at the CIA, Sally Rogers. She'll need to get me an escort to the front lines. Will that be OK?"

"If you think it is best, Christopher, I will share everything. I trust you."

Wren shot Baxter a look, then nodded. "Thank you. I'll make my own way to the airport."

He pushed the rear doors open and stepped out into the rain.

Krakow was gray and dark around him. Wren let the rain rinse the dried blood from his hands as he strode along the road, scanning passing cars for a cab.

Alone again. He'd always worked best alone.

Then a voice pierced through the drumming of the rain.

"Chris!"

He turned.

Clara Baxter stood in the rain, eyes burning.

"I can't go with you," she called, "but I owe Hellion and B4cksl4cker. Maybe I owe you, too. If you'll have me, I'll be your operator. At least until we get Hellion back."

Wren gazed at her. They'd never trusted each other. Years ago he'd saved her life, and she'd just repaid him with manipulation and dismissals. But she'd changed, too, and there was no doubt in Wren's mind she'd make a better operator than Teddy.

"Deal."

22

KYIV, UKRAINE

It was still raining by the time Wren landed in Kyiv, Ukraine.

His Bombardier touched down in the small hours of the night, a full day since he'd first arrived in Europe; almost twenty-four hours of war already.

He strode down the ladderway. It was dark and the air felt muggy and heavy. Despite the hour, the airport was abuzz with activity: passenger planes bustling as long lines of evacuees tried to board; huge military cargo jets unloading tall pallets of aid supplies wrapped in plastic; Ukrainian military forces building fresh security fences around the airfield's exterior, instituting checkpoints for staff and passengers alike.

There was the stink of jet fuel backwash in the air, and the acrid stench of burning. Wren only had to look out across the drizzly skyline to see fires burning amongst the low lines of distant buildings.

Russia had stepped up its artillery barrage while Wren was in the air. Dozens of missiles had landed in Kyiv since then, taking out several military centers, a hospital, a school, a shopping mall and numerous residential buildings. Hundreds of civilians were dead. The news channels didn't know if these were purposeful collateral strikes or down to outdated intelligence or malfunctioning guidance systems.

Wren suspected it was the former, just like the Circassians. The cries of children carried through the rain; families destroyed overnight, first-world civilians turned into refugees on President Anton Burin's whim. Striding down to the blacktop, Wren felt like he was heading into hell.

An electric cart was waiting for him. A solemn-faced man ferried him to a tiny hut at the edge of the airfield, bypassing the main airport. Inside, a man sporting a bushy mustache and a highly doubtful expression studied his fake passport.

"I'm an American special agent," Wren offered. "I should have approval. You can check with your state department. Everything is approved."

The man stared at Wren. His left hand rested on his belt next to a holstered pistol. With his right hand he lifted a red phone handset and held it to his ear.

Wren could only watch and wait.

Upon boarding his Bombardier two hours back, around 4 a.m. US Eastern time, he'd succeeded in placing a call through to Sally Rogers, his ex-lieutenant at the CIA. They'd worked together on numerous prior occasions, defending the US from enemies both foreign and domestic. They had a good relationship, notwithstanding the time she'd dumped him in a Mexican black site. He trusted her.

"Agent Rogers," she'd said.

"Sally, it's Chris."

There'd been silence for a moment.

"Chris? What's going on? How did you reach me here?"

"I had a little help from an AI dog. But never mind that. I'm in the air, Sally, headed for Ukraine. Two of my team have been abducted, Hellion and B4cksl4cker, out of Luhansk by a Russian SOF troop. They were hunting the shadow line, Sally. It may be coming online to Active Function already, in which case, trans-Atlantic comms may become a challenge soon." He sucked in a breath. "I think my hackers may be key to shutting this threat down; they were hunting a control node called the 'Nexus'. Now I'm going to retrieve them and shut the line down. I need you to get me CIA access, logistics and resources in Ukraine, with an escort direct to the front lines of the war in Severodonetsk."

A long few seconds passed, then Sally cursed.

"What?"

"We're dealing with cumulative crises here, Boss, and this sounds like one more."

"Cumulative crises? What else compares to Ukraine?"

Rogers heaved a sigh. "Ukraine's the obvious one, but also there's a fresh X resurgence."

Wren reeled. The X movement was the culmination of his father's attempts to fracture America; the Texas idiots who'd tried to split off their state, only stopping when Wren blew up their secession plot on live TV. "Where?"

"We're still figuring that out. It's in no one place, it seems, but lots of uprisings. Not whole states, but we've got dozens of counties declaring themselves to be independent republics."

Wren put the pieces together. "That could be the impact of the shadow line. Apparently it's everywhere, even in the US in a limited way. Maybe enough to synchronize these smaller groups without you spotting them."

Sally cursed again. "That could explain it. They're not on any known comms channels we can find, no darknet or social media, but they're plainly working together. I've been in the air consulting with the FBI for the last two days, trying to put each rebellion down without fomenting another Waco. They're small but persistent."

"I haven't heard about it. The news isn't covering it."

"Just how we like it. We've got it wrapped up pretty tight, but doing that's absorbing just about all our capacity. It's not leaving much bandwidth for Ukraine."

Wren grunted. "That'll be their goal. I've heard a theory that Ukraine is a pivot point that the shadow line revolves around. If they can win there, they can take the whole Internet and half the world in one stroke. What you're saying plays right into that."

"Whose theory is that?" Rogers said sharply. "I haven't heard anything tying the shadow line to Ukraine. Here we're working on the presumption it's just another Russian power play, flex their muscles and reclaim old territories."

"Maybe. This theory did come from a robot dog, so I don't know how much I trust it."

"A robot dog? What?"

"He's a genius AI, maybe sentient. I'll get him to send you what he has, you can liaise and draw your own conclusions. In the meantime, I need that clearance and escort to the Severodonetsk front lines."

Rogers laughed. "You're really serious. Are you going to fight the war single-handed, Chris?"

"My hackers were there a day ago, Sally. Somebody took them, so I'm going to get them back. Simple. If you can dedicate resources to helping me pin down a precise location for their captor, that'd be very appreciated. We're looking at a Russian SOF troop, Special Operations Forces Battalion 3, headed by a General called Brezhny Volkov. He won't be an easy target; last I heard he's on the move with an armed SOF convoy called the 'Red Right Hands'."

"You don't ask for much, do you? General Volkov, is it? Look, I'll try. I can't say much else. We're swamped here."

Wren could hear it in her voice. She very rarely showed stress. Even when one of Wren's fellow ex-Force Recon Marines had taken her captive a few years back, on the verge of burning her alive on a video livestream, she'd kept her cool enough to launch a surprise attack and break free. The coordinated X attacks must have really rattled her.

"Thanks Sally. I'll be on the ground in Kyiv in two hours. It'd be nice not to be arrested."

"You'd just escape," Sally said grimly, and from experience. When she'd dumped him in the Mexican black site, he'd escaped by authentically faking a heart attack. It had been a rocky point in their relationship. "I'll try to get you approval and an escort. I'll also be in touch if we get any intel on Volkov. Good luck, Chris. I hope you find your hackers."

"Good luck with the uprising."

Now the man with bushy mustache spoke in low tones into his red phone. His eyes didn't stray from Wren, but his left hand twitched by the pistol grip on his belt.

Wren stood immobile, gaze fixed on the phone, while scanning the small hut with his peripheral vision. One lunge and he should be able to secure the man's weapon. From there he could escape onto the airfield. Hijacking a helicopter to Severodonetsk might be possible, but with the amount of flak in the sky and terror on the airwaves, he wouldn't put it past the Ukrainian air force to shoot him down.

A bead of sweat rolled down his left cheek. He resisted the urge to wipe it away.

The man was silent now, just listening to the phone while staring at Wren. His knuckles were white around the pistol. Was that the sound of sirens drawing in? Could they be reinforcements to take Wren into custody?

A plane took off nearby and surged overhead. The little hut shook. The man nodded. His eyes bored into Wren. Then he put the phone down.

"You have permission to travel east," he said in his lyrical accent. "To Severodonetsk. There is a helicopter waiting for you. You will join an active battalion. Ukraine thanks you for your help, Mr. Nash."

23

EAST

The helicopter was a Mil Mi-8, a twin-turbine Soviet construction kitted out for transport. Wren boarded the 24-capacity rear compartment, where a wealth of gear from his Attack Crate 2.0 was waiting for him, spread out in tactical bags. He pulled on a steel-plate-reinforced para-aramid bulletproof Twaron jacket, thigh-plate tactical pants and a utility belt, prepped his usual Sig Sauer P220 ACP .45 and an M4A1 carbine rifle. He strung twin bandoliers of .45 hollow point magazines across his chest, overlapped them with a strip of grenades and flashbang grenades, then hooked a radio and tool kit into his tactical belt. Last he closed out with his earpiece and a combat helmet.

"Ready, sir?" asked the pilot, rotors already whirring up.

"Hit it," Wren answered. Within seconds they were airborne. The rotor blades became a deafening roar barely muted by the helmet's padded headset.

"Two hours in the air," came the pilot's voice through the headset. "Hot insert. I'll dump supplies, evac some wounded then the escort team will take you deeper. I'll be on call for your exfiltration too."

"Understood, thank you."

As the helicopter rose, Wren got a better look at the airport below. It was thronged. The highway from Kyiv to the north burned with the static white lights of an unbroken traffic jam, backed up for miles. All civilians trying to escape. In places the lights of emergency services spun like tiny Catherine wheels, forming up around dark patches torn into the highway.

Missiles had landed here too. Had they been targeting civilians, or had they been aiming for the airport and fallen short?

"We have missile defenses," the pilot said over the comms, noticing Wren's gaze. "So far, it's enough to protect major targets. But not for much longer."

Wren had nothing to say to that. In minutes they were speeding over Kyiv itself, where he saw the greater devastation. Fire crews gathered far below, encircled by police cars, ambulances and media trucks, each a swirl of lights and activity around a dozen different strike points; looked like residential buildings, parks, schools. The view from above felt obscene, like he was a giant overlooking a toy battlefield.

Except this wasn't a battlefield. These casualties were civilian, just like the Circassians before them.

Wren refocused his gaze on the horizon. East. What he needed now was a precise location for General Brezhny Volkov.

He brought up his phone, routed it through the headset and secured a private channel, then made the call back to Clara Baxter, his new operator. It rang several times and almost died in a static burst before a shaky line connected.

"Chris, where are you?" came Baxter's voice.

"In the air, Clara. Tell me you've been liaising with Sally Rogers and you have a current location on Volkov."

A few seconds passed, broken by flurrying static. "The signal's bad. That could be shadow line interference. But yes. We have a location on Volkov, though the situation is fluid. CIA overwatch is loose, as their satellites can't easily pierce the screen of dust rising over the Russian advance. They have drones in the air, your Foundation does too, but they don't last long before the Russians bring them down. Generally, reports indicate Volkov's facing strong Ukrainian resistance on the eastern edge of Severodonetsk. I'm forwarding coordinates. There's a trail of devastation behind his Right Hands, though. You should be warned, Chris, it looks like they're up to their old tricks. They ..."

The signal faded out again.

"Any sign of the hackers?" Wren shouted.

"... nothing. We don't think they're with Volkov, though. It looks like he sent multiple vehicles out after the initial snatch. We're trying to track where he sent them through Ukrainian CCTV, but the records are poor, as you can imagine, with the whole city getting shelled."

It had been a long shot. "So I'll take Volkov and get answers from him. How's my approach looking?"

"Lethal," Baxter shouted back. "He's traveling in a convoy of several tanks, three Ural trucks, two troop carriers and three large mobile artilleries. I don't know how you're going to get near him. He's dug in two miles behind the front line, directing the flow. There's no way you can fight through to him and take him in combat."

"Didn't think so," Wren said. "It'll have to be something else.

"How, Chris?" Baxter asked. "And when you do reach him, how are you going to make him talk? He won't buckle easily."

Wren just grunted.

"A man like that, nothing will work," she went on. "I've

interrogated dozens of Real Boys. Most were weak. They gave out at the first threat of pain. Of death. But Volkov? He's another caliber. You could skin him alive and he won't say a word if he doesn't want to."

Wren knew exactly what she meant. He'd known many men like that; men for whom the battle with their torturer became all that mattered. Men who would count refusing to answer a victory. You had to respect them. It took incredible grit to push through that kind of pain.

"He's on the spectrum of true belief," Wren answered.

"What? True belief?"

"Call it a measure of extremism. True believers, whatever the cause, may never break." Wren thought for a moment. "On our side, we call them heroes. Amongst the enemy, they're the most dangerous kind of zealot, because they're willing to die for the cause."

A moment passed. "OK, like kamikaze pilots or suicide bombers. You think Volkov's on that spectrum?"

Wren thought back to the guy who'd tried to grift him, two days ago by the gates of his kids' school in Delaware. He'd been on the spectrum, too. Not far, and not to any great cause beyond his own enrichment, but it was all a spectrum.

"Let's hope not all the way. Halfway would be good; willing to die for the cause, but not keen to do so."

Baxter snorted. "Have you got a way of handling a man like that?"

"Sure. He has to think he's going to win. He may betray the cause briefly,. If he thinks he can make it up later."

Seconds passed. "So you have to lose to get him to spill? Is this like a James Bond situation, you're strapped down with a laser pointed at the family jewels, while the villain expounds his whole plan?"

"Something like that. Without the laser. There's an element of the con in there, too."

The helicopter rotors hammered above. They had already left Kyiv far behind and were hammering away over dark fields studded with far-off towns.

"Sounds complicated, Chris. Color me skeptical."

"Best place to be," Wren countered. "True belief's a bitch."

Baxter laughed.

"Just watch him as best you can. Let me know where he goes. I'll do the rest."

"Roger that, Chris. Just be aware that comms are getting progressively worse. We've switched satellites three times to keep this line open. We'll try to keep it going for as long as we can; maybe we can piggyback a signal off the drones in the ..."

The signal faded away. This time Wren let it die, looking out at the dark land below and thinking about the Circassians.

This war had to be stopped before Russia destroyed another civilization.

He surveyed the contents of his Attack Crate 2.0 spread in tactical bags around him, and ideas began to develop in his mind. As the Mil Mi-8 beat east, he opened up his tool kit and set to work.

24

SEVERODONETSK

The helicopter approached Severodonetsk with the dawn, pale blue light rinsing through a sky awash with drifting smoke. A thick fog of brown blast dust obscured the city like the approaching wall of a sandstorm, through which the winds opened and closed jagged seams of visibility. Wren glimpsed pockets of fire where gas lines had burst, now jetting their contents upward like flamethrowers; tall buildings were shredded like cardboard torn down the middle, spilling their masonry guts across the blacktop; ant-sized figures in white helmets were spread across mounds of brick, cinder block and mangled rebar, digging for survivors.

Artillery boomed in the distance. Sparkling rockets arced up through the shifting dust like thrown stones chased by stringers of black smoke, swiftly becoming urgent whines that climaxed in throbbing impacts. Buildings burst and collapsed, spewing more rubble and dust to thicken Severodonetsk's brown shroud.

"This is the front line," the pilot called, then pushed forward on the cyclic control, initiating a fast dive. Their descent sent dust skirling outward, revealing flashes of the

Ukrainian resistance forces. Wren picked out vehicles, some already shelled and smoking, others pumping out men and materiel, some driving east into the smoke.

The figures seemed to be a jury-rigged combination of special forces and army battalions in urban camo, outfitted with rifles and ragtag armor. Some wore helmets, some didn't. They were dug in along a ragged line of blast craters and smoking trucks marking the front range of the Russian artillery. Beyond them lay the wall of brown dust, concealing the devastation that had once been their city.

Wren's blood boiled as the helicopter landed in a section of low rubble; once a children's playground, judging by the colorful sprays of mangled steel rising from the spongy blacktop. Instantly figures poured toward them, some unloading pallets from the back, others carrying in stretchers upon which grievously wounded figures were laid out.

"I'll see you for exfil," the pilot called.

"Good luck," Wren shouted and sprang out. In moments the helicopter took off, hammering him with its gritty downdraft. He watched it ascend for a moment, willing none of the incoming missiles to pick it out of the sky. Soon it disappeared into the brown smog, fate unknown.

"Are you him?" came a voice.

Wren turned.

It was a young man, thickset and bulked out with bulletproof urban camo armor. His face was barely visible beneath layers of black gun oil, smeared soot and a tactical gray helmet.

"I'm him," Wren answered, holding out his hand. "Call me Wren. You're my insertion team?"

The man nodded and shook Wren's hand. "Lieutenant Gorky, Seventh battalion. Good to meet you, Wren. They say you're our best hope of ending this thing soon."

Wren grunted. "That's the plan. You get me close to General Volkov and I'll do what I can."

The man's face soured at the mention of Volkov's name and he spat into the dust. "That pig's a murderer and a rapist. Tell me you plan to kill him."

"Questions first. Then I'll kill him. I swear."

Gorky nodded. "Make it slow. Here's my team."

More figures emerged from the dust. There were five in total: one tall and gangly with no helmet and long ropes of dreadlocked hair; one built like a bull and nearly Wren's height with a jet-black beard; two so encumbered with straps of gear and bandoliers of ammo he could barely see their faces, and one who'd already taken a hit in the temple. His right eye was bandaged and bloodstained beneath his helmet.

They'd all seen combat already.

Nearby a rocket whined in then erupted amongst buildings barely a hundred yards away. A blast wave of dust washed over them too fast to take cover, chased by the thumping of shrapnel. One piece spun to a halt by Wren's feet; it looked like a fridge magnet depicting a green-domed cathedral.

"What's our approach?" Wren asked.

"Circle south and east," Lieutenant Gorky answered, already starting away into the folds of dust. Wren followed. "We have vehicles cold to go, because the Russians are targeting sources of heat; must be via satellite or drone overwatch. We'll get some impact warning from the onboard radar. If that happens, we ditch the vehicle and proceed on foot. The Russian front line is a few hundred yards that way." He pointed directly into the dust. "Past that, the smoke clears and you can see. Everything's rubble. They hit the suburbs like a tornado with hardly any warning, even though we never put up a fight there. We'll shoot a path through their front line, then you're on your own." He paused a second, looking back at Wren appraisingly. "I hear you have overwatch capacity of your own?"

"I should have it," Wren answered. "Comms are patchy though."

"I understand. Even talking to Kyiv's getting harder. Here." He pulled a slim black block from his gear belt, extended an antenna from its side and handed it to Wren. "It's a booster, you can sync via Bluetooth. It'll route you to our mobile satellite array."

Wren took the block and slotted it onto his tactical belt. He brought up the first of his specially adapted two-way radios and synced it to the booster. Almost immediately, he heard the sound of keystrokes clattering in his ear.

"Clara?"

"Chris, I'm here," Baxter responded swiftly. "I hear you clearly. Are you in position?"

"About to insert. It's chaos here, Clara. Minimal visibility, broken comms, rockets inbound. Tell me you have eyes-in-the-sky on Volkov still?"

Seconds passed marked by rapid keys tapping. "Rex has him via high-altitude roving Reaper drones, yes. He's camped out in a residential district two miles northeast of your current position."

Wren frowned as Gorky led him up to two waiting vehicles, a wide brown Humvee and a squat green Ural. The troop split between the two, hanging off the sides with their rifles at the ready.

"He's not moving?" Wren asked, climbing onto the forward station of the Humvee, his own M4A1 rifle at the ready.

"It seems not."

"Any idea why?"

"Our best guess is that he's conducting interrogations,

Chris. We have footage of his men dragging people away. Could be soldiers, could just be civilians."

Wren grunted and turned to Gorky. "I'm ready."

The lieutenant nodded. He was a young man, but after 24 hours of war looked like he was already in his forties. "We are ready. Thank you for coming to fight with us, Christopher Wren."

Wren nodded. "I wouldn't be anywhere else. Let's go kill some Russians."

25

FRONT LINE

The Humvee fired up and led the Ural rumbling into the dust. Visibility was minimal. Wren leaned out from his berth, watching the murky ghosts of broken structures pass by. A shattered barber's pole lay on the sidewalk, candy-cane spirals stilled. A lamppost tilted inward like a sapling uprooted in a storm.

The team spoke on their comms in Ukrainian behind him. Wren caught none of it but it was strangely comforting still. He wasn't alone for this dive into hell. Every second they rumbled closer brought him a second closer to Hellion and B4cksl4cker, to taking the Nexus and killing the shadow line, and along with it men like Volkov.

For several minutes they navigated steadily through the city's outskirts. Some roads were blocked by bombed-out traffic snarls, others by wreckage of tumbled buildings. Gorky rerouted them smoothly. Wren saw malls and market stalls and dead bodies half-smothered in dust. The rage was cold now, burning like dry ice in his chest.

A raised voice came from behind. It sounded like, 'Nadkhodzhennya rakety.' Wren didn't know the first word, but he could make a guess at the second.

"Incoming rocket," said Gorky, already springing from behind the wheel. "Run."

Wren dropped off the Humvee and ran; five big steps up onto the sidewalk and leaping through the blown-out window of a designer bridal shop, where he dropped to the floor amidst tumbled white mannequins wearing thousand-dollar wedding dresses.

The rocket whined in then struck.

The earth bucked like a mule's kick, rolling Wren onto his side. The sound was disruptive and disorienting, chased by the hard patter of shrapnel raining off the shop's front wall.

"Come on! called the lieutenant, and Wren surged to his feet. His balance was shot, the equilibrium of his inner ear temporarily overloaded, but together they ran across the fresh mushroom of smoke. "They will fire again."

The vehicle convoy was gone; Wren picked out the Humvee's chassis half-sunk into a blast crater, shards of bodywork blown outward like sharp petals, then the dust sealed itself over. Another rocket whined in, there was the blast of impact, then the pop-pop of rifle fire.

"Down!" the lieutenant shouted, and took cover behind a parked vehicle by the roadside. Wren dropped to one knee beside him, head on a swivel. There was no sign of the rest of the troop in all the dust, but ahead muzzle flashes erupted; at least seven.

"Incoming from two o-clock," Wren said, focusing briefly on Gorky. "Give me covering fire and I'll take them."

The lieutenant stared at him for a moment, then nodded and surged up, firing over the car's hood.

Wren ran hard right, in seconds clearing the road and passing into another fractured storefront; some kind of bakery. Behind a glass counter sweet patisserie delights were still arrayed, looking pristine, while around them the walls, floor and ceiling looked like they'd been put through a paper shredder. Gunfire ripped nearby. Chairs and tables lay scattered and he darted between them, passing through what had once been a wall into what looked like an ice cream shop. The gunfire grew louder.

The Russians were likely holed up a few shops over. The walls here were intact, so Wren ran through the kitchen into a brick-walled back yard spotted with picnic tables. He stepped up onto a table by the wall, jumped to catch the top of the wall and pulled himself over. He dropped down to his feet in a square café courtyard, encircled by Russian soldiers.

Three were hunched over a small cookfire, boiling what smelled like MRE spaghetti bolognese packs. Two lay prone on their backs, bandaged and immobile. Two stood toward the front of the café where it butted the street, rifles at the ready. There were crates of ammunition and materiel everywhere, stacked amongst delicate white metal tables and filigreed chairs.

He'd dropped into a forward operating outpost.

The soldiers stared at Wren. Wren looked back. They scrambled for their weapons, but he'd already stripped a grenade off his chest bandolier, pulled the pin and dropped it. It hit the concrete floor with an unsettling clank, and Wren took three big steps and dived over a stack of MRE crates.

The grenade exploded.

The blast deafened him and blew a rain of bricks and body parts out, up and falling back down from above. A hand struck Wren in the back and bounced in front of him. More explosions followed as the various ammo crates popped off as Wren crawled away. Blood and dust splattered the walls. Cries filled the air. Wren estimated the three men at the cookfire had been decimated. At best the two men with rifles up front had been disoriented.

Wren rose to his feet in an offshoot corridor leading

toward the WCs, where he beaded his M4A1 back on the courtyard.

The first man to run through took one shot in the chest and one in the head and went down like he'd been sucked into quicksand. The second stumbled into Wren's line of fire and tried to back up, but it was too late. Wren fired on automatic, pinning him to the wall.

For a moment there was something like silence. Barely even any cries and no gunfire. Then came the clank of an answering grenade tumbling back through the café. It spun across Wren's passageway, and he flung himself into the ladies' WC just as it blew. His legs were hoisted by the blast and his shoulder hit the toilet tank and cracked the porcelain.

Water disgorged up over Wren. He slipped down into the gap between the toilet and the wall, found purchase and managed to pull himself out. A Russian officer stood in the entrance, pistol pointing down. Wren jerked sideways and the pistol discharged, cracking off the remnant of the toilet tank. Wren tried to bring the M4A1 around but too late; the Russian officer's head blew to the side like a piece of rotten fruit.

"Christopher Wren!" came the shout of lieutenant Gorky.

Wren breathed a sigh of relief and answered. "It's me."

He stepped out into the passage and saw Gorky standing in the courtyard.

"Are you OK?" the lieutenant asked.

Wren scanned his chest and his feet. His armor looked unbroken. "Fine. But-"

The lieutenant jerked sideways. For a split second Wren had no idea what had just happened, as if some invisible hook had been sunk in the commander's left shoulder, spinning him like a top.

Then came the explosion, further rearranging the

wreckage in the courtyard and spraying a large proportion of it back into the Gorky's face. He flew back toward the street on a tide of shrapnel.

A rocket. It had struck Gorky a glancing blow then continued to explode.

Wren broke from cover with his rifle up, running with the outflow of dust. The commander's broken body lay to the right. Ahead Wren picked the rocket crew out: four men behind a large armored truck, dropping a new rocket into the chute of a portable launcher.

Wren underhand pitched a second grenade toward them, like a bowling ball at nine-pins. There was no time to run. It blew.

Afterward there was silence.

Wren advanced with his rifle up, to find Russian soldiers lying in pieces. Several were still alive, albeit missing limbs. He put single shots into their heads then called out.

"It's Wren, all clear!"

Then he ran to lieutenant Gorky. He lay still where he'd fallen. Wren cursed, closed his eyes then stood up.

The troop arrived.

"He saved my life," Wren said. "I'm sorry."

The boy with the dreadlocks stepped forward. "This is the front line," he said. "You're on foot from here."

Wren nodded, thanked him then ran east, out of the wheezing river of dust and onto a residential street with no street signs. Gunfire chased him. Civilian bodies lay amongst burning vehicles and buildings, bullet holes in the backs of their heads.

Wren ran.

After several minutes Clara Baxter's voice came in his earpiece, cutting through the noise and static. "Target is within range."

The gunfire picked up and Wren chanced a glance over his shoulder.

A dark-green Ural 4320 Russian military truck skidded through an intersection fifty yards back. Its tarp-coated rear bed was stripped back and four figures hung out over the 6x6's bare frame, spraying AK74-M's in Wren's direction.

26

RED RIGHT HANDS

Thirty minutes later, after battling through a burning building and taking out an T90-M tank, Wren kneeled before General Brezhny Volkov's Red Right Hands. Their rifles were in his face. Their chests displayed their Soviet allegiance; painted red palms with golden stars at the center.

Wren raised his arms and the few words of memorized Russian spilled from his lips.

"U menya yest′ informatsiya! Ya podchinyayus!"

I have information. I surrender.

A rifle butt smashed into Wren's temple. Colors burst in his head and he smacked sideways onto the blacktop. The Right Hands hauled him up with ease. There was blood in his eyes now, blinding him, and he tried to blink it clear. Strong hands slapped his face, cuffed his wrists tight with a thick zip-tie and dragged him away.

Artillery boomed to the right. Voices called in coarse and mocking Russian. A rifle muzzle jabbed into his back. Wren stumbled on steps leading up, then the quality of sound shifted; he was inside.

He was shoved through what looked like the entrance hall

of a home, bounced off a wall then thrown forward into an open space, like a den. His left thigh hit something soft, maybe a couch, and his momentum carried him over too fast to get his hands up. He hoped for a soft landing, then his face crashed into and through a horizontal pane of glass. Pain roared up through his nose, cheeks and mouth.

A glass coffee table.

Laughter sounded behind him.

"Ty eto videl?" a rough voice asked.

'Did you see that?'

Wren groaned and tried to roll to his feet.

"Nyet," another deep voice said, hauling him to his feet. An unexpected punch came in his stomach like a piston blow, and the Twaron fibers did little to absorb it, freezing out his solar plexus. He resisted the urge to gulp helplessly at the air.

Something hit him square between the eyes, jacking his head back sharply. He staggered and fell, this time into a soft landing. An armchair.

His head rang like a bell and the urge to vomit rose up sharply.

A baseball bat? He blinked away blood and picked out the outline of a giant man above him. He was decked out in urban camo gear with the red right palm print and golden star daubed extra-large on his chest, 6' 7" and at least three hundred pounds. His face was carved with what looked to be fingernail scars. The marks of his victims? And there was a shiny red impact peach on his forehead.

A headbutt, then, not a baseball bat.

"On pokhozh na." he boomed. "Krutoy paren!"

Something about Wren being a tough guy.

There was more laughter.

"Kakova vasha informatsiya?" the big man asked.

What's your information?

Wren still couldn't breathe. He gulped for air and

managed to eke out a few more words he'd memorized in Russian.

"Ya pogovoryu tol′ko s generalom Volkovym."

I'll only speak to General Volkov.

The big man laughed, then pointed at Wren's left ear and the right side of his chest. Two men descended; one wrapped Wren's head in a tight embrace, shoved a slim length of cold metal into his ear and dug in. Seconds later he pulled back with Wren's earpiece, squawking still with Clara Baxter's voice. He dropped it to the floor and crushed it underfoot.

The other man opened Wren's chest pocket and pulled out his cell phone, which he tossed to the big man, who promptly activated it. "PIN?" he asked.

Wren glared back at him.

The big man stepped closer and slapped Wren across the face. His head jerked sideways and the pain was worse than a punch.

"PIN?" he repeated.

"Ya pogovoryu," Wren repeated through numb his lips, "tol′ko s generalom Volkovym."

The big man pocketed Wren's phone, then slapped him again, so hard the room spun long after the recoil was finished.

"You will talk to me, American," said the big man in rough English, then gave a signal and the others dragged Wren out of the couch and away.

Down a hall they went, into a dark, bare room, where some dozen naked bodies hung from their wrists like slabs of meat in a slaughterhouse. There were men and women, young and old, all shivering uncontrollably.

Wren was shoved into their midst. Only faint gray light leaked through the drawn curtains, but Wren picked out holes torn into the plasterboard ceiling above. Ropes had been looped over the exposed beams, hoisting each prisoner onto their tiptoes by their cuffed wrists.

More war crimes.

This was torture by anyone's book, and the effects would be immediate, serious and long-lasting. Wren realized they weren't shivering because they were cold, but because their bodies had passed beyond the breakdown point of ordinary muscle function. Lines of blood ran down from their wrists, where they'd periodically let the cuffs take their weight until the pain grew too much, then hoisted themselves back onto their tiptoes until the muscles gave out again.

Two figures climbed onto a chair ahead and punched fresh holes through the ceiling. Plasterboard and dust rained down amidst the shaking prisoners. A rope line was tossed over then cinched tight to the beam. Wren's cuffs were knotted into the line then his arms were hauled upward, wrenching him onto his tiptoes. Instantly he felt the pressure in his shoulders, neck, down his back and into his calves. In moments he'd be shuddering too.

One of the Right Hands kicked Wren's feet out from under him, dropping his full weight onto his wrists. The plastic cuffs bit into his wrists and the pain was instant. He scrabbled for his footing. One of the Right Hands laughed while the other two went to work: one produced a pair of hand shears, which he slitted into the neckline of Wren's Twaron gear. He looked in Wren's eyes then ran the blade down through the tough fabric between the armor plates. The material was strong against impacts and even stab attacks, but vulnerable against cutting edges.

Wren's jacket unzipped and the Right Hands pulled it away, and the man with the shears started on Wren's pants. In thirty seconds flat they stripped him to the skin and stood back, assessing him.

"Jake?" one of them asked, reading the tattoos on Wren's chest. "Quinn?"

"Deti," said another.

Wren understood enough Russian to know what that meant.

Children.

The first man nodded. He stepped close to Wren and whispered with foul, ashy breath. "First you, American. Then your children. Thank you for their names."

He sent three swift punches into Wren's side and closed out with a hook to the face that knocked him off his tiptoes again. The pain was already indescribable.

"U menya yest′ informatsiya," he tried again. "Diya Generala Volkova."

I have information for General Volkov.

The man laughed, spat at Wren's feet, then sent an uppercut that knocked him out standing up.

27

WAR CRIMES

Wren woke with a gasp.

How long had he been out? He guessed at seconds but couldn't be sure. He brought his head up and fought for his footing, but it was hard. Already he was feeling the effects of the extreme stress position: his wrists tearing and burning; his body deforming under his own weight as his shoulders compressed and pinched nerves; his calves beginning to tremble; lightheadedness setting in from the constricted blood flow.

He surveyed the bodies around him. How long had they been strung like this? Hang for a day and a night and the circulatory system would start surrendering parts of the body it couldn't reach. Your extremities would rot alive. Sepsis would set in. Another twenty-four hours and you'd be dead.

Wren steered his gaze upward. A dozen holes had been punched through the white plasterboards, revealing the wooden joists and light filtering through gaps where the floorboards had been removed. He thought through the play. It wasn't going to be easy, but it was only going to get harder as the stress position wore him down.

He twisted his wrists to grasp the rope, achieving a half-grip that would have to do, then let his wrists take the strain. The zip-ties bit sharply into his skin. He wasted no time and pulled himself up as high as he could. His body locked out in a preacher position, elbows by his sides and wrists by his throat. He leaned back as much as he could, swinging his legs up and over until he managed to snag his right ankle around the rope.

For a second he hung upside down like a baby suspended by the umbilicus, then coiled his right leg twice around the taut rope above, locked it in place with his left foot, and let it take the strain.

The crushing weight came off his wrists. He took a deep breath. Blood dripped from his ruined mouth to the floor below. Any moment the Right Hands might come, so this had to be fast.

He pulled his legs in, lifting his body higher and earning some slack in the line to his wrists. He ran his hands up the rope some five inches, let them briefly take the strain again then pushed his right leg higher still.

Climbing like an inchworm.

He did it again. His wrists burned. His biceps burned. He completed one more pull then his right foot bumped against the ceiling and he kicked at the edges of the hole. Tufts of plasterboard tore and fell around him. He inch-wormed further until he'd pushed both legs up through the hole, then wrestled to get his upper body up through the ceiling and onto the floor above.

He completed the maneuver drenched in sweat, lying flat on the bare boards of what looked to be a child's bedroom. There was a sparkling hand-painted mural of the solar system on the ceiling. Light washed in through the open curtains and glowed off the yellow walls. There was a large white crib, a hanging mobile of assorted bears, a large mirrored cupboard and a chest of drawers that had been rifled through, with clothes tossed on the floor. Beside him lay the hole back to the pit below, and the beam atop which the twelve looped ropes for his fellow prisoners hung.

He rolled over to focus on the rope knotting him to the beam. It was a simple slip knot, and the work of moments only to untie. It did nothing for his cuffs, but that was a situation easily remedied. Wren pushed himself to his feet and stood unsteadily.

To his right lay an open window and a full-length mirror. Through the window lay a scene of war: Volkov's artillery pieces launching mortars to the west. In the mirror he saw himself, a big, naked man, spattered with dirt and blood, bruised and gouged. His wrists were red raw where the zip-tie had dug in, his eyes were bloodshot from hanging upside down, but all that Wren saw were the tattooed names of his children.

The Red Right Hands had spoken their names, and that sealed their fate.

He strode to the mirror and put a fist into the glass as the artillery boomed. It shattered. Wren picked up one shard, reversed it and cut the zip-tie.

The relief to his wrists and hands was immediate, chased by pins and needles as the blood worked its way back in. He rubbed his hands to get the feeling back then went to the remaining ropes, bent over and started cutting.

The ropes frayed and slit swiftly. Dull thuds carried from below as bodies fell. Perhaps some of them would survive. The sound was a risk, but-

The door thumped open below. A voice in Russian rang out. "Chto eto?"

What's this?

Wren stood and stretched. He readied himself. He looked down the hole through which he'd climbed. Fraught moments passed as their voices grew louder. Three of them, Wren thought. One appeared directly below him. He swore in Russian. Wren waited until his helmet tipped back and his features were revealed, peering directly up through the hole.

His face made a soft landing for Wren's heels.

28

SOFT LANDING

Wren's three hundred pounds flattened the man to the ground, cracking his ribs and playing his head off the floor like a spiked football. Wren rolled away the downward momentum and came up charging: two Red Right Hands stood staring at him, rifles in their hands just three yards apart.

Wren grabbed the rifle butt of the one on the left while sending a haymaker right elbow into the other's face. Rock-hard cartilage met his delicate temporomandibular joint and wreaked havoc, crunching in and dislocating. The man dropped without a sound, leaving Wren to wheel on the one man remaining. He yanked hard on the rifle and Wren simply let it go.

The man spun off balance. Wren leaped, wrapped his head at an angle and wrenched. The spine snapped.

He dropped.

Wren was left panting.

There were footsteps in the hall outside. They'd heard.

Wren snatched the AK74-M and surged to the door. It opened just as he stepped behind the hinge and two grenades flew in. Wren pulled the door all the way open to shield him, screwed his eyes tight shut and covered his ears.

Flashbang light exploded; twelve million lumens blaring like a tiny sun, penetrating his eyelids, chased by one-hundred-seventy decibels of blasting sound.

In seconds three figures surged into the room. Wren could barely see and his balance was shot, but he tracked their silhouettes and fired. They went down.

He staggered out into the hallway beyond, disoriented and barely able to see a thing for the flashbangs' flaring afterglow. He navigated largely by memory, emerging into the den, where the walls and floor doubled and blurred. His ears thundered. He stumbled over a body; it looked to be a little girl with her throat cut. He hit the couch again and almost went over it, then abruptly vomited.

It helped.

He stretched up and turned slowly, taking stock. He was alone. Nobody else to kill. Then he saw him. The giant Red Right Hand stood across the room, with his rifle beaded on Wren. He looked pleased; his lips spreading into and warping the fingernail scars down his cheeks. His lips moved but Wren couldn't hear a thing through the ringing in his ears, and didn't need to.

He understood exactly what this man wanted. It wasn't a fair match-up, not after Wren had been shot, strung up, beaten and blown up but it was the best deal on offer.

Wren nodded once. The big Russian nodded back and held out his rifle. Wren held out his own. The Russian dropped his first and charged in, fists cocking back like giant piston heads.

Wren slipped under the first massive swing but the second came up from below like a surfacing whale, catching him full in the gut. A blast of wind expelled from his lungs and he rolled sideways on his feet, tumbling onto the oak dining table.

The Russian followed, looming like a bear. Pain and nausea rushed through Wren's system but he rolled as best he could. Before he could get his feet down on the other side of the table though, the Russian gripped the edge and flipped it with such ease and speed that Wren was flung through the air.

His head knocked a lamp off a side table, his hips and side struck the wall and embedded into the soft plasterboard, then he hit the ground awkwardly, splayed and disoriented. His head rang, his lungs burned, his ears boomed and everything hurt.

The heavy oak table fell atop him, slapping him flat.

He knew what was coming next before it happened, but there was nothing he could do but pull his arms and legs in close to guard his head.

A great weight thudded down on the table, crushing his hips sideways and flat. For a second the weight relieved, then it returned instantly, this time pummeling his ribs into the ground and grinding his face into the carpet.

The big Russian was jumping up and down on top of him.

Each jump was exhausting and further twisted Wren's sense of his body position. In the series of slams and slaps and crushing thumps he fought to get free, but there was no time between jumps to earn any leverage.

The Right Hand was laughing now; a great booming crescendo. Wren felt his consciousness slipping. Take enough of these crushing blows and he'd be squashed flat like a minute steak.

There was nothing to do but go up.

Wren let one of the jumps bounce off his shoulder then rolled to his chest, let the next hit then pressed himself up onto all fours. The Russian made an uncertain grunt as he came down this time, his footing lost, and bounced off the wall. That was all the break Wren needed.

He exploded upwards, flinging the table across the room. He'd hoped to catch the Russian with it but the big man must have anticipated this and jumped clear; now he stood by the base of the couch, hands up and inviting Wren to wrestle.

Wren obliged, charging in with his mind pumping hard.

In a war of attrition against this giant, he'd lose. The Red Hand wore bulky armor while Wren was naked as a babe and slick to the skin with sweat and other people's blood. He was slippery. He'd be hard to grip. He had to leverage that advantage to the max.

Wren went in low and surged for the big man's throat and his armpit. The big Russian welcomed him in with a classic clinch, arms locked. In any ordinary bout, the bigger and stronger man would bear down on his opponent and muscle him down.

This was no ordinary bout, though, and just as the Right Hand was setting his stance to break one of Wren's arms, he abruptly slipped out of the Russian's grip and followed up with the biggest elbow he could muster, square to the big man's occipital bone at the back of the skull.

Five thousand pounds per square inch of raw Newtonian force, focused in against the weakest part of the skull. It hit like a hammer on an anvil and rocked the big man's head to the side.

On a smaller man it would've caved his skull in like a pinata. The Russian only staggered one step to his right.

Wren plunged back in with a midriff tackle. All the force in his thighs drove his mass into the Russian's, which drove him further off-balance and backwards into the wall, which unfurled like it was made of paper. Wooden studs splintered and plasterboard burst and then they were tumbling through the wall cavity into a small white bathroom.

The Russian's calf hit the bathtub and he fell inward. His head cracked off the white-tiled wall, his arms splayed to catch his weight but there was nothing to grab except a plastic shower curtain, which pinged off its mounts and wrapped across him as he dropped into the tub.

Wren fell after him, a dozen fresh splintery scrapes down his arms and thighs welling blood, and snatched the showerhead. As the Russian fumbled to get out of the tub, Wren brought the tip of the showerhead down hard on the big man's head like the blade in Psycho.

It was blunt and plastic but the angle of attack forced the transfer of mass and damage through the thin rim, bursting a welter of blood from the Russian's mouth that spurted up onto the translucent plastic curtain. He kept struggling for purchase but now Wren brought his own weight into play, pinning the big man's chest flat into the enamel coffin with his right knee while he brought the showerhead down again.

It hit and rocketed the man's head against the tub with a deep clang, bursting more blood free. Wren hammered two more tooth-crunching blows before the big man forced his way up, shrouded by the blood-soaked curtain.

As he climbed free, Wren wrapped the shower head cord around his neck twice and yanked it tight, pinched off the man's head like the filling in a neat wonton dumpling. He began to shriek, high-pitched and awful. Wren only squeezed tighter, but the big Russian was becoming manic, weaving and thrashing so hard it became near impossible to control him.

Then he lost control.

The big man managed to hammer a kick squarely between Wren's legs. Instantly everything shifted and Wren's arms went weak, his legs gave out and he sank backwards. His hip caromed off the sink and carried it down with him. Porcelain shattered on the floor and water sprayed out of the ruptured faucets.

Wren hit the tiles amidst the ceramic shrapnel and squirmed, trying to displace the incredible, overwhelming pain in his crotch, even as the huge Russian ripped the bloodied curtain away with a roar and a suck of breath.

His face was a ruin; it looked like one eye destroyed, blood everywhere, his upper lip torn revealing cracked and missing teeth. His one good eye was ablaze. He stepped out of the tub and waded over to Wren.

"Ya vyrvu tvoi legkiye!" he bellowed, something about lungs, then brought his foot down on Wren chest. Wren managed to slip the full weight of the blow and wrapped both arms around the big man's ankle. The Russian dropped his left knee into Wren's clavicle, wrapped one hand into Wren's hair and raked his head back to expose his neck, ready to stave in his throat.

But the mistake had already been made.

With his feet thrusting off the wall, Wren's shoulder rammed into the Russian's right knee cap, forcing it into backwards hyperextension. The patella cracked under the massive conflicting weights, the Anterior Cruciate Ligament popped like a torn guitar string and the Russian toppled.

All the force went out of his blow at Wren's throat as he hit the wall, dislodged tiles then came down across the basin's jetting pipes. Wren let go and rolled up to his knees as the big man fell, then clambering atop him.

Hot water slashed across his face and steam filled the air. The Russian kicked and his hands roamed for Wren's face, but Wren was too fast, and in seconds he caught the big man's right arm in an arm bar.

Wren's calves dropped across the Russian's chest, he held the man's wrist in both hands with his arm extended up

Wren's body, then thrust up with his pelvis. The big man's elbow popped.

He screamed. Wren let the ruined limb go.

Wren pushed his flopping, flailing body aside, heaving for breath in the steam. The Russian tried to pull a knife from his tactical belt, but it was easy now for Wren to steer him. Two limbs and one eye down, it didn't matter how big or strong he'd once been. He didn't stand a chance.

Slowly, carefully, Wren took up position by the big man's head, wrapped his face again in the shower curtain and started asking questions.

29

VOLKOV

When it was done, Wren opened the window and let the steam vent. Everything hurt.

Outside, Volkov's convoy waited.

The big Russian had told him a lot in his last minutes of life. Volkov's habits. Volkov's predilections. Volkov's commands. Like his reputation boasted, he practiced an extreme form of sadism under the cover of guerilla tactic. He'd led the charge against Circassian uprisings in the Caucasus mountains, and against democratic rumblings in Chechnya, and he'd been at the forefront of the 'invisible' war for the Ukraine, which had begun with the invasion of Russian SOF 'little green men' in the Crimea back in 2014.

Terrorism was his tactic. Violence against the civilian population was his weapon. Scorched earth devastation was his preferred tool for a generational land grab.

He'd known nothing about the thing that really mattered, though: Hellion and B4cksl4cker. Either that, or he'd held out longer than Wren was prepared to wait, which wasn't long.

Reinforcements were coming. Clara Baxter had said as much. It had to be soon, and Wren gulped at the fresh air as it poured through the window and trying to shake off the hunger in the big man's dying words.

"All of this," the big man had croaked. "This country. It is ours. It was always ours."

Wren exhaled low and slow, letting his racing heart settle.

Volkov's M-90 tank sat fifty yards away across the churned-up front lawn. The troop carrier was there. The artillery were still firing. It seemed that no one yet knew their SOF unit had been routed.

They soon would.

Wren turned back to where the big Russian lay. Stripped naked, he looked pale and sad under his plastic sheeting, his limbs malformed and joints swelling up with bruises even in death. His ATACS tactical armor lay in a pile by the door, topped with Wren's retrieved cell phone.

In the cool hallway, near where the little girl with the slit throat lay, Wren pulled the armor on. It was chunky, heavy and solid; some Russian-made para-aramid bulletproof weave. There were two blades set in sheaths, one at the hip and one at the ankle.

In the kitchen, Wren found a cache of weapons, ammo, first aid kits, comms equipment and rope. He bundled a kit and some rope into a rucksack and armed himself with two heavy all-steel MP-443 Grach pistols. His twin two-way radios lay on a side table alongside the Ukrainian signal booster and he scooped them both up; one he slotted into his new tactical belt, the other he dialed in.

"Clara, can you hear me?" he asked.

All he got back was scratchy static.

He checked the time. 3:32 in the afternoon. It felt like a lifetime, but just fifty minutes ago she'd warned him about reinforcements. Ten minutes left. He had to grab Volkov now.

On the way out, he ducked his head into the prisoners' room and surveyed their still bodies for a moment. Nobody was moving. Some lay on the ground. Some still hung by their arms, but none groaned, none shook, none shivered. None breathed. The flashbang grenades must have finished them off. Wren cursed, but he didn't have time to do any more.

He left the torture house behind.

Volkov's tank rested at a crossroads, on rutted blacktop marred with thick bars of clay dropped out of the tank's treads. The rain had blurred the road into a sandbar, spotted in places with bodies. There were no uniforms on the dead.

A Russian infantry soldier was leaning against the tank's treads, smoking a cigarette. He waved as Wren approached. Wren smiled back, drew one of his Grach MP-443s and fired. The heavy gun pulled left; three shots missed but the fourth landed in the man's belly. Wren covered the rest of the distance and executed him with a shot in the back of the head.

The artillery still boomed nearby, providing near-constant covering sound. Nobody came running.

Wren circled the tank. The troop carrier lay ahead. An awning had been stretched out from the side, and beneath it lay a matching stretch of black linoleum, fitted with an unexpected array of office furnishings: a wooden podium desk laden with an in-tray and out-tray; a laptop computer and several unfurled maps; two large gray filing cabinets in the rear and a potted plant.

Sitting at the podium desk, sipping from a bone china cup, was General Brezhny Volkov.

He was a burly man, tall and barrel-chested, wearing a green officer's tunic resplendent with medals. In his mid-forties, he had a shock of slicked back gray hair with a thick salt and pepper beard; the hair made him look civilized while the beard made him look wild, like a wolf caged by his uniform.

He was studying a paper printout while sipping tea. On

his right stood a tall, thin man, a colonel by his pips, likely Volkov's aide-de-camp. To his left, on a pullout section of the podium desk, sat a diminutive man taking rapid minutes on a second laptop. A private secretary.

Wren shot them both. His aim with the Grach was getting better, taking the aide in the head and the secretary in the throat.

Volkov looked up. He didn't even seem alarmed, and the cast to his olive-green eyes halted Wren in his tracks. There was an intensity in them that commanded attention. There was a demand for obedience. Wren had seen eyes just like them before, set into his father's face.

"You're coming with me," Wren said.

Volkov moved almost imperceptibly, bringing up a pistol with buttery smoothness. He almost got a shot off, but Wren's Grach beat him to it, slugging him in the right shoulder.

The General rocked back in his chair, then simply took the pistol with his left hand and tried again. Wren followed up with another shot in his left shoulder, and the pistol fell to the linoleum.

Volkov stared. Both shoulders were bleeding freely, but he showed no sign of distress. The pain didn't touch his eyes. If anything, the intensity within them only grew stronger.

"Who are you?" Volkov asked. His English was rough and guttural, British.

"They call me Saint Justice," Wren said, striding over with a pair of zip-ties in hand. "We're going to talk about the way you started this war."

30

INTERROGATION

Wren hog-tied Volkov, zip-tied him into the back of the Ural troop carrier then drove south.

Ten minutes passed. Twenty. He watched his rearview mirror throughout, but there was no signs of pursuit. Steadily they drew away from the front lines and the dust and the city, heading out into the suburban districts. The houses gradually receded from the road, as yards lengthened and sidewalks became wider and leafier. There were fewer missile craters, fewer bodies on the floor, fewer burning homes.

Fields of crops appeared in places. Off to the right a swathe of bright yellow sunflowers blazed in roiling black smoke. The stench was sweet and intoxicating. Wren drove until he found an abandoned residential neighborhood with a long, straight road leading south.

He stopped the Ural and sat for a moment, readying himself. On the seat by his side lay all the gear he'd taken from the Red Right Hands' torture house. His heart beat hard. He brought up his two way radios and checked them both. Nothing but static, and no link back to Clara Baxter.

That was OK. He opened the door and climbed out.

Smoke drifted over the yards, carrying the smells of cordite, spent jet fuel and roasting sunflowers. The pat-pat-pat of Russian cluster bombs mixed with the clatter of anti-aircraft fire in the distance, carrying through the encircling pall of orange dust, like a gathering storm just over the horizon. Occasional bright flashes sparked through the clouds like sheet lightning.

Wren studied the houses. Many still had cars parked out front. Curtains twitched when Wren's eyes roved across them. Most of the residents here hadn't evacuated, though several had. He picked out one home that was clearly abandoned. There was no car outside and the door hung open, with a trail of belongings strewn down the hallway.

It would do.

Wren felt eyes watching as he opened up the back of the Ural. Volkov was tucked under the seating, bound wrist and ankle with zip-ties to the seat posts. Wren reached in, cut the ties and pulled him out. The General's face was pale and his uniform was slick with blood from his wounded shoulders, but those eyes remained as intense as before.

"You will die for this," he said.

Wren dragged him out, rolled him up onto his shoulder and stood. The man was heavy and Wren saw stars, but walked toward the abandoned house. Eyes in neighboring homes watched his every step.

Inside the house, there was a hallway scattered with dropped clothing and smashed dishes. There was a living room in disarray. There was a dining room with the chairs toppled. Wren laid Volkov on the dining table.

"Just you and me," Wren said.

"Ty pomresh," Volkov muttered, his eyes blazing.

Wren didn't understand, but it sounded like a threat. "Don't give me that bullshit. Speak English."

Volkov said nothing further. Wren nodded, then stood on

a chair and started punching through the ceiling panels. It didn't take long to find a beam. He fed a length of rope up and around.

Volkov's eyes narrowed as Wren brought the rope down, looped it around his wrist cuffs, then pulled, taking in the slack and lifting Volkov's arms up into the air. He grunted as Wren hoisted him up off the table, then again as Wren pushed the table over to the side to leave him hanging from his wrists, barely balanced on his tiptoes.

Wren knotted the rope. He fetched a chair, placed it in front of the hanging man and sat down to watch.

"When you started this war, you took two of my friends. Now you're going to tell me where they are."

Volkov stared. The intensity in his eyes only burned brighter, though now it was mixed with something else. Maybe curiosity. The pain of the stress position didn't seem to touch him, other than in the short, sharp pants for breath it forced. The wounds in his shoulders pulled tight and oozed blood.

"Hellion," Wren said. "B4cksl4cker. A pair of hackers in a mobile supercomputer truck. You took them. Where are they now?"

Volkov said nothing. The silence between them stretched with deeds unspoken. The air tasted of ash and emptiness.

"There's a lot of things I can do to make you talk," Wren said, speaking slowly and clearly. "Tricks. Techniques. Some of them you'll know. Some you won't. " He paused, not breaking eye contact with Volkov. "I've learned a lot over the years. Pain can be very persuasive. We both know that."

Volkov said nothing. Wren let the silence stretch out. He'd expected this. Clara Baxter had predicted it. A man like Volkov was no stranger to pain. In Wren's experience, torturing others either broke you or made you harder, and Volkov looked as relentless as obsidian.

"I could take pieces," Wren went on, his voice the only clear sound in the silent house. Narrow bands of gray light sifted through the half-drawn blinds. The detritus of a life lay discarded around them, knocked over in the owners' flight: photographs in frames; a decorative brass owl; the broken pieces of a glass vase. "Fingers, one at a time," he went on. "Toes. Your nose, ears, eyes, your cock. Select portions of skin. Your belly. Your face."

Volkov didn't bat an eye. None of this was news to him.

"It'll be lonely work," Wren went on. "Hard. Grinding. Just you and me. It will take hours. But still, I don't think you'll tell me what I want to know. Will you?"

Volkov's jaw didn't budge. He barely even shifted on his tip-toes, though Wren knew the stress position had to have him in agony already.

"Or I can just leave you here. Maybe hang some weights around your waist. I'm sure you've tried that before. Hang someone like that for long enough, and the weight will tear them apart before the sepsis kills them." Wren breathed in a slow breath. "Still slow, but infinitely more painful. Within hours your legs will give out. Your shoulders will dislocate first, then your elbows, then your wrists. Soft tissue like ligaments, tendons, they'll rupture one by one. Next up is skin, muscle, fat. They'll stretch then tear. At some point, maybe later tonight, one of your shoulders will rip through, right around there." Wren pointed at the gunshot wounds. "Not pretty. That will probably be enough to kill you outright. A lot of blood, and you don't have much left. But you might live long enough to feel your other arm go. It'll be taking twice the strain by then, and it'll tear clean through." Wren sat back in the chair. "You'll be deboned like a chicken."

Still Volkov said nothing. There was only the sound of his labored breathing coming as a whistling wheeze. His eyes burned like hot coals. Wren had rarely seen intensity like it. If anything, Volkov was daring him to go ahead.

Wren smiled. "But that doesn't scare you either, does it? Maybe it intrigues you." He paused, leaning in. "I know you, General. Men like you. All the years you've spent at this work, you've wondered. It's a kind of fantasy for the torturer, isn't it? How you might hold out. How you might bear the pain. On some level, you're looking forward to this. To the contest. You're confident you're not going to break. Frustrating me will be your last victory. Am I right?"

Volkov remained silent, but there was something else in his eyes now. A recognition, perhaps. Maybe an appreciation, that here was a worthy foe, someone who understood.

"So I won't do that either," Wren went on. "Torture doesn't work anyway; it causes the knowledgeable to lie and the ignorant to confess. I know you know that. You still do it, of course, but for other reasons." Wren narrowed his eyes, reading Volkov's steely glare. "Maybe because it's fun? Hmm. Definitely because it's an effective terror tool. In that sense, it works a treat." Volkov said nothing, but Wren saw the confirmation in his eyes. "It cows the populace. But as a tool for extracting real intelligence?" Wren stood and moved closer to the hanging man, stopping within an inch of his face, eye to eye. "It's useless."

Still Volkov said nothing.

Wren stepped back. He spread his arms.

"So let's try something different. I'm going to offer you a choice; just how much do you believe in the cause? How willing are you to die for it?"

The curiosity in Volkov's eyes deepened. "So let's take ego out of the equation. This is not a contest with me. I'm just a fork in the road, that's all." Wren mimed weighing the choice. "It's your decision to live or die."

Volkov's eyes shifted slightly. The curiosity was replacing the rage.

"I'm betting you want to live. All this rah-rah Soviet BS, you may roll around in it like a dog in its own filth, but only because it serves your needs. Anywhere else, you're a serial killer. But with the Soviet wind behind you? You're a hero. But would you sacrifice yourself for it? I don't buy it. You're a man of urges. A man with unusual needs."

Volkov hawked then spat a glob of thick red phlegm right at Wren's face.

Wren let it hit. He didn't care. He wiped it away and continued as if Volkov had done nothing at all.

"Here's the plan. I'll take you back out there," Wren said, pointing to the street. "I'll give you this radio." He plucked one of the two-way radios from his belt. "Then I start walking. Straight down the street. Off into the distance. At a hundred yards out, I'll ask you a question. We'll make it an easy one. A test. At this point, I can still run back and find you easily. We both know that. You're wounded. I'm less wounded. When I find you, I execute you. Simple, easy, clean, no second chances. Clear?" Volkov said nothing. "OK. We're just warming up here. The next question comes at five hundred yards. At this point, if you choose to run, it'll be harder for me to find you. But I most likely will, and when I do, I'll kill you." Wren paused. "If you answer, however, then the final question comes at a thousand yards out. At that distance, you've got a real shot at escape. I'll be honest, I'll struggle to find you. I'll certainly look. I may get lucky, you may. But if you give me the answer I'm looking for? That's it. I walk on. Two paths diverge in the woods. I'm on the clock here, and I don't care about you. I just want what you know. Once I have that, we're done."

Wren watched Volkov taking it in. Maybe he believed it,

maybe he didn't. Either way, it was a chance, and what was the cost? Some Soviet secrets he didn't really care about?

"Are you game?" Wren pressed.

Now Volkov bared his teeth, lips pulling back to reveal the wolf. He couldn't resist having the last word.

"This is mistake. I will come for you, American. I will make your death slow. I will kill you for years. Every day, I will take more. I will take everything. I will strap you on front of my truck as mascot, head and body only, screaming but alive. Everybody will see this."

Wren stared flatly. "So that's a yes?"

Volkov hawked and spat again, this time on the floor. "Da."

"Deal," Wren said. "Let's get you outside."

31

WALK

In the middle of the street outside, in the thick of the dust, Wren put Volkov on a chair, cut the cuffs on his wrists and ankles and placed the radio in his hands.

"One hundred yards until the first question," he said, then started walking.

Ahead the road stretched into orange dust, lined with silent homes. Bombs fell far away. He counted the strides and didn't turn. There was time to think. He tried to empty his mind but it was hard.

He saw again the little girl, lying in the torture house with her throat cut. She couldn't have been older than seven, between Jake and Quinn. As each step carried him further away, he registered details he hadn't consciously noticed before. She'd been wearing a tinseled pink tutu over a white leotard. Maybe just back from ballet practice. Maybe those were her princess pajamas. First thing in the morning, she'd come downstairs to find armed men in her house.

Now she was dead. Her parents were dead, most likely still strung up in the torture room, where Wren had failed to save them.

Blood stained her white leotard.

And Wren had just promised to set her killer free.

Ninety-five yards.

Wren stopped on a hundred, heart racing, and turned. Volkov remained on his chair. He was far enough away that the spreading smoke obscured him a little, but still his eyes cut through like razors.

Wren raised the radio. For an opening question, his only goal was to build trust. That began with verification. "Three days ago you captured two people," he said. "Hellion and B4cksl4cker, a pair of brilliant hackers in a convoy of trucks." He paused for a moment, chewing on the question. "Are they still alive?"

Seconds passed. Artillery thundered. Then Volkov stood. He raised the radio to his lips.

"Hackers," came his raspy voice, heavy with disgust. "Creeping rats, hiding in shadows. I am ordered to capture them in Luhansk. Are they alive?" He paused, stringing the moment out. "Last moment I saw them, yes, they are alive. Is this why you have come, to find vermin?"

Wren's heart skipped a beat. Volkov was trying to make him angry and force a mistake, but all Wren heard was the confirmation. "How did you know where to find them?"

"I was ordered."

"Ordered by whom?"

"Walk now," Volkov answered. "Five hundred yards. Ask second question after walk."

Wren grunted. Those were the terms of the deal. Volkov might be toying with him, but there had to be trust. He turned and resumed walking.

Four hundred yards was a long way. A quarter of a mile. Maybe four or five minutes to walk. Volkov's voice through the radio made it feel a lot longer.

"You have children," he rasped. "I am told this. Tattoos on your chest. Boy and girl. Do you want to know what I will do with them?"

Wren didn't say anything.

"Slow deaths," Volkov went on. "Piece by piece. Wife also. You will watch. I also know many tricks." He paused, as if savoring the word. "Techniques."

He went on to describe some of the worst. Wren tried to shut his voice out but couldn't. These were the worst things one human could do to another. Volkov listed them easily, like these were always top of his mind.

Four hundred yards was a long way.

By the end Wren's knuckles were clenched and his jaw clamped tight. He'd already bitten his mangled lip, sucking on the iron tang of blood like an obscene pacifier. Every instinct commanded him to run back the way he'd come and beat Volkov to death with his bare hands. The world would be better off.

But then Hellion and B4cksl4cker would be lost. The shadow line would be lost, and with it the war.

At five hundred yards Wren stopped and fought to control his breathing. He turned. This time he couldn't pick out Volkov's eyes anymore. The drifters of smoke were thickening. He could just see the dark shadow of his outline, a man standing against the odds.

"What is it?" Volkov taunted. "Are you having doubts, American? Thinking this has become bad deal?"

Wren ignored him. He had his second question ready. Unlocking his tight jaw took an effort, but he'd done harder things. "Who gave the order to capture Hellion and B4cksl4cker, and why?"

Moments passed.

"You sound weak," Volkov said. "Fading. You seem like

sad man. Man full of fear. Far from family, far from friends. I am not sure I will answer this. Perhaps I will escape now."

Wren stared. The smoke stung his eyes. Volkov's dark shadow didn't move, but the threat was there. Would Wren catch him?

"It's your decision. We made a deal. You run, I follow, you die. No more questions, no more deals. Just a bullet in the head."

Volkov considered. "Yes. I may not find and kill your children if deal ends now. This would be great pity. You are right. This is better. And answer is simple. Order comes from same place all orders come from. Head."

"Head of what?"

"Head of my country. You know who is leader of my country, yes? Very strong man, powerful leader."

Wren's jaw tightened. "You're talking about President Burin? You're saying he personally ordered you to come out here, start the war and take my hackers?"

Volkov laughed; the sound was rich and smug. "Nyet, of course not personally! There is system. Order comes through system. This is great strength of Russia; faith in system."

Wren snorted. "Great strength. OK. But you're giving me bullshit. You know that's not the name I want. Who gave you the order? Who did you deliver the hackers to, Comrade Volkov?"

"Comrade?" he spat. "You do not understand meaning of this word. You do not understand Russian brotherhood. But you will be dying soon. Perhaps I will educate you then." He took a long breath, and his wraith-like silhouette flickered in the distance.

"Volkov," Wren prompted.

"Da, dying man," the General snapped. He was angry. "I will answer, but you will regret this. Order came from GRU

Commander of Twelfth Directorate. This man's name is Vladimir Deynekin."

Wren's pulse accelerated. He didn't know Vladimir Deynekin, but he knew about the GRU; Russia's equivalent of the DIA, the military foreign intelligence wing. He knew it was broken into numbered 'Directorates', the heads of which reported directly to President Burin. The first several were responsible for geographical locations; Europe, the West, Asia, Africa. The latter Directorates were organized by function: military intelligence, signals intelligence, NATO, war economics, and so on.

"What's the Twelfth Directorate in charge of?"

"Information operations."

Information operations. It synced up. The shadow line. The shadow war.

"And Vladimir Deynekin is the Commander?

"Da."

"Why did he want the hackers?"

Volkov laughed down the line. "Is this third question? Fourth question? Already you ask two questions each time. Are these new terms of deal?"

"It's an extension of the second question. Why would Burin want these hackers just as the war was beginning? Were they such a threat to the shadow line?"

Volkov laughed. "You are trying very hard, yes? Answer is, I do not know. I follow orders. Ask many questions in many ways; this answer will not change."

"I don't believe you," Wren barked, growing louder. "You were shot out before the war even began, just to take these two people. You had to know why."

Volkov grew louder too. "American, you are lost. Dying man in wilderness, in country far from home, asking vulture for help. Come fight now or walk more and ask last question. This is your choice."

Wren's knuckles tightened around the radio. Maybe Volkov was toying with him, but there was nothing he could do about it. For the deal to work there had to be the semblance of trust, and the most important question still remained.

"One thousand yards," he said.

"One thousand yards," Volkov repeated.

Wren started walking in silence.

Volkov was not silent, however.

"Do you know Novichok nerve agent, American?" he asked, the heat dropping from his voice and continuing almost conversationally. "Let us discuss merits. Is excellent poison. Russia leads world in development of such poisons, did you know this? Application of Novichok agent is simple. On tip of umbrella. On bottle. On door handle. Once I am free, I will make one call to good friend of mine, very high in GRU. This friend makes many calls. Within hours, everyone you know will be target. Your friends. Your soldiers. In America. Around world." He paused. "All will die in days, thank you to Novichok. Most painful death. This is how grateful I am to you."

He went on. His voice became a drone in Wren's head, pushing through the tinnitus of past explosions and the drumbeat of falling bombs. Every word stung, and Wren doubted none of them. The names of Russian poisoning victims had splashed across the headlines for years: Viktor Yushchenko, democratic candidate for Ukraine's Presidency in 2004, poisoned with TCDD dioxin; Alexander Litvinenko, a KGB defector, poisoned with radioactive polonium-210 in his green tea; FSB double agent Sergei Skripal and his daughter, poisoned after the briefest exposure to Novichok on British soil; Alexei Navalny, most recent democratic challenger for the Russian Presidency, poisoned and almost killed with Novichok on a flight to Moscow.

Volkov went on, listing the symptoms of the various poisons: the crooked limbs as nerves spasmed to ghost signals via Novichok; the pockmarked skin as cells fried beneath a microgram of polonium-210; the shortness of breath as lungs filled with fluid thanks to TCDD dioxin.

Wren reached a thousand yards.

He stopped walking and Volkov stopped speaking. Wren turned but there was nothing to see now. The thick brown smog of dust and smoke had drifted over them like a shroud, obscuring the distance.

"You still think you can find me, American?" Volkov taunted. "Catch me?"

Wren didn't know. By now Volkov could be in the Ural he'd come in, hot-wired and ready to run. But Wren didn't think so. Not after all this. Volkov wasn't the kind of man to run from a contest like this. His threats had become a game he'd want to play to the end.

"Third question," Wren said. "Where are the hackers now?"

For a long moment Volkov said nothing. It was the pivotal question. The question that shifted everything. Wren held the radio close and listened to the man breathe.

"You think this is real war, don't you, American?" Volkov asked finally. "Battle for Ukraine. You think this matters."

"Why don't you tell me what matters."

"Belief," Volkov said, growing louder. "Loyalty. Respect. You are fool who will die for nothing. Family, friends, children, all will die for nothing! You do not believe in anything."

Wren laughed. "Like the greater glory of the ex-Soviet Union? Don't try to kid a kidder, Comrade Volkov. You don't care about that either. Not really. You're in this because you're sick and the system you're a part of serves your urges. You like to kill. You like to maim. You like to torture. Now where are the hackers?"

Volkov hawked and spat loudly. "Remember you have said this. This is deal I will enjoy." Seconds passed. Wren feared he had run. "Last time I saw hackers, I delivered them to mobile command unit of Commander Vladimir Deynekin. Location was Luhansk Air Museum. Where they are now? I do not know. Perhaps Luhansk. Perhaps some other place."

Wren's breath stilled. "You handed them directly to Deynekin? He was in Luhansk personally?"

"Yes. That is now three questions, American. I will call my friend. Enjoy last moment before your world is destroyed."

The static died as Volkov ended the call. Wren's heart pounded in his chest. Too late. He'd squeezed something from his questions, but he needed more. Why had Deynekin, head of a GRU Directorate and surely engaged with heavy matters as his shadow war began, come to collect two random hackers?

Wren considered breaking the deal and chasing Volkov down. Maybe he could find him, but it wouldn't be fast enough. Wren had given him a working radio, after all. It would only take seconds for Volkov to send a warning and order the assassination of everyone Wren knew.

He couldn't allow that.

There was no time to waste, and he swiftly pushed a combination of buttons on the radio, spun the volume dial to the top and a silent signal went out. Far off, perhaps a thousand yards distant, a fresh explosion added its small, subtle boom to the thunder of war, as the two-way radio in General Volkov's hands exploded.

Wren had adapted it on the Bombardier; the guts of a grenade packed into the radio's case, designed to trigger on a unique signal from its twin. Volkov would have been holding it up by his face, preparing to bring hellfire down on Wren; now his head, shoulders and upper body would be pink mist, lost in the dust of war.

Wren couldn't hear the sound of his legs toppling to the ground, but he imagined them falling all the same, two muted thuds.

Justice was done. Volkov was dead.

He didn't feel any better.

32

CLARITY

Wren lurched back into the dust, mind working on the blur of plots and possibilities. For the last twenty-four hours he'd felt like the hammer was hanging over his head. Now it had fallen and it left him worn and dizzy.

Volkov had talked. Wren had answers, but no clarity.

He had a location to start looking, the Aviation Museum in Luhansk, and a man behind the curtain, Vladimir Deynekin, and that was good, but something essential was missing.

Volkov's shadow war.

Steadily the adrenaline of the last hours faded from his system, and his body paid the price. His injuries throbbed and his mind felt like slow-moving sludge forcing itself through a too-narrow pipe. Each footstep came harder than the last, as the exhaustion of his rush through the Russian frontlines caught up to him. He could feel a crash coming and struggled to focus, homing in on the one concrete detail he had.

The Air Museum in Luhansk.

He brought up the radio and ran the dial around to Clara Baxter's frequency.

"Clara, do you read me?"

He got only static in return. He kept trying for several minutes, stumbling through the dust, then shifted frequency and this time got through.

"Agent Rogers," came a voice with stark clarity, as clear as though she was standing on the street beside him. It disoriented Wren. "This had better be good."

"I, uh-"

Seconds passed. "Chris? Is that you?"

"Yes," he managed, fighting through the fog in his head. "It's me. I've got..." he trailed off, forgetting why he'd called.

"Boss, you don't sound good. Are you OK?"

He squeezed his eyes tightly shut and forced his numb brain to focus. "I'm fine. Just beat up. Listen, I'm on the ground in Severodonetsk. I took out General Volkov and now I have a location for where he sent my hackers. Something in Luhansk. An Air Museum?"

"An Air Museum, in Luhansk?" Keystrokes flew in the background. "OK, got it. You do know that Luhansk is one of the first places they took, right? It's basically on the border. It's got to be crawling with Russians by now."

Wren had trouble following what she was saying. He had to parse the words down to get to the meaning. "Was it? OK. I've got a name too: Vladimir Deynekin. Volkov said he's commander of the GRU's Twelfth Directorate, Information Operations. Does any of that ring a bell?"

"Deynekin?" She sounded surprised. "Of course I know him. Twelfth Directorate I know even better. They've been implicated in just about every meaningful cyberattack we've suffered in the past ten years." She took a few seconds, more keystrokes rattling down the line. "Propaganda, disinformation, false flag attacks in Donbas and Crimea. They're a black-hat state media outfit bending hearts and minds against us with memes and fake news. But then you know all about that."

Wren caught about half of it. "Yeah. I'm heading to Luhansk now, see if I can pick up their trail. I'm trying to get through to my operator, Clara Baxter, in Poland, to coordinate. Comms are out, though. Can you help with that, Sally? Also, can you share whatever intel you have on Deynekin? It could help."

A few seconds passed. "You're not seriously saying you're going to hit Luhansk now? Boss, you sound half dead, like a zombie."

"It's not far from here. Fifty miles, maybe."

"May as well be five hundred, if you're a zombie."

"I'm not a zombie. I just lost some blood. It's OK. I lose blood all the time."

She let out a high laugh. "It's a bad addiction, Chris. You've really got to get that seen to."

"Sure. I'll go into rehab, uh, when all this is done."

No more laughter followed. Wren wasn't feeling it either, and silence hung between them until it was broken by the sound of gunfire and shouts from nearby. He'd covered maybe four hundred yards back toward the waiting Ural.

"I have to go, Sally. Can you help?"

"Of course. Yes, Boss. I'm thinking. I'll get hold of Baxter. I'll get you whatever I can on Deynekin. How do I reach you direct?"

"I don't know. Try this frequency? Otherwise I'll reach out." He squeezed the bridge of his nose, shooting silver sparks across the darkness.

"Chris?" she asked. Not for the first time. He'd missed something.

"Sorry. Everything's muddled. There's something else going on here, Sally. More than just the war in Ukraine. The shadow line. Active Function." He thought for a moment, feet trudging through drifts of rubble and dust. "I know you had the X outbreaks. Maybe that's the 'real war'. Are you seeing anything bigger?"

Rogers grunted. "That's the question, isn't it? The X mini revolutions are dying down, but you're right. The 'shadow war' is all anyone here is talking about. The Joint Chiefs, the Intelligence Directors, the President. For the past few hours we've been getting field reports that read like the storm of the century, Chris. There's a viral tsunami of disinformation out there, and it's getting swallowed down in dozens of countries unchallenged."

"Disinformation about Ukraine?"

"It starts there, yeah, but it goes far wider. Have you been paying attention to the news coverage of Ukraine out of Africa?"

Wren laughed, but it tailed off lamely. "Not lately. I don't have great access here."

"Of course. Well, here's some representative headlines out of Nigeria, Kenya and South Africa." She took a second then started to read. "'10 vile Ukraine Nazi atrocities' is one, then there's 'Ukraine's false flag attacks brew fake sympathy,' then 'Russia fighting for freedom of all Slavs', and also 'America sides with Neo-Nazis.'"

Wren played those back in his head as he trawled through a barren intersection. Maybe he could see the shadow of the Ural ahead. "A lot of Nazi stuff. They're blaming Ukraine? Blaming us?"

"En masse, Chris. Everywhere."

"And those are, where, on fringe websites?"

"Not fringe, Chris! These are mainstream. We're talking about blanket coverage. It's all anyone's saying across the whole continent of Africa; every media outlet, newspaper, blog, TV show, personality, Iota account, NameCheck page, they're on the same page. It's a wall-to-wall echo chamber on how evil we are, and how evil Ukraine is, and how righteous Mother Russia is to finally us both in our place. There's absolute consensus on that, which we both know is impossible under normal conditions. There's never that much agreement. And it's not only Africa." She sucked in a breath. "The media whitewash covers large chunks of developing Asia and South America. We're talking about more than half the population of the world."

Wren tried to absorb that as he slumped onward. It sounded like the first stage of attacks Hellion had predicted, in that phone call so long ago. "That's got to be the shadow line. They're using it to block every other narrative. To take control of the media."

"That's our working theory, but do you really think one shadow Internet line could do all that?"

"How many would it take?" Wren mumbled. "It's one button to launch a nuclear strike, right? Massive infrastructure to launch it, but just one button."

Sally sighed. "Good point. It's working so far. We're already seeing the real-world response to this level of propaganda: there's a torrent of money and arms heading to Russia from these client countries, as well as fresh target locations getting lined up. Apparently Taiwan is next up for invasion. The articles are already going live. 'Grotesque medical experiments on Han Chinese in Taiwan' is one. 'Taiwan practicing cultural genocide against mainland China,' is another. They're everywhere."

The Ural grew clearer and sharper ahead. He could pick out the chair he'd sat next to it. "They're establishing pretexts."

"Pretexts for war, exactly. And there's so much more. It's a field day for autocrats out there, Chris. They're trying to turn the tables of what's true around on us, and countries are moving fast, taking sides under this tsunami of bullshit. We're already losing ambassadors."

That shook him out of his fog. "We're what?"

"You heard me right. The situation is changing by the minute. We're trying to stem the bleeding, but they're not listening. Brazil. Colombia. Nicaragua. Belarus. Vietnam. They're poised to close their embassies and end diplomatic relations with us. They're branding the US a war criminal."

Wren could only stare out into the dust. Perhaps this was the true power of the shadow line. Everything else paled in comparison.

"It's all coordinated, Sally. It's Russia. China. Maybe-"

"It's all of them. They must've been planning for years. I can hardly believe it, but it's happening right now. They're trying to isolate us."

He didn't know what to say. "I'll stop them. I'll find Hellion and B4cksl4cker. I'll get Deynekin."

Rogers sighed. "By going to Luhansk? Into the belly of the beast?"

"Fastest way to the heart," Wren answered. "I go, I rip it out, the war ends. Simple."

For a moment Rogers said nothing. "OK. Maybe you're right, maybe it really is that simple. It's more than any of us here has. The Air Museum in Luhansk. I'll brief the President. If there's anything else we can do for you, let me know. I think there's going to be some suicides before the night's out, amongst the heads of intelligence. None of us saw this coming."

Wren didn't know what to say. He hadn't seen it coming either. He'd chosen not to look. But the storm didn't care whether you looked at it or not.

The Ural was dead ahead now. Volkov's legs lay by the chair. His upper body was gone. "It's OK, Sally. We see it now."

33

LUHANSK

Wren drove.

The path east out of Severodonetsk passed in a fraught and sleepy blur. There were columns of tanks heading west, and backed-up roads filled with empty civilian vehicles, abandoned by refugees. There were craters in buildings and in the blacktop. There were bodies and burned-out machinery.

Soon the creepers of dust and smoke peeled back and the Ukrainian countryside spread out on either side. It was cartoonishly bright and unreal. Sharp yellow wheat fields stretched to the horizon under an acid blue sky. The intensity of colors hurt his eyes.

Luhansk crept up on him like a hunter stalking its prey, slow then sudden: farm buildings on the outskirts, small roadside homes with neat lawns, then he was on the main street weaving toward a brutalist concrete town hall. There was no devastation here, but the sidewalks were empty. There were no soldiers, no people, no bodies.

It was a ghost town.

Tourist street signs led him toward the Aviation Museum. A mile on, it lay behind a chain-link fence; three gray decommissioned hangars linked together by a tall glass atrium. Decrepit planes spread away in shades of polished steel and rust across grass grown atop an old runway. There was no guard at the gate, and Wren rolled Volkov's Ural up to the main compound. Wren killed the engine and stepped out.

There was no sign of a GRU mobile command unit. There was no sign of anything. The stillness and silence were striking.

Wren glided into lobby, past the ticket desk and over the turnstile, passing through one, two, three hangar halls of aviation history. A Wright Brothers imitation plane hung from the ceiling, alongside several World War 2-era fighters and a steel-gray Sukhoi Su-7 fighter jet.

Nothing to suggest Hellion and B4cksl4cker had ever been here.

After the final hall he stepped out onto the grass. There was a play area for children, and picnic tables, and a trail leading to the planes; a range of Cold War fighter jets, a large old widebody Pan Am 747, a bulbous-winged Yakovlev Yak-28 bomber, various long-bladed military helicopters.

Still no sign of his hackers. No sign of Russian mobilization or the GRU.

Maybe Volkov had lied. Maybe Deynekin had just left.

Wren sat on one of the picnic benches and gazed out at the planes. Some had moss growing on their wings. He was exhausted.

What now?

His eyes defocused. At least it was quiet. He brought up the radio and tried Clara Baxter and Sally Rogers again, but only got static. He kept tuning, trying for a radio station, but caught only scraps of an automated emergency warning system broadcasting in Russian or Ukrainian.

He switched off the radio and lay back. His head throbbed. He needed something to eat, something to drink, he needed medical treatment, but he was too tired to get back up. How long since he'd eaten? Rested? Was it as far back as Clara Baxter's new home in Poland, snatching mouthfuls of bacon and pancakes while debating with Rex?

It felt like so long ago.

He'd get something soon. The trail out here felt cold. Maybe he'd just rest his eyes for a moment.

When he woke it was growing dark.

He sat up, rubbing his eyes. The array of planes had fallen into shadow, outlined faintly by the setting sun. In the skies to the west the clouds were red, reflecting the fires of war. Another war in another place, it felt. Wren stood, and his injuries sang and tweaked. His mouth was painfully dry and his stomach pulsated with hunger.

The lights in the Aviation Museum were on. He walked back past the kids' play area and the automatic doors shushed quietly open to admit him. There was a café in a glass-walled conservatory section. In a still-humming fridge he found meals ready to microwave and picked two; a spaghetti Bolognese and a sausages and sauerkraut. While the microwave nuked them, he trudged back to his Ural and collected the first aid crate he'd taken from the Red Right Hands' torture house.

He sat down at a lonely plastic table looking out at the old aircraft, with two hot meals before him and a belly full of several pints of water, and started stripping off his armor. It hurt, peeling away from bruises and dislodging dried blood. Between mouthfuls he cleaned and treated the underlying wounds: the cuts on his thigh and hips from a Right Hand bullet and a razor wire fence back in Poland; bruises across his chest and arms from grappling with the big Russian; purple zip-tie 'bracelets' around his wrists from hanging.

He cleaned, sutured and bandaged as he ate. The injuries

stung, but none seemed to be infected. He gave himself an antibiotic injection to be safe, then focused on eating.

The food was delicious. Not good or healthy by any standard, but salty, sweet, fatty and hot. He downed forkfuls of pasta slathered with dried parmesan, gulped a strawberry milkshake, then bit into the sausages. Oils exploded in his mouth.

When the meals were done, he washed the big Russian's outfit out in searing hot water in the sink, then left it to dry on a row of metal radiators, taking his seat again naked. It was pleasantly warm and drowsy in the cafe, gazing out at the planes and slowly eating a fudge toffee brownie alongside a tall mug of strong, hot coffee. He didn't think. There were no thoughts to have, anyway. Go back, was all he could think. He still had the lead on Deynekin, if that wasn't a lie too. Sally Rogers might shake something loose. And who knew what Clara Baxter had found?

He checked the time. Closing on 9 p.m. He finished his brownie, feeling a little better. Stronger. Soon he'd get back in the Ural and head out. Back through the warzone to Poland, and from there…

He didn't know.

Abruptly, a field of bright lights flickered to life outside. Wren was momentarily on edge; they'd found him. Deynekin had come for him. But no. The clock said 9 p.m. These were automated uplights for the planes, stretching left to right like the buried runway was back in service. The old machines took on new shapes and contours as the floodlights embraced them from below.

It was strangely and intensely beautiful. Wren found himself rapt. These weapons of war now swelled and rolled like huge twinkling jewels, their hand-beaten curves and faceted glass windows catching the light at shifting angles. Here were tens of thousands of hours 'worth of craftsmanship, research and human ingenuity. There could be such beauty even in war.

Before Wren knew it he was pulling his armor back on and heading out into their midst. He felt dwarfed by their undulating profiles. He admired the way the lights had been thoughtfully placed to catch their boldest features. Propellors, rotors and bomb carriages all took on a new meaning. These were swords beaten into plowshares, serving an educational, inspirational purpose.

At the end of the field he was turning to go back, climb into his Ural and roll away, when he heard something. A buzzing sound, like an electrical substation or a distant drone. He scanned the dark and silvery skies but saw nothing, and felt no need for alarm. There was no other noise. No voices, no vehicles, no cries, no gunfire. The night was peaceful and dark here.

The sound was unmistakable though.

He kept walking, drawn by the sound into the darkness and away from the lights. At the edge of the field he climbed over a low fence and stumbled on a broad spread of deeply rutted tracks. The earth was raw where it had been churned up recently, revealing shiny white roots. Heavy machinery had passed this way.

Now a trickle of adrenaline shivered into Wren's system.

Could this be evidence of Deynekin's convoy? Was the head of the GRU's Twelfth Directorate still here?

The buzzing grew louder and Wren drew his Grach, tracking the churned earth across the dark field. Ahead lay a low rise of recently upturned earth and he crested it. His feet sank into the mounded loam, looking out over an answer he'd never thought to find.

The Grach dropped slack by his side, then fell from his hand. He was too late to use it. The buzzing wasn't what he'd thought. It was far worse.

It was the drone of millions of flies.

Before him stretched a deep, wide pit, filled with the faint outlines of human bodies. His eyes adjusted to the moonlight and ran desperately across their great expanse. There were men, women and children. They looked like a dark human sea, limbs draped over each other and interweaving, hair tangled, clothing rumpled and bloodied, pale faces staring up to the night sky cold and alone.

Wren's strength gave out and he dropped to his knees.

The flies buzzed all around him. They settled on his face and arms, as the slow and sickening realization descended. He was looking at the whole of Luhansk. This was the Circassians all over again. This was how you destroyed a culture and took their territory, once and for all.

This was genocide.

He felt sick.

The pit was huge. Deep, wide, and partially filled in. The work was only half done.

That meant they were coming back.

34

LOADER

Wren was ready.

It took two hours for them to return, closing in for midnight. There were five of them, dressed in dark green camouflage gear. They looked like common infantrymen. They came in three vehicles with all lights blazing: two large semi-end trailer dump trucks and a yellow front loader with a bucket shovel. The two dump trucks reversed into position, backing onto the pit. From his position dug into the mounded dirt, Wren could see they were filled to high peaks with fresh bodies.

Two men emerged from each truck. One of each pair went to drop the back hatch and shoot the brace posts into the ground, while the other went to the pneumatic hoist to dump the load. Both carried rifles slung over their shoulders, but neither were alert. There was an air of weariness about them. While they prepared to offload, the front loader skidded down into the pit.

Wren crawled through shadows beside the crest of dirt. The soldiers weren't looking and didn't see him coming. Five yards out from the nearest one on the hoist, Wren rose to his feet. The mechanism lifted, metal groaned and bodies tumbled. Wren's blade plunged into the man's left kidney. He fell screaming, but it didn't matter. The second man took the blade in his chest just below his heart and dropped.

The tumbling of bodies ceased but the screaming continued. The next pair of soldiers were no more alert, though. They just gazed numbly out at the bodies they'd dumped, looking for the one that was alive. Doubtless they'd heard plenty of screams. They didn't even look behind them.

Wren stabbed the man at the hoist in the back, on the right side to avoid his heart. He dropped. His partner at the back hatch finally realized something was off, saw Wren and drew his weapon. Wren fired first, twice into both of the man's thighs, and he dropped.

There was a rumbling to the left, and Wren turned. The front loader was climbing the crest of dirt toward him, its lights bright and blinding, its bucket rising. Wren felt nothing, only the cold flow of combat rage. He climbed three steps up the dump truck then jumped, clearing the bucket to come down on the cab as it crashed into the truck.

The driver surged forward, eyes wild and swinging a screwdriver. Wren leaned away then dropped his blade into the hollow of the man's clavicle. He screamed. Wren left the blade where it was and kneed him in the face, knocking him unconscious.

Screams filled the night.

They didn't touch Wren.

With five ropes, he tethered each man by the ankle to the loader then dragged them fifty yards around the pit, to a spot where he'd dug five deep holes into the loose earth. One-by-one Wren untethered them and directed them feet-first into the holes. They cried and begged but Wren didn't listen. He didn't care. When they resisted he forced them in.

Soon all five were planted deep in their holes, looking out over the pit. Wren packed them in. Loose dirt poured down their sides. They wailed. They cried. Wren didn't hear it. It didn't matter. It was nothing next to what they'd done.

When they were packed in snug, immobile as apple trees in Morozov's garden, he stopped. He ran one of the dump trucks down into the pit and turned it so the headlights shone in their faces, then returned to the crest. For the first time, he looked into their eyes. The fury he felt was incalculable. Beneath that merciless gaze, the men fell silent. One seemed to be dead already. Wren checked. No pulse.

A shame.

He looked at the remaining four one by one. He waited until they were all shivering, and babbling, and begging. Then he spoke.

"Who did this?"

The men bleated like animals. Answers poured out. Mostly they were names that Wren didn't recognize. President Burin's name came up several times. Wren pulled the phone from his pocket and brought up the photograph of Hellion and B4cksl4cker, battered and bruised in the back of their own server truck.

"Have you seen these people?" he asked, holding the phone close for each of them to see. That was when they clammed up. Wren read the fear in their eyes. A greater fear than they felt for him.

"What is it?" he asked. "Who are you afraid of?"

They said nothing but their eyes were wide.

Wren got back in the loader and started the engine. They couldn't see him approaching from behind, but they heard him as he rumbled closer. They cried out. Wren felt only fury. He lowered the bucket scoop and took off the heads of the two men on the right as cleanly as if he was slicing carrots.

Blood sprayed up. The dead man and one other. Wren left

the loader running and climbed out. The remaining three men were white with terror now, screaming themselves hoarse. One had managed to set himself partially free, and Wren kneeled down beside him, almost lovingly slotting his shaking arms back into the dirt and packing it down harder with repeated stamps.

"Who did this?" he asked again, holding out the phone. "Who took these people?"

They stared. They looked at their dead fellows, whose heads were missing. Their bodies had been planted. From such strange seeds strange fruit would bloom.

"Who?" Wren boomed.

One man said something.

Wren kneeled beside him. "Say it again."

"Deynekin," he babbled, growing frantic. "Vladimir Deynekin! Deynekin, Deynekin, Deynekin."

Confirmation struck Wren like steel loader bucket. He moved to the next. He showed him the photo. He asked the same question. This man was weeping.

"Vladimir Deynekin," he said. "Twelfth Directorate, Da. He, uh..." He paused, searching for the words. "Came here. This place. He gave, uh... orders."

"These orders?" Wren shook the phone.

"Da! Yes!"

"And these orders?" Wren pointed at the sea of bodies behind him.

"Da, yes, yes! Deynekin gave orders! Only orders!"

Wren wanted to beat the phone into his head. How many atrocities had been committed by men just following orders? "So you're GRU? Russian Intelligence?"

The man shook his. neck so hard Wren thought his neck might snap. "Nyet! We are, uh, soldiers. Only soldiers."

Wren looked at the body pit. He looked back. "You're not only soldiers."

The man began to sob.

"Where is Deynekin now?" he asked, shaking the phone again to capture the man's wavering attention. "Where are these two? Did you bury them here?" He waved behind him.

"Nyet! No. Not here."

"Are they dead?"

"Kakiye? What? No. Not dead."

Wren sat back on the dirt. It felt like the hammer was falling again. For two hours he'd dug his holes and prepared his interrogation, barely allowing himself the thought that Hellion and B4cksl4cker might still be alive. It had taken everything he had, every minute, to avoid running out and starting to dig through the bodies looking for them.

"You're sure? They're alive?"

"Da. They were alive. Now? Ya ne znayu. I don't know."

Wren grunted. It was the best news he'd heard in days. "Where are they? Where did Deynekin go?"

"Ya ne znayu! Don't know! I don't. We are soldiers only."

Wren stood. He believed him. He moved to the third man along. His head was lolling and pale. This was the man who'd taken the knife in his kidney, and couldn't have long left. Wren lifted his head by the sweat-drenched hair and looked into his misting eyes.

"Where is Deynekin?"

The man drooled. He whispered sounds that Wren couldn't pick out over the drone of a million flies. Still, he leaned in. He strained.

"Rossiya," the man whispered.

Russia.

"Where in Russia?" Wren asked.

The man whispered empty sounds, barely even syllables, then he died.

Wren stood. He surveyed the two men remaining, their

heads barely protruding from the dirt like strange, pale mushrooms.

"First one to tell me where in Russia, I let him live."

They stared at him. They stared at each other. Then they both started shouting out places. Wren caught Moscow, and St. Petersburg, and Vladivostok. They kept on, sometimes repeating the same answer and other times shifting, just watching Wren's eyes to see if he'd bought any of it.

He didn't. This was the problem with torture.

"You don't know," he said.

They protested loudly. He'd hung out a life raft and now they were jumping all over it.

"But he's not here."

"Nyet, no, da, not here. He is not here!"

Wren turned away. He looked at the pit of bodies. He'd come looking for one thing, and he'd found something altogether different. The 'real' war, maybe.

"Shh," he said absently, and the two men quietened. Wren waited, then he held up his phone and started filming. He captured the sweep of the pit, then walked down into it. He walked amongst the bodies. It was silent but for the endless buzz of flies and the moaning of the men. Wren moved carefully and respectfully. This wasn't only evidence of a vast crime, now. This was last rites; likely all these poor souls would ever receive. This was all the confirmation of death their families would ever get.

He circled in silence. He captured faces. Finally, after something like twenty minutes he turned the camera on himself.

"My name is Christopher Wren, and I'm standing in a mass grave of Ukrainians. These are the people of Luhansk, murdered by Russian Special Forces troops under the command of Twelfth Directorate commander Vladimir Deynekin."

He went on, describing the date and the time along with key recent events of the war, to help with verification. He described his rush through the front lines, his interaction with the Red Right Hands and General Volkov.

Around ten minutes in, the words ran dry. He ran one more panorama around the bodies then ended the footage. He followed that with photographs, knowing full well that as soon as these were released to the world, more Russian soldiers would be ordered out to unbury the dead and move them. This field would become just a field again. The war crime would disappear.

At some point, there came the sound of engines in the distance.

Incoming vehicles.

Wren stood on the crest of dirt and glimpsed them. Far off still, but drawing closer. Two more dump trucks and two troop carriers. If they were filled with troops, there would be too many for Wren to take. He was exhausted anyway; too drained to fight anymore.

There was nothing more to gain here. Deynekin was in Russia, the general on the hill orchestrating his war from the heart of some digital shadow line kingdom. The best thing Wren could do was get his evidence out, then locate Deynekin and launch a precision strike.

On Russian soil.

The two men in the dirt began shouting in Russian. "Pomogi mne!" one shouted repeatedly. Help me. Another focused on Wren. "They are coming. You will die!"

Wren looked back at him. He'd planned to leave these men here, gazing out over their works until time and blood loss took them. Now that plan had to be expedited.

"You first," he said, and climbed into the front loader. He ran it back, changed the angle, then ran it forward. The men screamed until they didn't. Wren took all three remaining heads in one neat slice. Blood geysered. Then there was just the droning of flies and the nearing burr of the engines.

Wren walked back along the rutted line of dirt, between the planes and through the brightly lit hangars to his Ural, which he drove away, back through the empty streets of Luhansk and west, toward the front lines.

35

DUST

Wren came back to himself in dust and darkness.

He was sitting at an odd angle, leaning forward and caught on his seatbelt. Outside it was night still and the air was thick and gritty. The truck's hood gushed smoke and fire. Ahead there was a bent lamp post, with the Ural buckled around it.

He'd crashed?

He didn't remember any of it. Reaching the city. Pushing through the clouds of dust. It was all a blank lost in a tide of exhaustion.

He hit the seatbelt release and pushed open the door. His chest was tight. His head pounded. Shops lined the road to his right; each still had their lights on. Voices shouted nearby, gunfire rattled.

Where was he?

A truck raced by, swerving madly. Troops in the back fired weapons wildly at the buildings. Somebody laughed loud and long, the sound dopplering like a receding ambulance siren.

Wren had to get off the street, and staggered forward. A coffee shop twenty yards ahead looked inviting. More vehicles raced through the gloom, closing in, and he pushed open the glass door and entered.

Inside there was no smoke or dust, a box of clear air somehow preserved in the midst of chaos. For a nauseating moment Wren stood in the doorway, a sitting duck entranced by this vision of normality. He could almost be back in Frederica, picking up coffee for Masako and shakes for the kids. Soft wall lights with teal shades cast a golden glow across the dark oak flooring. The dozen or so tables had glossy walnut tops married with black cast-iron frames. There was gentle geometric art on the walls, in vivid but comforting colors.

But nobody was here.

Porcelain coffee cups sat on tables, their contents half-drunk. It felt like he'd climbed aboard a ghost ship, decks empty while its tattered sails flapped overhead, roaming the ocean alone. He circled behind the counter, feeling like a ghost himself. Where even was he? How had he come to be here?

To his left the milk foamer buzzed. The espresso machine hummed. The fridge pumped out a wave of cold air. He glanced over the sandwiches, rolls, muffins and milkshakes on display, stomach rumbling, but he didn't think he could keep anything down now; not after the things he'd seen.

The gunfire and shouts outside grew louder.

He slumped against the counter and tried his radio. He tried Clara Baxter and Sally Rogers and Theodore Smithely III, but nothing went through. It was useless. Outside another truck raced by, barely visible but for the hot flash of a mounted machine gun ripping chunks out of unseen enemies.

There was a landline phone beside the bean grinder, and Wren grabbed it. It was a long shot, but when he held it to his ear, there was a dial tone.

Another truck whipped by and Wren dropped behind the

counter, sinking to the floor and cradling the phone in his lap. The cold tiled floor felt like heaven. For maybe thirty seconds he just sat there, listening to that dial tone like it was a lifeline to the real world. Only the boom of bombs rattling the cups on the shelves pulled him back into the moment.

He dialed.

Clara Baxter's number was busy. Sally Rogers' went through and rang. A minute passed and he read the motto written on the wall. COFFEE IS LIFE. He watched the clock as a second minute ticked by. It was the small hours after midnight, 3:32 p.m.

The mad hours.

His body slumped lower against the cupboards. The line rang. Another minute ticked by, then finally an answer came. This time the line was terrible, raspy and scratchy, but her voice reached down as if from on high.

"Agent Rogers."

"Sally, it's Chris," he said. "I went to Luhansk. The town was empty, but I found a mass grave. There were hundreds or thousands of bodies. That's what they're doing. It's the Circassians all over again."

A second passed. "Circassians?"

"Tribal peoples the Russians have crushed for generations. It's genocide, Sally. Mass destruction of civilians." He paused, battling for the words that should come easily. "Deynekin wasn't there, but he had been. He's back in Russia now, and he has my hackers. We need to..." He paused, trying to push through to the next step. "We need to find him. End this. Uh..." He trailed off."

Seconds passed, long enough for Wren to worry the connection had been lost, then Sally Rogers breathed out. "My God, Chris. Genocide. OK." She took a moment, steeling herself. "Have you got any evidence of that?"

"I've got photographs. Video."

"OK. I'll send someone for you. Where are you, Chris? You sound worse than before. "

"I feel worse. I'm exhausted, Sally. And I don't know where I am. I drove west out of Luhansk. Maybe you can track this line and tell me."

"You don't know where you are?"

"I crashed. I don't remember any of it."

A few seconds more passed, then the business-like tone came back. "One moment."

The line clicked. Wren drifted on the rat-a-tat sound of small-arms' fire outside.

"Boss," she came back, a cold dread in her voice. "You're back in Severodonetsk. You really didn't know that?"

He hadn't. It wasn't good. He cursed.

"Exactly. You're in the heart of Russia's staging post for all of eastern Ukraine. This is very bad, Chris. They've converged dozens of battalions around it. They have it enclosed on all sides. I don't know how you got in, but I don't know if it's even possible to get out. The place is more rubble than it is buildings by now."

Wren wavered. "The front lines can't be far from here. I can break through."

"But you don't even remember driving there. How are you going to break through?"

He rubbed his temples. "I'll make it." He looked around. "I'll drink some coffee. I'm in a coffee shop, after all."

She let out a panicky laugh. "Coffee's not going to save you, Chris."

"Let me rig up a drip line and see."

She didn't laugh again, and silence hung between them until it was broken by a woman's screams from the street.

"Listen, Chris. I'm going to do everything I can to get you out. I have your position and I'm working up an exfiltration route. You say you've got evidence of a mass grave?"

Wren blinked. Had he said that? "Yes. It's all on my phone. If you put a satellite over..." he reached for the word, "the Aviation Museum in Luhansk, you'll see the pit. It's huge."

"Not happening, Chris. Our satellites are getting blocked by theirs. Low orbit jamming, Chris. We need that evidence." She sucked in a breath. "It's going to hell out here. We're fighting a losing public relations battle. Evidence might help us punch through. And we need you. We need Deynekin." Keys clattered in the background. "There's no clear route through Russian lines, so I'm going to try to create a corridor for you. I'm dialing in Army, Navy, the Ukrainian Special Forces. We'll launch some distraction attacks. I'll give you a bearing, you follow it, and I think we can briefly break the cordon." More seconds passed. Wren floated. "You'll need to stay put to receive the bearing though, Chris. We have no radio comms anywhere in Russian-held territory. It's a miracle you found a working landline. I need you to stay in that coffee shop, right by the hard line, and answer when I call. Can you do that?"

He didn't know. The shouting in the street was getting louder. "I'll try, Sally."

She exhaled hard. "OK. Good man. I'm working on it. One more thing you should know; comms could die completely at any moment. For the last few hours we've been going steadily blind, losing huge swathes of our comms lines, including military. We prepped for a data bomb when the shadow line hit Active Function, we ramped up digital security as much as we could, but this..."

Wren let his eyes lapse closed and focused on her voice only. "But what? Are we losing more ambassadors."

She laughed. "Way worse than that. Someone's actually cutting our physical infrastructure. We've got a dozen undersea cables offline already, and do you know how they're doing it? It's disgustingly efficient, like slamming our own planes into the damn towers."

Wren bristled, trying to picture that. Underseas cables were by definition highly inaccessible. "How?"

"They're using small tug ships on the open ocean, each one trawling long, deep anchors." Her voice dripped with contempt. "It seems they drop the anchors to the sea floor and rake the sediment. The location of most of our trans-Atlantic and trans-Pacific undersea cables are broadly known. Even if these tugs take just a best guess, then rake those anchor lines far enough, they'll trawl up the cable and snap it. Simple. Cheap. Almost impossible to detect on radar. You know how hard it is to locate and bomb a tug ship on the open ocean, Chris?"

Wren's body felt like it was sinking into the tiles. The odds were astronomical. He knew spotting a single tiny ship in that expanse was a task beyond even Rex's capacity, and there had to be tens of thousands of ships at sea around the world. Thousands of them would be within range of an undersea cable at any given time. Detecting which ones were dragging an anchor would be functionally impossible.

Wren didn't know what to think. He hadn't expected that. "We were vulnerable," he managed.

"Our whole ass was hanging out!" Rogers barked back, jolting him. "We're going deaf, dumb and blind, losing our ability to communicate, and if we can't see and we can't talk to our people overseas, to our nuclear submarines or our overseas bases, then we can't project force. And if we can't project force…"

She trailed off. There was no need to finish the statement.

"We've lost," Wren said.

The words resonated through the empty coffee shop.

"We've already lost," Rogers agreed "Our eye was off the ball. Right now we're trying to locate and bomb ships that might be trawling anchors, but it's a crapshoot." She sighed. "If you came across a register of those ships in Luhansk, you'd let me know, right?"

He smiled even as he felt the crash rearing up over him like a wave. "Scout's honor, Sally."

"OK then. Gotta respect that. Just hang tight, Chris. You're my priority. I'll get you out. I'm making calls right now, but I'm on the line still, OK?"

"OK," he mumbled, and laid back on the tiles. The gunfire from outside dimmed as darkness rolled in and he was swept under by the tide.

36

TIDES

The ringing of the phone dragged Wren back up from the depths. After a few seconds of dizziness and confusion, he realized where he was: gazing up at exposed ceiling ducts, laid out behind the counter of a coffee shop in the depths of Severodonetsk.

Sally Rogers was calling, the phone shrill, but there were also voices just yards away, barking orders.

Voices inside the room.

"Ono prishlo ottuda," one of them ordered. "Posmotri!"

Wren didn't understand the words exactly, but it sounded perilously like, 'It came from over there. Go look!'

He froze. The phone kept ringing. Footsteps slapped closer.

"Posmotri na eto mesto!" the voice shouted. "Eti zhirnyye ukrainskiye svin'i."

Wren guessed some of that, something about fat Ukrainian swine.

The laughter grew. Wren had nowhere to hide and no energy to run. His hand went to his waist but the Grachs were gone. He glanced to the side and saw his utility belt shoved against the cupboards. He vaguely remembered pushing it away in his sleep.

Too far.

The footsteps stopped. The quality of light shifted as a figure leaned over the counter.

Wren looked up and saw a young man above the counter. His blue eyes were wide in an oval face, with sweat, soot and blood stains running down his smooth cheeks. His helmet was battered. His Russian uniform was filthy. There was no telling what crimes he'd committed in the last twenty-four hours.

His eyes darted between Wren's prone figure and his belt, loaded with twin MP-443 Grach pistols. Seconds passed that felt like an age. Wren was helpless. One shot and it would all be over, and not a thing Wren could do about it.

"Chto eto?" came the shout from in back. 'What is it?'

That broke the deadlock.

Wren pushed off the cupboards and slid for the Grachs. His sleep-addled hand stubbed the nearest holster, fumbled the heavy pistol once, twice, then a shot rang out behind him.

Something ruptured and Wren felt the impact along his side, then managed to lift the Grach and swing the barrel around to-

The young man was gone.

Wren lay absolutely still, heart thumping with both hands wrapped around the Grach's grip, shaking and sweating while he tracked the barrel along the line of the counter. Where was the boy? What had been shot? He wasn't sure. His body felt like a foreign land to him, every part of it hurting.

"Nichego," came the young man's surly voice, footsteps stamping away now. "Nepravil'nyy nomer."

'Nothing,' Wren understood, and was the rest of that, 'wrong number'?

The other man laughed.

"Zhirnyye ukrainskiye svin'i," repeated the second voice. Ukrainian swine, again. Gunfire rang out and glass nearby shattered, then the men were gone.

Wren lay still, trying to understand what had just happened. The boy had definitely seen him. He'd fired. Something had taken the hit. Wren heaved himself up onto his elbow and scanned the length of his body. There were shards of red plastic across his lap that looked like hard crystals of blood. But not blood. Then he realized the ringing had stopped and looked sideways.

The landline phone lay in pieces where the boy's bullet had shattered it. A great shot. Enough to silence the ringing, enough to placate the figure in back, enough to prevent a shootout and keep Wren alive.

Had that been mercy, then?

Wren rolled to a sitting position, stars shooting behind his eyes, and strapped the tactical belt back around his waist. He tried not to think about the look in the boy's eyes. He couldn't think about that now, not on the battlefield. Mercy would get you killed.

Slow and steady, he stood and looked out through the glass. The dust from outside was spreading into the coffee shop like an infection now, pouring through the shattered doors. Wren cast a hungry eye over the espresso machine and the fridge full of sandwiches, but pushed that thought aside too. He'd be even less able to keep anything down now.

Then he became aware of a distant ringing. His ears pricked up. Not on this floor. Next door? No. Upstairs?

He walked back along the counter. A fire door in the back led to stairs and he climbed. Every step ached. At the top there was a small corridor which led to a sturdy metal door, locked. The ringing was coming from the other side.

Sally Rogers with his exfil plan.

Thoughts raced through Wren's mind. Maybe this was an office. It could be an apartment.

"Stand away from the door," Wren shouted through the metal, waited twenty seconds, then fired at an angle into the handle. The Grach pushed its full-metal jacket slugs through the metal frame and into the mechanism. In three shots something inside sheared. Wren stepped back, took a deep breath and shoulder-barged the door. The frame shrieked and separated and he tumbled into an apartment beyond.

He caught his footing and spun. A living room. There was a beige couch bed against the wall, a woven rug on the floor, shelving filled with books and DVDs either side of a dining table, a large-screen TV playing an animated kids' movie with the volume muted, and two children staring back at him from behind a low coffee table.

Wren stared back.

The kids couldn't be older than five or six. A boy and a girl. A sudden ache in his chest hit, and he thought of the little girl in the tutu back at the torture house, her throat cut. These children were wearing their pajamas, one showing an ice princess, the other a green monster eye. Their pajamas were stained with food. Wren felt the world outside falling away, even the sound of the ringing phone disappearing.

"Strashnoho," Wren said, summoning the few lines of Ukrainian he'd memorized. "Nichoho strashnoho."

'It's OK. Everything is OK.'

The little girl whimpered.

The phone kept ringing, set on a side table beside the couch.

Wren dropped to one knee, holstered his weapon and held out both hands, palms out. "Where are your parents?" he asked, trying to make his voice soft, but it was rough with smoke and dehydration. "Where's your mom? Your dad?"

The little boy began to cry.

Wren cursed under his breath. How many homes across Ukraine were like this one, now? Children abandoned by circumstance. Alone. Maybe their mother had just stepped out to talk to a neighbor. To ask what was going on. To collect food. Or maybe she'd been at work downstairs when the first Russian brigades swept through. Maybe their father had gone out to fight in the first call up.

Now they were both gone.

Fresh anger burned in Wren's chest, adding to the ache.

"Nichoho strashnoho," he soothed again. "I promise. I'll get you out of here."

He stood and edged slowly toward the couch. The children flinched tight to each other and began to wail, their eyes bugging wide and spilling tears.

"It's OK," Wren murmured, then reached the phone. He dropped back to both knees, feeling dizzy from the exertion. The wailing stopped briefly, and they watched closely as he lifted the phone from its cradle.

37

ELSA

"Chris?" said the handset.

A fresh wave of weariness came on Wren with her voice. "Sally. Tell me you've got a way out."

"We'll get to that. What took you so long to answer? Is everything OK?"

Wren looked at the children. The wailing had stopped abruptly when he'd answered the phone. For some reason he thought of the soldier with the blue eyes.

"Everything's fine. But I've picked up an entourage. Two children."

"What? Kids?"

"There's probably children all around me. Every building here must be full of them. But these two are alone. Maybe these two, I can save."

A few seconds passed. The little boy snuffled and wiped his nose with his sleeve, and Wren couldn't help but smile. One more stain.

"OK. Well, kids notwithstanding, you need to leave right now. What reports we can gather say the Russians are leveling the city block-by-block. They can't be far from you now."

Wren's heart sank. "Like the Circassians."

"I can't argue. It looks like you're right, Chris; Russia is clearly targeting civilians. This whole thing is a genocide and a war crime, conducted under cover of the shadow line. Now they're salting the earth. But I've got a corridor lined up for you. We have almost no visual over the city, so it's going to be tight and you'll need some luck. There's dust and smoke, and our drones getting shot down. I've got artillery fusillades along the route, some bomb drops lined up, plus some skirmishes planned to pull the Russian front lines apart. The best I can do is give you a bearing of best fit to squeeze through the gaps; you'll have to read the lie of the land on the fly."

Wren grunted. "What's the bearing?"

"Two-seventy-three. North-west, basically. As long as you stay close to, but don't cross, the Siverskyi Donets River, you should be good. Once you hit two miles out you'll be able to pick up the P66 highway. Russia's bombed it but latest intel says it's passable. It's likely the last chokepoint they'll have. But you need to go now, Chris. Get a fast car and drive."

Wren's mind spun. He looked at the children. He thought about all the other families in nearby buildings, destined to be reduced to rubble. He couldn't save them all. He couldn't save any more than these two, and that was only a hope right now.

Jake and Quinn came to his mind unbidden.

"Have you got someone there who can speak Ukrainian?" he asked. "Ideally a woman?"

Seconds passed. On the TV screen the ice princess was splashing bright colors and shapes across the darkness, singing a song about venturing bravely into danger. Wren thought he might have to explain why he needed a translator, then Sally came back.

"Yes. What do you want her to say?"

Wren smiled. Sally understood. "That I'm a friend and I'm

going to help them. That there's bad men outside and they need to be quiet and follow me. They need to trust me. They need to stay with me. If they run now, that's it. Can she say all that, in the nicest way possible?"

"Yes." Sally answered. "Give me a second."

Wren remained on his knees in the living room of a family he'd never meet. The two children gawped at him. He had some idea of how he must look; a hulk of a man covered in dust, blood and mud, heavily armed and armored, with a bedraggled face, lips busted, bruised and scraped. A soldier who'd just exploded into their living room and spoken to them in a language they didn't understand.

They had to be beyond terror. Terror made you revert. Made you needy. Made you put on your favorite old DVDs and try to ride it out.

He set the handset on the table and raised both hands up to cover his face, held them there for a few seconds, then opened them outward.

"Peekaboo."

The little boy flinched. The little girl stared stonily. Wren tried a smile, careful not to show his teeth, and tried again.

"Peekaboo."

The little boy began to cry. The little girl hugged him close. Wren took that as progress. At least it was a connection.

"Nichoho strashnoho," he said. "It'll be OK."

"We're ready, Chris," came Rogers' tinny voice through the handset. He picked it up and held it to his ear.

"Hello?"

"Hello. I'm the translator."

"What's your name?"

"Beatrice Smith."

Wren considered. He looked at the screen. "Call yourself Elsa."

"Elsa?"

"Just trust me. It'll help. Keep them on the line until I'm back. OK?"

"OK. Elsa."

"Now tell me, how do I say, 'This is my friend, Elsa'?"

"Simple. 'Tse moya podruha, Elsa.'"

Wren turned to the kids and gave it a try. "Tse moya podruha, Elsa."

The little boy stopped crying at once. Wren held out the phone. They looked from the screen then back to Wren, but made no move to take the handset.

"They're terrified," Wren said. "Start talking, try to lure them in. I'll be back." He laid the handset on the coffee table close to the children, then pushed himself up and backed off, bulling through the dizziness. He heard the translator's tinny voice speaking through the phone and watched the little girl flinch.

That was another connection. She was listening.

All he had to do now was get a car.

38

ESCAPE

The street outside had fallen quiet, the dust thick and muffling the sound of distant bombs. The soldiers were gone, it seemed. Wren padded back the way he'd come, past Volkov's smoking Ural, scanning the road for a vehicle he could jumpstart.

After a block he turned left and chanced upon a parking lot. To the right a building was on fire, belching smoke into the air. Wren advanced through the lot, picking out first another Dacia, a Lada, a Toyota. He wanted something fast. Then he saw something unexpected and surprisingly pristine. A gleaming silver Tesla.

He picked a stray brick off the blacktop and covered the last few steps to the driver's side window and pulled back the brick to break the glass.

Only at the last moment did he see the face looked out from within.

Wren almost dropped the brick.

It was the young man with the blue eyes. He stared up at Wren. Wren stared back. It was a moment of peak unreality. In any other life, Wren would turn and walk away.

"Zavesti chertovu mashinu!" came a shout from Wren's right.

'Start the car!'

He spun and saw a man emerge from the smoke barely ten yards off, zipping up his flies. He saw Wren. They stared at each other for a second, long enough for a breath of dust to pass between them, then he went for his weapon.

Wren flung the brick. It crossed the distance and hit the man in the face with a solid crack, knocking him backwards. Wren chased it, falling on the soldier with his Grach drawn. The man spluttered blood, and Wren hammered him in the temple with the gun's grip.

Gunfire cracked from behind. Wren threw himself sideways, came up on one knee and fired.

Instantly he regretted it.

The young soldier with the blue eyes stood beside the Tesla, holding his chest. Even through the curtains of dust Wren could see the blood pumping between his fingers. He brought his hand up and looked at it, like he couldn't believe this.

A moment ago he'd been showing mercy. Now he was dead.

With what little life he had left, he refocused the gun on Wren, but Wren fired first. The bullet clipped him dead-center between his blue eyes and spun him back against the Tesla. He went down.

The dust sealed over.

No voices came clamoring after them. The soldier beside Wren gulped for breath. Wren put a shot through his skull. The sound was muted. There was no response.

He walked over to the young man. He was long gone, blue eyes staring sightlessly into the brown mist. Wren cursed. This was what mercy brought you.

The Tesla door hung open and Wren dropped in. The engine was already on, humming low with power. The battery gauge was full. He didn't see a key fob, and no effort had been made to hotwire the cables, which would have been a non-starter anyway in an electric car. The young man must have the key. Wren dropped by his side and searched his pockets.

There was a wallet with a family photo inside, and a picture of his sweetheart; a. sweet-looking dark-haired girl. The key fob was there, too.

Wren took it and climbed in the Tesla, closed the door, shifted into drive and pulled around the lot, careful to avoid the two corpses. He stopped outside the coffee shop, left the engine running and entered. By the fridge he gathered two large paper takeout bags and filled them with sandwiches, yoghurts, drinks, bottled water and candy. He dumped these in the Tesla's back seat then jogged back into the shop. Up the stairs, a fresh fear bit into him. What if the children were gone? What if they'd been taken? What if they'd already been murdered?

He shouldn't have been gone so long.

By the time he ran through their open doorway, his heart was slamming and he'd envisaged a dozen awful scenarios.

The living room was empty. The children weren't there and the animation movie was no longer showing on the TV; now there was some half-dressed female pop star prancing on a stage. Her skimpy leotard was made of red and gold, and featured a large five-pointed star prominently across her chest.

"Hello!" Wren shouted, and ran to the table where the handset remained. He snatched it up but the line was dead. He scanned the room for signs of violence, then broke for the three doors. The first was a tiny bathroom, empty, the second was an adult's immaculate bedroom, and in the third he found them.

They were getting dressed, pulling on an assortment of jackets and shoes. The little boy was there, trying on hats. The little girl was struggling to pull a pair of jeans over her filthy pajamas.

The relief almost felled Wren.

"Nichoho strashnoho. Let's go."

As they finished up, he cast an eye around the walls, then went back into their parents' bedroom. There was a dresser table and he quickly rifled through the drawers.

There were all manner of papers and documents inside, neatly filed in clear plastic wallets. He glimpsed at least one passport and some academic transcripts and gathered them all into a cloth bag hanging off the bed's corner post. The kids would need them; all the ID Wren could muster for their new life.

The little boy and girl were waiting for him by the couch. Hand in hand. The translator had worked miracles. Wren nodded smartly, like he was inspecting them. "Very good. I'm impressed. Let's go."

He ushered them out. They walked. On the way out Wren paused by a side table and scanned several framed photographs. He saw a family; father, mother, children, now fragmented. A day out at a theme park. A day at the beach. He grabbed all the pictures and stuffed them into the bag. This was all these children would have of their parents.

He led them down the stairs. They were scared by the dust, but he mimed holding his breath and ushered them through to the car. They all ran together. When they saw the goodies in the back seat, the little girl squealed with glee.

"Knock yourselves out," Wren said, then put their seatbelts on. They shrank away at his presence and he didn't blame them, but in seconds everyone was secure, he was back in the driving seat with the door closed and the engine humming its fake sound. The Tesla's dash had GPS that wasn't operating and a compass that was. Wren marked 273 on the dial, gently pushed the gas and pulled away.

39

REFUGEE

The drive through the dust-swamped streets and alleyways of Severodonetsk took far longer than Wren expected, and was conducted in a constant state of nerve-fraying tension. The children shifted, squabbled and cried; children Wren couldn't meaningfully communicate with, could only shush and lull and attempt to soothe while the world around them collapsed.

There were multiple Russian foot patrols to evade, along with a tank column grinding steadily west, a mobile artillery outpost booming from the grounds of a middle school, and countless roads jammed with fleeing civilian vehicles or blockaded by Russian Urals.

At moments he caught glimpses of the Siverskyi Donets River through the dust, and did what he could to track its contours. Occasionally he was aware of the distractions Sally Rogers had timed to his escape: bombs bursting off to the left; surging battle to the right. It helped, but still Wren had to turn around often, speeding through hairpin three-point turns on streets clogged with debris while soldiers approached, weapons raised, only to take long, winding detours off his bearing. Throughout he kept one eye on the car's battery.

With every moment it faded further, and Wren dreaded the moment it finally died, leaving them stranded in the dust and searching for another vehicle.

They came closest to disaster when a figure suddenly lurched out of the fog before them, dressed in torn clothing and shrieking at the top of her lungs. It was a woman no older than twenty-one, with a bloody face and clothes. Wren hit the brakes, killed the engine and turned to the children.

"Stay here, stay low," he whispered, gesturing them to drop flat in their seats. He opened the door, then a gunshot rang out.

The woman fell onto the car's hood and spat up blood. Another shot came in and took her in the back, and she slumped off the car to the blacktop below.

The voices of men speaking Russian rang through the smog. They were laughing. Four or five of them at least, perhaps more. Every instinct in Wren itched to stalk the dust and kill them, but he was in no fit state, and he had the children to think of. Instead, he silently shifted the car to reverse and drifted backward like a cloud, thankful for the silent electric engine. Only two hundred yards away did he carefully close his door and take another street.

After something like four hours, with the sun rising through the smog, they finally emerged from the cloud of dust. By then the children had fallen to fitful sleep in the back. The car's battery was down to the dregs and Wren himself was running on fumes.

A makeshift barricade lay ahead, with a long line of civilian vehicles backed up before it. Above the barricade fluttered the blue and yellow of the Ukrainian flag.

The Tesla chose that moment to die. Wren stepped out, leaned into the backseat and slung the bag of photographs and paperwork around the little girl's neck, then plucked them both up, cradled them in his arms and limped along the line of abandoned cars to the blockade.

Everything after that was a blur.

The children were taken from him by medics with the Ukrainian flag patch on their arms. In a triage tent they stripped his filthy armor, stabbed sutures into his wounds and swabbed him down with iodine disinfectant. At some point he must have said his name, because minutes after that they packed him onto an evacuation helicopter.

The rotors fired up and the helicopter ascended. Sitting in the all-consuming thrum of the rotor blades, surrounded by fellow escapees of the war zone, many of them bandaged and all of them filthy, Wren gazed out at the carnage of craters, fire and dust below. From all this, he'd saved two children and evidence of genocide.

It hardly seemed enough.

He looked at the packaged lunch in his hands. A ham and cheese sandwich, a fresh green apple, a small bottle of banana-flavored milkshake. He dimly remembered a nurse with haunted eyes but the prettiest smile pressing them into his grip moments earlier. He'd tried to tell her he didn't need them, that other people needed them more, but she'd wrapped his shaking hands around them still.

"You need them," she'd said in smooth and firm English, accepting no further resistance. "they're for you."

He ate the sandwich numbly. He slurped down the milkshake. He barely tasted anything. His ears still rang. His eyes burned. His body ached and stung and throbbed in equal measure, as his mind tried to make some sense of the events of the last twenty-four hours.

The little girl in her tutu. The dead victims in the torture house. The commander who'd saved Wren's life then taken a rocket to the shoulder. The beauty of the Luhansk Aviation Museum by night, chased by the pit filled with the Luhansk dead. The boy with the blue eyes, killed for showing mercy. The dead woman in the road.

Nobody but Wren could tell their stories now. The war had swallowed them all.

The pilot said something but his voice was a gnat in Wren's ear. He pulled off the headset and welcomed the crushing white noise of the rotor blades. Improbably, like a babe cocooned in arms, the rhythmic beat lulled him to sleep.

In dreams, he was back on the hilltop of his Delaware farm with Masako.

The stars shone brilliantly. They stood side-by-side and hand-in-hand, looking out over the gentle mist rising off the trees toward the velvet sky, where a flurry of shooting stars arced across the black. This time, no drone dropped from the sky.

Wren reached down into his pocket. He found a small box waiting for him, and dropped to one knee. He recited the short speech he'd prepared, something suitably poetic that passed in a blur, then held out the box and opened the lid. The ring inside sported a faceted diamond as big as a cube of ice.

Masako gasped. She dropped to her knees and wrapped him up in her arms, kissing his face everywhere, even on his wounds, and then she said-

40

POZNAŃ AIR BASE

Wren woke as the helicopter came down.

Masako was gone. He peered out into bright sunlight across a long gray runway to a blocky line of large gray hangars, flanked by squat block buildings. For a moment he thought he was back at Luhansk Aviation Museum, but there wasn't any drone of flies or the scent of death in the air.

He rubbed his gritty eyes and sat up straight. The vertebrae in his back clicked and a host of scrapes and scratches stung against their stitches and bandages. This was a different helicopter from the one he'd evacuated in, he realized; smaller and faster, with seats for only four. Maybe he had the phantom memory of swapping over: his arms spread over the shoulders of porters, shifting him to here, putting a drip in his elbow and...

He looked down to find the clear plastic tube leading to a needle passing into his skin. The bag on the other end was empty. He pulled out the needle and held the hole.

Getting too old for this.

He pushed open the helicopter's door as the rotors wound down, blinking against the light, and saw someone waiting for him that he hadn't at all expected. He swung his legs off the seat and leaned out, hardly believing it was real; like a vision from another life.

"Clara Baxter?"

She smiled. "Welcome back to Poland, Christopher Wren."

It was bizarre to see her, but also strangely comforting. It brought back a part of himself that he'd put on hold in the dust of Severodonetsk. He couldn't have spent more than twenty-four hours in the war zone, but it felt like a lifetime.

"I thought you'd retired," he managed.

She snorted. "I did. But love does strange things to us, doesn't it?"

Wren puzzled over that for a moment, climbing out of the helicopter. His body pulled and stung, but he felt better than he'd expected. "You're saying Gabriel told you to come?"

"Not exactly. He's on the run, Chris. He took the girls and they fled into Slovakia."

That alarmed him. "What? What happened? Are they all right?"

"They're fine, at least I think so." She sighed. "With comms down it's hard to check. Rex predicted Bratva or the SOF or some other assholes would keep coming for me, and I couldn't stay with them after that. I was making them a target. All that left was for me to come here and try and end it sooner."

Wren grunted and stopped before her. She did look different; something about her eyes. "It's your fight now," he said softly.

"It's my fight," she agreed. "What about you, are you ready for more?"

He shrugged. "Sure. Why not?"

"I only ask because you don't look ready."

He laughed. "I'm falling apart, but that doesn't matter." He let out a deep breath. The sun was low in the sky, and he couldn't tell if it was morning or afternoon. He checked his wrist, but there was no watch there, only his purple zip-tie bracelets. "How long have I been out?"

"Around seven hours since you left Ukraine, I think. Apparently you were out cold for all of it. The initial evac dropped you at Kyiv Airport, where you were treated by a secondary medic team, who plugged you up with more fluids then redirected you here."

"And where's here?"

"Poznań Air Base, on the western edge of Poland. The military bases in Ukraine aren't safe." She gestured around at the empty runways. "It's quiet here because Poland's mustered all its planes east, in case Russia goes for a clean sweep of old Soviet states."

Wren looked at her. She really did seem different. The same dark black hair, the same tactical strike suit, but a new light in her eyes. "I'm glad you're here, Clara."

"Where else would I be, as the world comes apart at the seams?"

He grunted. "Did you speak to Sally Rogers?"

"Yes. Last reliable contact was three hours back. Half the undersea lines are down now, and what's left of satellite comms is corrupted with disinformation. Rex can't maintain a single clean connection to the States. We're functionally cut off. But Rogers told me what you found."

That threw him back into the dark and the drone of flies. "Luhansk."

"Luhansk," Baxter agreed heavily. "I'm sorry, Chris."

"Me too. But now we know who's behind it. Vladimir Deynekin. Tell me you've got something on him."

Baxter winced slightly. "I got everything Sally Rogers could muster. Since then we've been working every lead we can think of, trying to come up with a location for him and where he's keeping Hellion and B4cksl4cker."

"And?"

"A lot of ghosts and supposition. The man's a cypher, Chris. A genius, undoubtedly. With the shadow line cutting comms and pumping out BS on everything left, he's winning the information war, hands down. Half the world thinks we're at fault here, that we're the ones throttling the flow of data while Russia and China are the good guys trying to set the Internet free. We're struggling to get any counter narrative out." She sighed. "Have you got the Luhansk footage? That could really help."

Wren gritted his teeth. It was ugly to use a pit full of dead innocents as a weapon in the data war, but ugly was where they'd come to. "On my phone."

"Good. There's things we can do with it even with the Internet dying. Servers we can upload to, places we can start spreading the word and hope it'll push back Russia's support."

Wren said nothing. That sounded like a pipe dream, especially with half the lines down. "We need Deynekin."

"Rex has prepared a full debrief. There's food waiting, too." She pointed toward one of the large gray hangars. Its main bay door was rolled down, but a side entrance hung slightly ajar.

"Rex is here too?"

"He's been invaluable." She started toward the hangar and Wren fell in beside her. "You look like you could use a good meal."

He snorted. "I think I had some spaghetti bolognese and a sandwich in the last twenty four hours. A couple of milkshakes, too."

She smiled. "Then you're in for a treat."

41

STEW

The door in the hangar led to a narrow office partitioned within the larger space. There were three gray couches arranged in a U shape around a large projector screen, beyond which lay desks and monitors occupied by seven people. They all looked up when Wren entered, and in their eyes he saw the fear. It was palpable in the air around them, like the dust of Severodonetsk, like it had followed him here.

"This is Christopher Wren," Baxter announced brightly. "These are top local CIA assets, each an analyst with field experience, the very best Rogers could pull in before reliable comms fell apart." She pointed to the couches. "Take a seat, Chris, I'll get some food and we'll debrief."

Wren grunted and scanned the people at their desks. Nobody he recognized. They were all young; typical for active CIA agents in overseas roles. Baxter headed for a door and Wren walked over to the analysts.

"Where are we with the war?" he asked.

The analysts looked amongst themselves.

"It's OK." Wren focused on one young man, mid-twenties

with a dark sweep of hair standing proud atop his head. "What's your name?"

"Welby Bohannon, Krakow Station, specialist in explosives. Mr. Wren, uh. I'm sure Ms. Baxter has told you comms have been decimated?"

"Good to meet you, Agent Bohannon. And I'm aware. What about physical advances?"

Bohannon nodded. "We believe Kyiv fell four hours ago. There are no clear reports. Ukraine's President has fallen silent. There's nothing in or out of the Presidential Office."

That came as a punch. Wren had feared it, but the reality was worse. If Kyiv fell, then why not the whole country? Why not other countries?

"What are we doing about it?"

A woman with big ear rings and tight corn rows popped to her feet, holding out her hand. "Agent Evita Brock, sub-head of Vienna Station, with experience in Paraguay, Germany and Iran."

Wren shook her hand. "Report, Agent Brock."

"Yes, sir. We're functionally blind out there. Our command structure's in pieces. EUCOM, that's the US European Command, may be sending out strike orders but we don't know if they're getting through, and we can't trust anything we do get. We've already received fake orders to retreat, to fire on friendlies, to advance into traps. The shadow line is sowing chaos."

Wren grimaced. "What about expansion of the theater of war? Is China on the march? Did they go after Taiwan?"

Clara Baxter came back through the door, holding a tray laden with a large steaming bowl alongside three thick slices of chunky brown bread. "I see you're getting your debrief early," she noted.

"Agent Brock," Wren pressed.

"Taiwan fell seven hours ago, Mr. Wren," Brock

answered. "It's gone. Last intel suggested China was exploding beyond its borders, eating up territory in Nepal, Kyrgyzstan and Mongolia, along with huge swathes of the South China Sea. Russia's expanding beyond Ukraine as well, into Moldova, Tajikistan and Turkmenistan. Maybe more that we don't know about."

More punches. Wren didn't know what to say or how to roll out of the way, so he took each blow on the chin. The world order was crumbling and America was powerless to stop it.

Baxter set the tray down on the coffee table between the couches. "Better to think about what we *can* do, Chris. Not dwell on things far outside our ability to influence." She pointed to the couch. "That includes sitting down and eating up. You'll feel better, and you'll get a full debrief on Deynekin. We've not been sitting on our hands out here."

There was a glint of the old defiance in her voice, which was good. Wren didn't think he could take any more defeat right now. He grunted, went over to the couch and sat down, looking at the bowl before him.

"It's called 'Bigos'," Baxter said. "It means 'Hunter's Stew', a traditional Polish dish made with fresh, cured and smoked pork shoulder. There's mushroom and caramelized sauerkraut too. You dip the bread and-"

"I think I can eat a stew, Clara."

She smiled. He'd caught her mothering him, which was not a word or an action he would ever have associated with Clara Baxter before. "I'm sure you can."

He picked up one of the slices of bread. It was soft on the inside but crusty on the outside. He ripped the piece in half and faint whispers of steam escaped, then he dunked it into the glossy brown stew.

Fragrant vapors puffed upward. Golden button mushrooms rolled in the mix, as did shredded strips of pork;

some seared brown, some smoked a candy pink. The scents were intoxicating: the thick oiliness of meat juices; the sweet aroma of the braised onions; the unctuous richness of thickened gravy.

He brought the bread up to his lips and bit down. The first sensation was pain, as the salt in the broth bit into his torn lips, but that was rapidly followed by an explosion of flavors that made his eyes pop and his heart speed up. It was meaty, rich and hot. The bread had a little crunch and various seeds splintered satisfyingly beneath his teeth.

"Good?" Baxter asked.

"Amazing," he mumbled around the mouthful of bread, already dipping again while fetching up the spoon to chase it down. "My compliments to the chef."

"I made it myself."

The spoon and the bread halted halfway to his mouth and he fixed his gaze on her. It seemed quite a leap, but she had once hated him, and she was infamous for using the tools of an assassin.

She laughed. "You think I might have poisoned it?"

Wren studied the spoon. "You've done worse."

"Not this time. It's fine, Chris. Watch." She stuck a second spoon in and gulped it down.

Wren watched her a moment longer. There were no symptoms of poisoning. He grunted and shoveled the whole spoon into his mouth.

He did not regret it.

It was the same taste as the broth, but richer, deeper and explosive. Sweet and savory meat juices burst in his mouth, sending an involuntary shiver down his spine. He could almost feel fresh strength pouring into him.

"Good, right?"

"Don't watch me eat," Wren grumbled around his food, then chased the spoon with the bread, from there beginning a conveyor belt that served a continuous stream of stew to his mouth.

"I love to see a man with an appetite," Baxter said. Wren ignored her. "I'll go get Rex ready for the Deynekin debrief. You eat."

Wren swallowed another chunk of bread, only half-chewed. Maybe things weren't so bad, after all.

"Bring a second bowl," he called after her.

42

DEBRIEF

Wren felt better after the first bowl. After the second, he felt wonderful. It was amazing what ills a hot bowl of delicious stew could heal over. The pains scattered across his body were still there, but barely noticeable for the warm meat coma descending upon him. Just as he felt himself starting to slip backwards into the couch's warm embrace, Baxter appeared again with a large jug of black coffee and two mugs.

It finished the job, the perfect combination to leave him both satiated and awake. He took several long pulls of hot coffee then looked up at Baxter, feeling the caffeine rush into his system.

It was all happening now.

"OK, so what have you got on Deynekin?"

"Rex?" Baxter said, looking upward.

"Hello, Christopher," came the AI's smooth Californian accent, sounding from speakers mounted in the rafters. "I have conducted an exhaustive study of Twelfth Directorate Commander Vladimir Deynekin, including a thorough examination of any location he may be keeping Hellion and B4cksl4cker. Unfortunately, there is no satellite imagery and nothing captured via any form of CCTV on his current whereabouts. He is far too digitally adept to be caught out in this way. His physical location has been 'ghosted' from all records dating back decades, so we are left to make assumptions. The first and most obvious assumption is that he might utilize GRU headquarters in Moscow as his base of operations."

The projector overhead hummed to life, spilling light onto the screen. A map appeared showing Moscow. The city's layout was familiar to Wren, and visibly embodied the country's hierarchical political system: the Kremlin stood at the very center on a bend of the Moskva River, around which concentric circles of ring roads stretched outward like ripples in a pond. A spot northwest of the Kremlin lit up with a highlight and the letters GRU. The map zoomed in on a boomerang-shaped building highlighted in flashing red.

"The GRU is located in Khoroshovsky District," Rex narrated, "on 3 Grizodubovoy Street. Deynekin certainly could run his cyber war from here. There are likely tens of thousands of server cores here, a high speed trunk line to the Internet and doubtless to the shadow line. In addition, there are thousands of skilled spies, intelligence workers, strategists and bureaucrats to handle the war's logistics. But I believe Deynekin is unlikely to use the GRU as his base of operations."

Wren considered. "Why's that, Rex? It's got to be a secure location. The GRU may be an obvious target, like the Pentagon, but it'll most likely be bombproof, with most of its functions buried deep underground. It's a good location."

"The reason is not related to security, Christopher," Rex countered. "It is a simple question of Vladimir Deynekin's character and behavior. I have run a wide-ranging personality analysis with logistical and predictive capacity based on his past behavior. On the Meyers-Briggs personality scale he charts as a textbook unhealthy ISFJ, or Introverted, Observant, Feeling and Judging type. In essence he is an outward-looking introvert who deeply understands people's inner motivations, with the desire to exercise judgment over them at a distance, often through third-party means which he longs to control completely. The Internet is a prime enabler of such a man. When unhealthy, this personality type has been called a 'Puppet-master'." Rex was silent for a moment, perhaps giving Wren a chance to absorb all that. "His sensitivity to others allows him to manipulate them masterfully, often to highly destructive results. For your reference, other famous ISFJ puppet-masters include Heinrich Himmler, architect of the Holocaust, and Lavrentiy Pavlovich Beria, chief of Soviet security under Stalin and architect of the latter day genocide of the Circassians." Rex paused again. "In addition, Deynekin appears to exhibit profound narcissistic, sadistic and sexual depravities; he enjoys causing destruction via his position of power at the Twelfth Directorate. I found multiple instances where he has personally destroyed political enemies via state-empowered data attacks. A man of this character would never tolerate being personally exposed in any way. As such, I believe he would not accept the GRU as his main office, where he is just one Commander amongst twelve. He would be fully aware of the way his forbears, Himmler and Beria, were run to ground, and would consolidate his power base elsewhere, with multiple escape routes should he ever need them."

Wren grunted. That was a lot. "I don't put too much stock in personality tests. Did you get that one off the Internet, Rex?"

"It was not clickbait, Christopher," Rex replied, which was a more sarcastic response than Wren had expected. "This is as close to science as the study of personality allows.

Wren looked at Clara Baxter. "Do you concur?

Deynekin's a puppet-master and a control freak, so he won't be at the GRU? You could argue that his personality type would make him want to be at the thick of it, dominating his peers in the GRU with the success of the shadow line."

"Not at close quarters though, Chris," Baxter said firmly. "I agree with Rex's assessment, Chris. This war is highly personal to Deynekin, but I believe he'd try to perpetrate it at a distance. All reports indicate he is the creator of the shadow line, which basically embodies that approach."

"He designed the shadow line?"

"Designed and built," Baxter continued. "Think about that for a second. His personality drove him to build an entire personal Internet over which he has absolute control. That's more than just being a control freak. It's empirically megalomaniacal. This war is his, Chris, one hundred percent, just like the shadow line is his. I don't believe he would settle for anything less than absolute control over his physical location, too."

Wren said nothing. It was a lot to grasp. "OK. So if he's not at the GRU, do we have any idea where else he would go?"

Baxter took a breath. "One idea, Chris. Have you heard of the Naukograd program?"

43

NAUKOGRAD

"The what program?" Wren asked.

"Naukograd. Sally Rogers sent it over in a huge tranche of Deynekin's suspected activities." Baxter brought up her phone and started swiping through pages. "I fed it to Rex and he scanned it for highlights. It's tens of thousands of pages. A lot's speculation, but the gist is that the CIA believe Deynekin and the Twelfth Directorate are behind the 'Naukograd', or 'Science Cities' program; it's a whole range of new 'start-up' cities spread across Russia, each in their own special political and economic 'zone'."

Wren frowned. "Start-up cities?"

"Think mini wannabe Silicon Valleys. There's at least a hundred of them stretching from Moscow through Siberia to Vladivostok in the Far East, often built within or on top of the Cold War's existing 'closed cities'; Area 51-like zones blocked off from all travel." She kept swiping and reading. "Originally the closed cities were built and staffed by gulag prisoners doing forced labor in top-secret military factories, but most of them were shut down at the end of the Cold War. It seems the CIA have never got a good look at them." She looked up again. "Getting spies inside Russia is hard enough, let alone getting into a closed city."

Wren grunted. He'd had some experience with deniable black ops in Russia previously. "OK. Are any of these 'Science Cities' viable headquarters for Deynekin's war?"

"I think they all are, Chris. In the past decade or so Russia's flooded investments into each of the Naukograds, providing massive tax incentives to redevelop them into tech hubs. They build out the infrastructure in advance, so each of these new cities looks like an Iota or NameCheck campus, with dozens of cool buildings, bright colors, ping pong tables, fireman's poles, etc, while packing them with servers, supercomputers and optic fiber cable. The apparent purpose was to bring in foreign companies and kickstart an innovation revolution, getting a third leg going to the Russian economy going, beyond agriculture and fossil fuels."

Wren could see where this was going. "And how did that work out for them?"

"On the surface, terribly. Russia spent billions on the Naukograds and none of them have produced anything much: no disruptive new tech companies; no brilliant new ideas; no must-have apps. Until recently, all anyone thought they were good for was hosting troll farms and disinformation signal boosters, pumping out black-ops BS to fracture the world."

Wren grimaced. "They're innovative enough at that. Tearing things down. Russia's got the wrong culture for creativity, though. Too prescriptive, too hierarchical."

"Right, and perhaps innovation was never really Deynekin's aim," Baxter went on. "Some in the CIA argued that the Science Cities were really just loosely-concealed attempts at IP theft and corporate espionage. They sucked in Western tech companies offering cheap rates and funding, get them to share their existing code and ideas, then boot them out and steal the content. That's one theory. The other theory is that the Naukograds are actually the backbone of the global shadow line."

She fell silent. It was an impressive ending point.

Wren cursed.

"If that's the case," Baxter went on, "and the Naukograds are fundamentally criminal in nature, as backed by a totally corrupt government, it's possible they've actually served as massive money pumps for years, funding the spread of the shadow line."

"Money pumps?"

Baxter nodded. "Right. It's a well-known fact that some fifty percent of the world's financial hacks originate in Russia. We're talking billions in income there, highly under-reported. Western companies that do get hit often cover it up, and when they make some noise, the Russian government always passes it off as lone hackers, people they're actively hunting down. But there's a clear argument that it's all State-sanctioned, even State-sponsored. Picture the Naukograd cities full of militaristic hackers waging darknet attacks on the West." She let that hang. "Misinformation's a massive one too; even an export to other countries. Say I'm a small-nation African President and I want to destroy my political enemies to secure my election? Russia's the obvious service provider. They've got the expertise, like a reputational hitman."

Wren considered. "Billions, OK. But a global infrastructure project like the shadow line, reaching into every country in the world? It'd take trillions."

Baxter smiled grimly. "You're right. Perhaps Russia's biggest income stream comes from an innovation they co-opted and fed into their disinformation accelerator. Cryptocoins."

"Cryptocoins? You mean like Hitcoin?"

"Sure, but there's hundreds if not thousands of different kinds of coins by now, Chris, and the vast majority are

Russian pyramid schemes. The Science Cities are perfectly placed to pump out cryptocoins, since all you need is vast computing capacity to 'mine' them. They're also perfectly placed to produce the propaganda that cons regular folks into 'investing'. 'Get rich quick', you know? It seems Russia's got the market cornered." She paused for a breath and scrolled on her phone. "In the last few years, the CIA estimates the Russian government has made seven trillion dollars in foreign exchange currency off cryptocoins. It's a total money siphon. Easily enough to fund the Naukograds, the global shadow line, and then some."

Wren said nothing. It was a lot. It painted a picture of a corrupt country that had lost the Cold War on every level, and was left to turn to crime as its major industry. The alternative was simple, but to the Russian government likely unthinkable: Democracy. Free markets. Free speech. Unchain creativity, innovation and critical thinking. But that wasn't going to happen under President Burin's watch, and it wasn't conducive to giving men like Brezhny Volkov and Vladimir Deynekin what they wanted most: unalloyed power.

"And Deynekin's the architect of all this?" Wren asked. "He's behind the Science Cities?"

"All accounts indicate that. They started springing up right after he took over the Twelfth Directorate."

Wren thought about that. The pieces were starting to come together, and the picture they created was unexpected. He poured himself another mug from the coffee jug and sipped it hot. "So Deynekin built the shadow line from the ground up. He financed it with theft, hacks and cryptocoins. He grew it to a global level. Now he's using it to provide cover for a global transfer of power, the same way he used the darknet to transfer money. That means he could be using any one of the Science Cities as his personal HQ and throne." He turned back to the screen, still showing Moscow and the

GRU. "Rex, can you plot the known Naukograds on a map of Russia?"

"Of course," Rex replied.

The map zoomed out to encompass all of Russia, an immense country stretching across eleven time zones, complete with internal borders for the numerous 'oblasts' or states, with portions of its external borders shaded a slow-pulsing red where it had recently annexed chunks of its neighbors.

"Is this map live, Rex?"

"Yes, Christopher. I will feed reliable data in as we have it. Adding Naukograds now."

Red dots started appearing on the map, rising to over a hundred. They were clustered around the east and west, but there were some two dozen or so spread throughout the empty center of the country, and they formed a clear spine.

"That's the shadow line," Wren murmured.

"This is a likely supposition," Rex said.

"And Deynekin could be at any of these?"

"We believe they all have the capacity to host a shadow line control center."

Wren cursed. It was too many. "We have to narrow this down."

"If you have any suggestions, we are listening," Rex said.

Wren ran his gaze around the map. The pulsing red of the annexed territory made it look like the surrounding lands were bleeding. Ukraine was swallowed in blood. Portions of a dozen flanking countries had been bloodied as well. Every inch meant thousands or tens of thousands of casualties. Millions of refugees. The world had been thrown into chaos, soon to come under the vicious thumbprint of President Burin, Vladimir Deynekin and their allies.

Wren's mind spun. He thought back on everything he'd

learned about the shadow line and Deynekin. An unhealthy ISFJ. A puppet master.

Something shook loose.

He rose to his feet, picked up a black marker and drew a swift circle on the left of the map, then turned back to face Clara Baxter and the CIA analysts, who'd risen from their desks and circled up to watch.

"Moscow," Wren said, projecting his voice and looking into their eyes one by one. They were all pale and drawn. Perhaps they hadn't slept in days, hadn't spoken to friends and family in weeks. "If Deynekin is everything you say, Rex, then he'll want to absolutely control the source of his power. You say that's the shadow line, his own personal Internet? I think you're right. He'll need phenomenal computing capacity, server farms for days and the fastest Internet trunk line possible to run his cyberwar. The Naukograds can provide that. But also, his power stems from the political."

He turned to Clara Baxter. "You mentioned Himmler? I've studied him. He held the rank of 'Reichsführer-SS', second only to Adolf Hitler, for twenty years. He orchestrated the entire concentration camp system. He built the rail lines, and the gas chambers, and the SS to enforce them." He paused, thinking ahead. "These were immense feats of transnational infrastructure. As for Beria, he ran the vast national Gulag system, encompassing millions of forced laborers. Both sound like Deynekin, right? But neither of these men achieved any of this just by their will alone. Without Hitler's support, Himmler wouldn't have gotten anywhere. It's the same with Beria and Stalin. They both gravitated to the central wellspring of power to fuel their own. History says Himmler scarcely ever allowed Hitler to even leave the room, let alone the building or the city, without hanging on his coat tails. Beria was first in the room when Stalin collapsed, and first to kiss the dear leader once he was pronounced dead."

He paused to let that settle in, then stabbed Moscow with the pen.

"For Deynekin, that center of power is President Anton Burin. It's the Kremlin. All political power in Russia flows from here." He drew a circle around Moscow. "A man like Deynekin would not operate far from that center; let's say within a hundred miles of Moscow, even two hundred to be sure. That's less than an hour in a helicopter, close enough that Burin could summon him on a moment's notice."

He eyeballed the map's scale, then drew two concentric circles around Moscow. The map zoomed in accordingly, stretching as far as Smolensk in the west, Yaroslavl to the north, almost to Novogorod in the east.

It was considerably less ground to cover, but a vast amount of land still. There were few major cities but countless towns and villages, and around twenty Naukograd dots.

"Rex, get us all the details on those cities that you can. Everything. Their specs, the companies that have passed through them, the cryptocoins they make, the hacks they've waged." He widened his gaze to the analysts. "Take two or three each. When Rex pumps it out, you process it. We're looking for anything to signify a command center, or Deynekin, or the presence of hostages, or anything at all suspicious. We need it right now. Go."

The analysts broke for their desks, enthused with new purpose. Wren stood for a moment longer, trying to get into Deynekin's head, then looked at Baxter.

"It checks out," she said. "Deynekin would want to be near Burin. Rex, what do you think?"

"I concur," Rex said. "It is an excellent start."

Wren grunted. "We need more. We're also going to need a way to hit this place, once we narrow it down. Tell me there's some planes left in these hangars, something that can at least get us to the edge of Russian territory."

Curiously, Clara Baxter smiled. "I was waiting for you to start suggesting jumping out of planes. I think we can do a little better than the edge of Russian territory, though."

"What? How?"

"Rogers laid in a pleasant surprise. You're going to like this Chris."

"Like what?"

"Come on. I'll show you."

She started toward the side door leading into the main hangar.

44

INSERTION

Clara Baxter opened the door and Wren stepped through.

The main hangar was vast and dim, and it took a few seconds for his eyes to adjust, playing over the shape of the enormous craft ahead of him. It was all-black and looked like something you'd blast into space, a huge single wing with no discernible cockpit, fuselage or tail. More of a giant rounded triangle than any plane Wren had flown in before.

"It's a B-2 stealth bomber," Wren mumbled, in awe.

"That's right," Baxter said brightly. "Sally Rogers really came through for us. She said you'd suggest some kind of paradrop, once we knew Deynekin was back in Russia. I expect she took it to the President for approval directly. After all, what use is remote force locked away on a German air base if you haven't got the ability to direct it?"

Wren walked out under the giant craft, gazing up. Its name was emblazoned on the underside in paint barely discernible against the base gray.

SPIRIT OF KITTY HAWK.

"I didn't even know they had crew capacity," Wren said.

"They don't, there's only room for two pilots. It's basically a flat flying wing. But they do have big munitions bays."

Wren surveyed the giant machine. He knew something about their capacity and the program that had built them. In one sense, they were archaic; a multi-billion dollar program that reached its peak in the heights of the Cold War, with production discontinued around the turn of the millennium, when America felt certain they'd won. In another sense, they remained phenomenal pieces of engineering, pushing design and materials tech to their very limits.

"It can evade Russian radar? I mean, still?"

"Rex says it'll cut through with ease. They won't see us. The plan is to enter high, pushing up against the ozone layer, then release high wearing full oxygen gear and only deploy chutes low to the ground. That's around five minutes of freefall. No way for them to detect us. We regroup on the ground and strike."

Wren turned from the craft back to Baxter. "'Us'? So you're coming with me?"

Baxter smiled. "Sure. You didn't think you were going to hit Russia alone, did you? You and I will hunker down in one bay and the CIA team in the other. We'll need some heating gear, as the munitions bays will be hitting zero or below, but that's taken care of. When the moment comes, we'll all flush together right out of the stratosphere."

He studied her. "Stratosphere? That's pushing up to fifty thousand feet. Have you ever even sky-dived before?"

"Once or twice."

"From extreme altitude? Deploying from that kind of height is a different ballgame."

She shrugged. "I'll manage."

He accepted that and nodded, then went back to circling and admiring the B-2's wings, which were permanently spread like a blackbird sunning itself. "Two billion per plane," he said. "And they're giving it to us."

"I don't know about giving it," Baxter said, following behind. "I imagine it's more of a loan situation."

Wren reached up and ran his fingers along the plane's belly. Every contour of the underside was sleek and rounded, a perfect example of the 'continuous curvature' design that cutting-edge computer modeling had created way back in the late 80s, avoiding any sharp angles that caught the eye of radar beams. The flattened design ensured no vertical surfaces to trap lateral radar. The carbon-graphite material composing the shell absorbed significant amounts of radar, too, while being stronger than steel and lighter than aluminum. On top of that, the multi-spectral gray paint further absorbed radar, reduced heat output and blended in to match the appearance of the sky. Contrail-inhibiting technology and an ingenious combustion design that kept the engines buried deep in the shell to reduce infrared detection were just icing on the cake.

"Chris," Baxter prompted.

Wren turned. He had no idea how long had passed, just staring up at this beauty. "What?"

"I said, is this crazy enough for you?"

A slow smile spread across his lips. "I think it'll do."

"Good. So we come back to the question, where do we insert?"

Wren thought for a moment, then led the way back to the office area. The CIA analysts were hard at work, some tapping at their keyboards, some reading from their screens, some conferring over printed papers in hushed voices. The projector screen still glowed with twenty-plus Naukograds in the perimeter around Moscow.

"Anything yet, Rex," Wren said, addressing the speakers overhead.

"Not yet, Christopher. We're looking for some means to narrow down the cities further. We haven't found it yet."

"Keep looking." He turned to Clara Baxter. "In the meantime, maybe we can slow the spread of Russian disinformation a little." He fished in his pocket and produced his phone. It was dented, bloody and muddied. "There's video and photographs. Get it out there as well as you can. If it slows down the flood of support to Deynekin by even a few minutes, it's worth doing."

She took it without hesitation. "Will do, Chris."

"Have you got a phone I can use in the meantime? One that's secure?"

"Sure." She went over to the desks, pulled a phone out of a box and handed it to him. "The reach is abysmal, though. You won't get to the US, but there's some chance of getting through in Europe, if that helps. Who are you going to call?"

"I don't know yet." Wren took the phone and nodded his thanks, then poured himself a fresh coffee, turned and headed toward the main door.

"Where are you going?"

"For a walk. I need to think."

45

BOLT

The air was clear outside, the sky a shocking chemical blue, the sun startlingly yellow. Gray runways stretched away to distant chain-link fences. There were no planes, though, and no people out working, ferrying bags, waving batons. The airport looked abandoned and all the more peaceful for it.

Wren strode out on the ocean of gray asphalt, sipping his coffee as he walked, thinking about ISFJs, the Naukograds and the shadow line. There was something niggling in the back of his mind, something missing, but he couldn't figure out what it was. He tried to clear his thoughts to make room for it.

After maybe ten minutes of slow, steady trudging, he reached the edge of the runway. The chain link fence lay ahead, gray steel with green forests beyond. Wren picked out sweet chestnut, white willow, large-leaved lime and European Oak. Poland was beautiful, really.

He brought up the phone and started tapping out a message. There were two bars of signal, whatever that meant now. He didn't expect the text would get through, maybe not now, maybe never, but he wanted to send it anyway.

HI LORALEI. IT'S CHRIS. I'M SAFE.

He thought a while before writing more.

I KNOW THIS WASN'T OUR DEAL. PLEASE TELL THE KIDS I LOVE THEM AND MISS THEM.

He paused again. Once he would have typed I MISS YOU TOO, but not now. Maybe that surprised him a little. The romance with Masako had been a whirlwind for the last six months. Until it happened, he'd still harbored hopes of winning Loralei back. He hadn't thought of her that way since Tokyo, though. She was the mother of his children, the gatekeeper to him playing a role in their lives, but that was all.

He hit send.

A warm wind blew and he turned back to face the hangars. Far away, they didn't look like much. You'd never guess one of them held a two-billion-dollar feat of American engineering.

The phone was still in his hands. His fingers picked out the next number instinctively. The line rang. Wren started walking slowly along the fence, listening. It rang for a minute, then two, then gave out.

He rang again. Again at two minutes it gave out. He kept ringing and walking until finally the line answered and a familiar voice spoke.

"Agent Tanaka."

Her voice sent a bolt direct through Wren's chest, ramping up his pulse and pinning him to the spot like an anchor dropped through the blacktop.

"Masako, it's Chris," he managed.

Seconds passed. "Chris, is that really you? Are you OK?"

"It's me," he said, pushing through the tightening in his throat. He hadn't really expected the call to get through. "I'm OK. Did you, uh, get into Italy all right?"

She chuckled. "Sure I did, two days ago. The intelligence

confab was canceled almost immediately, though. They seconded us to Italian intelligence, hunting down nodes on the shadow line." She paused for a moment. "How are you even calling me, Chris? I heard all lines out of the US are down."

For a few seconds Wren didn't know what to say to that, and a wave of unexpected emotion rose over him. He'd seen too much, done too much, and those things couldn't just be washed away with adrenaline and Polish stew.

"Chris? The signal's bad. I-"

"I'm in Poland," Wren blurted. "It's, well… It's complicated, Masako. I… Maybe you heard that my hackers, Hellion and B4cksl4cker, were abducted by Russia?"

There was silence for a moment, followed by a soft curse in Japanese. "I didn't know that. I'm sorry, Chris. And you're in Poland? Are you looking for them?"

"Yes," he said, pushing through the clouding emotions. "I was in Poland chasing down Clara Baxter for a while, then Ukraine to hunt down a Russian general and his boss, now I'm back in Poland. I'm…" He trailed off. He didn't know what he wanted to say. "You were right about the real world, you know? It's all blowing up out here, and I shouldn't have hidden away. I need to be in it."

She didn't say anything for a few moments.

"Masako?"

"I'm sorry," she came back. "All that feels so long ago now. I didn't mean to hit you with any of it. It was a beautiful moment, Chris. I keep thinking about that hilltop, that view, and..." she sighed. "It's something to live for, you know? Something to fight for. And I ruined it. It was selfish. My own fears."

A shiver ran through Wren. He hadn't expected that. If anything, it strengthened the anchor through his chest, bolting him more firmly to this place and this time. He hadn't wanted to think about how strange it had been with things feeling disjointed between him and Masako. He'd been off-balance ever since that moment, he supposed.

Not now.

"I feel the same way," he said. "I just had a dream about the hilltop."

"You did?" she asked, and the tone of her voice was different now. It wasn't Agent Tanaka of the PSIA anymore. This was the voice of Masako in his arms, lying together in his cabin or her Tokyo apartment.

"It was beautiful, Masako. I miss it. It's something to live for, you're right."

She said nothing for a time, but Wren could feel her. There were hundreds of miles between them, wars and cyberwars and crumbling infrastructure, but it felt like she was right there beside him anyway.

It felt good. It felt wonderful.

"I'm sorry I tried to make you choose," she said eventually. "I'm sorry I applied pressure. Your kids deserve you in their life just as much as we do."

Wren rubbed his eyes. "Thanks. I think so too."

She laughed. It was more relief than humor, followed by a comfortable, intimate silence.

"I miss you, Chris," she said. "Are you really OK? And you said you went into Ukraine, into the war zone? What happened?"

Wren smiled. Just moments earlier he wouldn't have wanted to talk about any of that. Now, with Masako, he felt he could share it. She would understand. "It's bad out there. Lots of dead civilians. I'll tell you more, later, if you still want to hear about it."

"I do," she answered. "Later, of course."

Wren basked in the warmth of the silence.

"How's Italy?"

She chuckled, sounding breathy and exhausted. "Crazy. I'm currently in a seedy part of Mafia-held Rome, operating with an Italian SWAT team. I'm learning some Italian between raids, you'll be glad to hear." He smiled. Masako already spoke four languages; what was one more?

"That's good news on the Italian. I've always wanted someone to order my gelato authentically."

"I'll teach you." A few moments passed, taking stock of this new reality. "The hackers, Chris. Hellion and B4cksl4cker. Why were they abducted?"

Wren sighed. "It's the shadow line. They were trying to warn me, back with that drone. They thought there was some kind of 'Nexus', a central command unit that controls that shadow line. They thought if they found it, they could shut it down. That put them in the Russian's crosshairs."

"OK, I get that," Masako allowed, "but I mean, why *abduct* them?"

The words didn't really register with Wren. "What do you mean?"

"Maybe it's nothing, but doesn't abduction strike you as a strange tactic to shut them up? Why not just kill them? That'd be easier, right, if all they wanted was to stop them hunting this 'Nexus'? That's what Russia does with political enemies. Poison on an umbrella tip, take them out, over and done. So why were they abducted?"

Wren felt a second bolt pass through his chest.

This was it, the missing piece, and everything shifted. He'd been so blind. Head in wrapped up in anger and seeking vengeance. The world spun one-eighty and now he finally began to wrap his arms around the true breadth of Deynekin's vision.

"That's brilliant, Masako," he said, already starting back toward the hangar.

"What's brilliant?"

"Never mind," he blurted, mind racing ahead a mile a minute. "I'll explain it all later. Stay safe, OK? I love you."

He killed the call and accelerated to a jog without ever realizing that was the first time he'd said the L word.

46

GEAR

Wren slammed into the hangar with the pulse of a fresh lead thundering in his veins, drawing the eye of every CIA agent.

"Gather around," Wren called, striding over to the projected map of Moscow. "Let's work this thing one more time from the beginning. Rex, are you watching?"

"I am, Christopher."

"Zoom the map out to a global scale and clear it for me, please."

The map zoomed out and the circle around Moscow faded. Clara Baxter perched on the couch's arm as Wren snatched up his black marker and turned to face his new audience.

Baxter wore a quizzical expression. The others looked pale and drawn. It didn't worry Wren at all. He was buzzing with possibilities and dived right in.

"Just hours before the war began, my hackers Hellion and B4cksl4cker were taken here, in Luhansk, while hunting the shadow line." He scrawled a circle around the city on the eastern edge of Ukraine. "Not assassinated. Not poisoned. Taken. Vladimir Deynekin sent me a message threatening their lives and a photo. Rex, can you bring that up?"

In the corner the hostage photo appeared: Hellion and B4cksl4cker looking broken, battered and concussed amongst the server racks of their mobile supercomputer. Several of the CIA agents winced.

"Seeing that flipped me out," Wren said. "I came rushing out here without thinking too hard about the logic of it. But what if that was what Deynekin wanted, firing me off half-cocked?"

Wren looked at his audience. No one spoke.

"I never asked why he took them alive instead of killing them." Wren said. "I should have, but that photograph got in the way. He played me."

Clara Baxter looked doubtful. "You're reading a lot into that, Chris."

"Maybe, but his personality type is 'puppet-master' genius, right? We're reading into that plenty. I wouldn't be surprised he's playing the same game against us. My record's public domain; there's easily enough behavioral data out there to model what I'd do. Either he waits until I hear about it, and think about it logically, and come for him direct, or he freaks me out with that photo and I end up chasing my tail in circles for days, wasting time." He stabbed at it again. "He played me, Clara."

The doubtful look didn't shift. "That's a spun-sugar construction, Chris. Either way, what does it matter?"

"We're getting to that. Listen. Volkov even gave half the game away when he said Deynekin took receipt of the hackers *himself*. Personally! I guess I forgot about that in the rush to Luhansk, but it's pivotal. It changes everything. Why would the architect of this entire shadow war come pick up two hackers personally, if all he wanted was to shut down their search for the shadow line?"

Wren looked out at his audience. A light seemed to be switching on in Clara Baxter's eyes.

"I saw this photo, and I only saw hostages," Wren said, stabbing the screen again. "A way to compel, enrage and distract *me*. But these aren't just hostages. These are two of the greatest hackers in the world. If there was a hacker Olympics they'd take every gold in the individual contests, and together? They'd go platinum..." Baxter's eyes flared wider. She had it too, now.

"No," she said. "Seriously?"

"What if the hackers weren't just hostages, but the target all along?" Wren rushed on. "Who better to prosecute the first global cyber war than the best two hackers in the world?"

Nobody spoke, but now the looks on their faces said it all. This was something. This felt solid, and it sparked a strange and furious joy in Wren's heart, buoying him on.

He spun back to the map, marker pen hovering over eastern Ukraine.

"Check my logic here. Almost immediately after they were taken, Russia launched their war." He stabbed Luhansk. "That was odd but I didn't question it too much, though now I'm certain it's connected. Deynekin had obtained his secret weapon, and it wouldn't take long to compel them to work for him. The cyber war begins. Rex, play the invasion in slow motion."

A red tide began to expand across eastern Ukraine, beginning with the tiny blip of red over Luhansk, just as Rex had shown earlier. Now Wren read far greater depths into that tiny isthmus of pulsing red.

"Maybe Luhansk was a trap," Wren theorized. "Deynekin set bait and the hackers rushed in. Volkov grabbed them and Deynekin took receipt then flew back to a Naukograd near Moscow."

Wren drew an arcing line from Luhansk to Moscow,

studied the map for a moment, then drew another one zipping in from the far left, landing in Poland.

"I come into Krakow searching for Clara Baxter," he pointed at her. "I find Rex under attack and that leads me in circles fighting Bratva, looking for something real in the Real Boy mess." He drew spirals around Krakow. "At the same time, Deynekin's keeping America busy with X-based rebellions. Rex?"

Tiny red explosions began to pop across North America.

"Now America's chasing its tail, but I get the lead on Volkov." He stabbed the town of Severodonetsk. "Volkov gives us Deynekin, but now anchor ships are popping the undersea cables everywhere."

Explosions started blowing in the oceans, and Wren felt the urgency carrying him on, and stabbed Russia squarely in the middle. "Deynekin really is a puppet master. He played me and he played us all; he stopped us tracking the hackers as if they were hackers. That's what he needs them for." He took a breath and looked up. "Rex, have you detected any hidden patterns or messages in Russia's behavior?"

A few seconds passed. "No, Christopher. The data is structured, of course, but essentially random."

"The Russians could easily screen for encrypted messages," Baxter chimed in. "Patterns in orders too. Anything detectable, they could find it. Even Hellion and B4cksl4cker couldn't get anything through their screens."

Wren thought hard. The photo of his hackers was still there, battered inside their own supercomputer convoy, filled with world-beating floor-to-ceiling server racks.

Then it hit him. The answer had been staring him in the face the whole time.

"Their gear," he blurted. "Clara, Hellion and B4cksl4cker are super hackers, right, and hackers at that level don't use off-the-shelf models, do they? They build their own rigs and server racks, use their own operating systems, their preferred coding language, all of that, correct?"

Baxter was on the edge of the armrest, already reading where he was going with this. "Yes," she said. "And Hellion and B4cksl4cker, they're more custom than most. You think Deynekin-"

"Deynekin's a logistical genius," Wren rushed on. "Just like Himmler, he's put together this incredible feat of infrastructure, wrapping the world in Naukograds and the shadow line. Just like Beria, he's running them like his own personal Gulag system. For a man like that to prepare gear for Hellion and B4cksl4cker would have been child's play."

Clara Baxter was on her feet. "Rex, you know their systems well, can you bring up the full spec?"

"Yes, Clara."

The left side of the screen faded and in its place a long scroll of data appeared. To Wren it was an unintelligible list of letters, numbers and symbols jumbled together in detailed product specs, but it launched Baxter to the board.

"There," she snapped, stabbing a finger at the list. "That's their server configuration. And there, that's one of their unique macros." Wren held out the marker and she started highlighting lines one after another. "Here, here, here. All of these are unique in combination. This code. This designer server. This rack, this cooler. They rig them in parallel. Here. Nobody else uses this combination."

In a minute the list was filled with underlined and interconnected pieces of software and hardware.

"Why should this matter?" one of the CIA analysts asked, Welby Bohannon again. "So they use unique gear. As I understand it, every programmer does. But they're not prosecuting the war on their own servers, are they?"

"Aren't they?" Baxter asked, then looked at Wren, who gestured for her to go ahead. "Rex, process everything we've got on the Naukograds around Moscow through this filter. If Deynekin had the hackers hit the ground running his war just a few hours out, then he would've been ready. You wouldn't expect an Olympic athlete to perform with equipment they'd never used before, would you? That means he had the correct rigs, the correct software, everything just as they like it." She started circling gear on the list again. "Some of this gear is extremely rare, only available from single manufacturers. That'll leave a trace we can track. Rex?"

There was silence.

Then the highlighted list flushed from the screen, leaving only the map, which began to move. It scrolled and zoomed. As they watched, the red lights of the many Naukograds around Moscow began blipping out. Within seconds the east was eliminated. The west followed, then the north, then the south. After twenty seconds there were just five lights remaining in the vicinity of Moscow, and the map zoomed tight on them. Then there were three lights.

Then there was one.

The map closed on it; some kind of campus facility around twelve miles out of Moscow. A dozen buildings.

Wren's mouth went dry, his heart hammering fast.

"This is the only Naukograd within range of Moscow that fulfills all the chosen criteria," Rex said calmly.

"One hundred percent?" Baxter asked.

"One hundred percent," Rex confirmed. "The nearest match is below the fiftieth percentile. As you say, this equipment is highly unusual and eclectic. Statistically, this provides absolute proof. Hellion and B4cksl4cker are here."

Hope burst in Wren's chest like an uncorked champagne bottle. They had a target Naukograd. He read the name.

"Skolkovo."

47

B-2

From Poznań, Poland to Moscow, Russia was a nine-hour flight in any conventional aircraft. Tucked away in the depressurized munitions bay of a B-2 Spirit Stealth Bomber, wearing oxygen helmets and clustered around heating filaments, it was an hour faster but felt like longer.

Wren lay flat on his back, gazing up at nothing while his new team chattered nervously on the back channels.

The engines roared. His breath sucked in and out inside the helmet. His mind drifted, pulse slow and relaxed, catching on moments and slipping loose again.

"Skolkovo's infamous," Baxter had said, ten hours earlier as they prepared to strike. "Apparently the CIA have had their eyes on it for years, one of the biggest Science Cities. I could name the US tech entrepreneurs who've passed through it and you'd recognize half of them. Some went on to build household brands, but get this." She scrolled through her phone. "Not one of them produced anything valuable at Skolkovo. You may have noticed, there is no Russian Iota, no Russian NameCheck, no Yangtze, other than cheap knockoffs. There's nothing new. These entrepreneurs talked about the 'hidden rules' at Skolkovo, everything that was unspoken. It was supposed to be a free speech, free politics, free idea zone, but it wasn't. It was a mental strait-jacket."

Wren said nothing. That was no surprise. The Russians could ship in all the tech gurus they wanted and pay them astronomical sums, but they'd still be restricted in the way every other Russian was; the Naukograd was a gilded cage but still a cage.

"What about layout and security? It's a big campus, I'm seeing twelve buildings." He surveyed the layout; the twelve buildings were organized into clusters of three and shaped like a low, flattened X. "What's the likely location Deynekin's holding Hellion and B4cksl4cker?"

"I am working on this," Rex had answered. "Above ground the layout and security are very simple. Satellite heatmaps dating back several months indicate the twelve structures are all energy-intensive server farms, pumping out vast amounts of heat. The compound seems to be guarded loosely, with fences and guard towers at the four gates, manned by a rotating team of twenty soldiers."

"OK, so that's above ground. Does that mean there's something below ground?"

"Yes. Skolkovo was built atop a closed city, Christopher, a highly unique one. It was a Potemkin village."

Wren grunted. He'd known his share of Potemkin villages in the past. He'd grown up in one; his father's fake town in Arizona had started out life as a film set for a Sam Peckinpah wild west movie that was never made.

"What kind of Potemkin?"

"Intelligence is scarce, but during the Cold War it seems this entire area was mocked up with the shells of civilian buildings, designed to obscure what lay beneath; a sprawling nuclear fallout bunker for Soviet authorities in the event of a doomsday scenario. Defector testimony indicates the land is riddled with a maze of tunnels, shelters and command and control facilities. I am attempting to collate maps of this network, but Internet access is poor and the data available very limited."

"So Hellion and B4cksl4cker are underground?"

"I believe this is highly likely."

"What about security down there?"

"I know very little. I have found one mention of a secret program called 'Minotaur'."

"Minotaur? Like the Greek myth?"

"Yes. There are associated hints of a robotic deterrent, automated gun emplacements and the like, triggered by movement, heat, other indications of an incursion."

Wren frowned. "Maybe that's what they spent their Naukograd budget on developing."

"I suspect you are joking, but it is quite possible, Christopher. The US Army has multiple mobile arms platforms, one example of which is the SPUR Special Purpose Unmanned Rifle robot 'dog', a four-legged mobile sniper automaton capable of accurate shots at three quarters of a mile out. It is very likely Russia has a parallel."

Wren didn't want to think about that; charging blindly up dark tunnels into oncoming rifle fire sent by a giant robot dog. "I've tackled similar dog units before. They're big but dumb. We'll need Black Hornet drones to survey ahead and explosive rounds to take out the dogs; regular bullets won't cause enough damage. As for the maze itself, we're going to need an Ariadne." He turned to Clara Baxter. "That's Rex."

Baxter took a second, then seemed to grasp what he was suggesting. "No, Christopher," she said firmly. "I can't permit Rex to go into combat. Under no circumstances."

"Maybe under these circumstances," he countered. "Can you track a real-time map of a vast Cold War bunker in your head? Can you calculate possible hostage locations on the fly, all while monitoring robotic 'Minotaurs' charging through the maze?"

She shook her head. "It doesn't matter. Rex is too valuable to risk. Right now he's maintaining a darknet shield over all of us. Gabriel and the girls. Your family. Your Foundation."

Wren blinked. "What?"

Baxter's jaw and brows tightened like she was holding something back, then released. "I didn't tell you everything, OK? With Hellion and B4cksl4cker gone, last reports said your Foundation had fallen. There is no place on the darknet to hide. Rex is currently protecting them as best he can, and without him running some level of interference, they'll all be easy targets. Gabriel and the girls. Your ex-wife and your kids. Everyone."

The world spun around Wren. "You're serious? Why didn't you tell me about this?"

"I thought you had enough to worry about."

He laughed. He took a step back then looked up at the speakers. "Is this true, Rex?"

"I am afraid so, Christopher. The shadow line is everywhere. I am currently fogging their vision, but it is a temporary defense only. I apologize for my part in this misdirection."

Wren let his gaze drop to Clara Baxter. She glared back at him defiantly. As ever, there was no trust. She'd tried to play him again, manipulate him, and now his kids were on the verge of becoming targets. The whole Foundation was a target. Once he would have gotten angry. Maybe he still would, at some point.

"It doesn't matter right now," he said.

That surprised her. "What?"

He pointed to the map of Skolkovo on the screen. "This place is the Nexus, Clara. It's what allows Luhansk, and Severodonetsk, and every other atrocity. We have to go all in, and that means committing Rex. I'm no hacker; I don't know how to switch off the Nexus, and you may be good, but I guarantee Russia has better. We need our biggest gun on offense, and that's Rex."

Baxter opened her mouth to argue, but Wren bulled on. "You already said Rex is better than you; like Deep Blue against Kasparov? We need that skill now. We get Rex to the Nexus and plug him in, and he has the best chance of shutting it down."

Baxter closed her mouth. Seconds passed.

"OK," she allowed. "You're right. So we go all in with everything we have."

Wren didn't say anything, unwilling to trample her as she backed down.

"It should be up to him, though," she added. "Rex, would you be willing to airdrop with us, perhaps just with your core server synced to some bodycams and Black Hornets, relaying maps to our helmet Heads-Up-Displays? And how confident are you about shutting down the Nexus, if we can plug you in? It'll be a risk, of course, but-"

"Yes, Clara," Rex answered easily. "I will join you. Mapping through the HUDs will be a simple matter, and I also believe I can take control of the Nexus. This is my primary function, after all; reduce harm to the people I care about. My calculations concur that this is the best course. I must join you."

Wren looked at Baxter. She clearly wasn't happy, but shrugged it off. "I'll start writing a guidance program, Rex. There'll be vast amounts of information to attack and counter-program in the Nexus." She looked at Wren. "I doubt it'll be as simple as plugging him in, though. Deynekin will have passkey protections."

"Then we need to get that passkey."

They looked at each silently for a moment, considering

what that meant. "Do you think you can pull another Volkov on Deynekin?" Baxter asked. "How far along is he on the true believer spectrum?"

Wren grunted. By all accounts, Deynekin was as extreme as they came. "Far. This is his baby. He'll be ready to die to protect it."

Baxter made a face. "So how do we get him to talk?"

Wren had no answer, and a heavy silence spread between them. Nobody needed to point out how unlikely success seemed. They could all feel it.

"What about exfiltration?" one of the CIA analysts asked; Agent Evita Brock. "We can't climb back into the B-2, that's for sure."

"We'll figure that out," Wren said.

"So we'll, uh…" Brock trailed off. "We'll just make our own way home?"

"We'll destroy Russia from the inside out," Baxter said, looking at Wren. "That's the gamble here, right? Take the Nexus and turn the shadow line against them. If it works, it'll cut *them* off. Isolate *them*." She turned to Brock. "He's hoping that with Rex's help, Russia will collapse overnight and there'll be no resistance in our way."

Wren said nothing. He hadn't gamed it through all the way, but she was essentially right.

"All in, then," Brock summarized. "Ride or die."

"Oorah," Wren replied. "Rex, there's some other things I need from you. If you can-"

A buzz on the open line pulled Wren back to the moment. The hard carbon graphite of the B-2's munitions bay door lay cold under his back, and the hiss of his own breath cycled through the suit's air system.

"Chris, are you ready to drop?" Baxter asked. "That was the call from the pilot. We're approaching Skolkovo."

He took a deep breath and looked at Clara Baxter, lying to

his left. Rex's core five boards were strapped into a server rack in her backpack, providing a wireless connection to Wren and the team. She was looking back at him, and there was that familiar mixture of emotions in her eyes again; anger and mistrust.

"Ready," he said. "And Clara?"

"What?"

He searched for the right words. She'd always been an angry young woman. That was understandable, after what she'd been through. He understood why she'd lied to him, and why she'd done everything she could to protect Gabriel and the girls first and foremost. But there were no right words. She understood what they were facing just as well as he did.

"I'm glad you're here," he settled on.

"Me too," she said.

"Rex, open the hatches."

There was a loud clank as the bay door locks disengaged. A moment passed then the doors opened, and Wren, Clara Baxter and their team were dropped out into the midnight skies 50,000 feet over Skolkovo, Russia.

48

LZ

The air ripped around Wren. In freefall, he felt free. Everything else was forgotten at the boundary to this latest war. Family. Friends. Responsibilities. All that remained was the mission.

He made no effort to slow his fall or glide, adopting a head down missile posture toward the designated LZ, or landing zone. The skies all around were dark but there was little cloud cover below, allowing a clear view of the spread of land. At this height he had a rapidly diminishing fifty mile view. He could see all of Moscow spreading out, the arteries of its many concentric roads pumping white and red. Directly below lay the gleaming speck of Skolkovo, the jewel in the crown of Deynekin's Naukograd program.

"Forty thousand feet," came Rex's calm voice in Wren's ear. "Four minutes descent remain."

The world began to shrink as his vantage point closed in. Maybe forty miles.

"Christopher, you are on target. Clara, please adjust course."

Rex went on, directing each of their team. For Wren it felt

like nothing. Like autopilot. This was what he did. He was good at it. He could almost do it in his sleep.

"Clara, you are off course," Rex repeated.

"I'm trying," she shouted back. "I can't quite…"

Thirty-five miles visibility. Wren made the decision on autopilot.

"Direct me to her, Rex."

"Yes, Christopher. She is approximately half a mile away, one-hundred-and-thirty degrees, three thousand feet higher, on a course leading her away from the LZ."

Wren immediately opened his body and caught the full force of air friction, instantly putting the brakes on his fall. With simple adjustments of his arms, legs and body angle he rotated and soared off at approximately one hundred and thirty degrees.

Thirty miles.

"Direct me, Rex," he said calmly.

"Five degrees further, Christopher, and slower."

The world rushed below and Wren splayed his arms wider, shifting angle and ripping across the night sky.

"I can't see her. Put on her suit lights, Rex."

"She will be visible from below, Christopher."

"Doesn't matter, just do it."

A new star appeared in the sky. Wren reoriented by the growing lights of Skolkovo below, calculated Clara's trajectory and reworked his approach to intercept. She was heading swiftly out of the zone Rex had calculated as their clearest approach through ground radar systems, seemingly unable to change angle.

Twenty-five miles.

"I can't get a fix on anything!" Baxter shouted down the line. "I can't even keep a straight line!" The star of her lights began to reel.

"It's OK, Clara," Wren said gently, zipping closer like a missile on a targeting wire. "I'm coming."

She cursed back at him, but it didn't matter. Everybody needed help sometimes.

"Rex?"

"Christopher, you are approaching the cut-off point of no-return. Reorient now or you will both miss the LZ and risk visibility on low ground radar from Dolgoprudny base."

"Hold tight, Clara," he said, and closed the gap.

Twenty miles visibility.

The star zoomed in. Wren shifted position to brake his approach and avoid a spiraling entanglement. "I'm on your right," he said, "Clara, I'm going to steer you in."

She cursed at him.

"Three seconds, two, one."

He hit her in the trunk like a hard tackle on the QB and together they spun. She lashed out automatically, like a drowning swimmer pushing their rescuer down, but Wren was ready.

He slipped around the blows, all the while speaking softly and calmly through the comms link. "I'm going to reposition your body, Clara, and I need you to stop fighting me."

"Two minutes, Christopher. You have ten seconds to reorient. You are already risking detection."

"Lights off," he said, and tugged to swing Baxter around onto the correct glide path. She still resisted but didn't know how to leverage against the faint friction of the air.

"Here," Wren said, putting her limbs in position even as he oriented himself right beside her. "Like this. You're doing it."

The kicking finally stopped. The thrashing ended.

"You are on course," Rex said. "You will land short of the LZ but you can make up this distance."

Through the comms line Wren heard Clara Baxter

whispering prayers. He hadn't expected that. He held one hand on her shoulder strap. She held to his. Together they soared in. Visibility constricted. Ten miles and falling.

"Thirty seconds," Rex said.

Wren reached across and located Baxter's pullcord. He guided her hand to it and held it there. "Pull when I pull," he said, looking into her face mask where her eyes would be, obscured by the dark.

She just nodded.

"Twenty seconds."

Wren watched Skolkovo below zooming closer. It was encircled by dark forests, fields and the countless bricked-up nibs of old bunker entrance points, but none were as promising as their original LZ.

"Now," Wren said, and pushed away slightly, just enough to ensure their chutes would not tangle. After a further two seconds separation he pulled his rip cord. The chute blasted out and cranked hold of the sky, yanking his terminal velocity descent abruptly short.

To his left he heard Baxter's chute blow too, then there were ten seconds of drifting, swaying fall, then he was tumbling through trees, legs bouncing off branches, and coming to a thumping halt on the ground.

He rolled to bury his momentum and was on his feet in seconds, every part of him thrumming with adrenaline. He hit the release button and the chute peeled away, then he spun.

Forest lay all around him; not the LZ, far from an ideal landing area, but good enough for this. Branches could pierce skin as readily as bullets even at chuted re-entry. He spun, searching for Baxter, but saw nothing, though he heard the rough sound of her breathing through the comms.

"Rex?"

"Clara Baxter has landed two hundred yards away, fifty degrees, Christopher. I think she may be unconscious."

Wren ran. Trees whipped by in the darkness, barely illuminated by the silver moonlight. He hit his suit lights, heart now banging in his chest.

"Fifty yards," Rex said. "She is unresponsive, signals indicate she is unconscious."

Wren put on a burst of speed, whipping between tree trunks and over gnarled roots. "Put her lights back on."

A sudden shock of white light burst to his right. Wren redirected and charged. In seconds he was there, dropping down by Clara Baxter's side, ripping off her helmet and his own and dropping his head close to her lips to listen for breath, even as he snuck two fingers to her carotid artery to check her pulse.

It pounded.

She was breathing.

He leaned back.

"Clara," he said, but she was out cold, eyes closed. He angled his own suit lights over her body, swiftly running his hands down her arms and legs and down her ribs, checking for injuries. There were no breaks he could detect, no wounds. He tipped her on her side and checked her back, and just then she sucked in a hard inhalation.

Wren let her back down.

"You're fine," he said gently, feeling far from it himself. "You're uninjured, you just took a hell of a thump coming in. Clara?"

He peered into her eyes, and the furious, fearful look there flung him back into the past; back to Pleasure Island when he'd rescued her from a sacrificial death atop the Pinocchios' iron altar.

She'd lashed out then; an all-encompassing ball of rage and terror that marked everyone as her enemy.

Now it was different.

Now there was something like trust in her eyes.

"Thanks," she rasped.

Wren smiled, even as a familiar feeling welled up inside him. This was what it felt like with his kids; teaching them how to ride a bike, or kayak alone, or handle a fishing rod. It required trust.

"It's nothing," he said. "I do that all that time."

She laughed, then unexpectedly punched him on the shoulder. "You do not."

"I'll admit, I could have used a more cooperative partner. Fewer punches and kicks. But I've had worse."

She peered at him, then laughed again. "Christopher Wren, mid-air redirection service."

"I'll have cards printed up."

She snorted. "I just wish I hadn't been screaming my head off on the open line."

Now Wren laughed.

"I took the liberty of excluding those moments from comms," Rex chimed in, his voice emerging tinnily from the helmets they'd left on the ground. "You were on a private line with Christopher Wren alone."

That hit Wren in the chest. Baxter just nodded. "Thanks, Rex. OK, let's go."

49

POTEMKIN

Wren and Baxter ran through the dark and tangled forest, heading for the LZ and designated entry point to the Cold War tunnels. There were no sirens incoming. No helicopter blades.

"We remain undetected," Rex confirmed.

Several times they ran up against brick and plaster structures left to rot and crumble amongst the thickets of new-growth trees. Each of these had a front door, and windows, and some still had portions of their tile roofs intact. At the first of them Wren peered through the gaping front door, only to see raw emptiness inside. No flooring other than dirt, no internal walls, no hints of furniture or plaster surfaces atop the brick. The only hints of inhabitation were a few rusted cans and the bulbous lines of amateur graffiti on the walls.

"Fake," Baxter said. "Like a stage set."

They ran on, along the thin skin of a mossed-over tarmac road, burst through in many places with tentacle-like roots. Larger buildings loomed in the darkness to either side, and Rex kept them informed in a low voice.

"The school. The library. The town hall."

All of them were Potemkin props. At one point the road ahead collapsed into a long, deep crevasse, revealing a capsized tunnel below, and they detoured around it through one of the taller structures: four walls reaching twenty feet high, with several doors and a range of tall, narrow windows admitting bands of silvery light. Only after they left did the outline become apparent; a 'church' with a tall tower.

Five minutes further on, they passed between the rusted iron railings of the village's fake cemetery, overgrown with real weeds and vines. Fake polystyrene graves lay in ramshackle rows, some with their headstones standing upright, some toppled as if by centuries of neglect. Each stone had the name and dates 'carved' into them, detailed enough that spy planes circling above forty years ago would be convinced. No bodies were buried here, though, at least not the ones whose names were listed on the stones.

At the center of the cemetery stood the five members of their CIA team, like ghosts in the moonlight, next to a tall, thick mausoleum that looked to be made of heavy gray stone. Wren touched the wall; unlike the graves it was reassuringly solid.

"What happened?" Evita Brock asked.

"I had a problem with my chute-" Wren began, but Clara Baxter interrupted him.

"I had the problem. Wren helped. We're both ready now."

Wren looked at her. She glared back defiantly. He respected that, and refocused on Brock. "Ready?"

"C4's in place," she said. "We're set to blow the door."

"Let me see it."

"Yes, sir."

She led the way through the mausoleum's open square arch, flicking her suit lights on casually. The interior was small and featureless; the same bare walls and ceiling as the church, except for the floor. It was solid poured concrete, as they'd suspected; a latter-day infill to block up one of the many entrance and escape routes to the bunker below.

Wren aimed his wrist-mounted light down, checking their work. They'd drilled four inch-wide holes five inches deep into the concrete, each now glinting with the shiny, bright pink 'prills' or pelletized beads of ANFO; an ammonium nitrate-fuel oil combination widely used as an industrial explosive. From each of the holes ran blasting wires.

"Looks good. Rex?"

"I am ready," Rex answered in Wren's ear. "Once we have a location for the Nexus, I will surge forces."

Wren didn't need to point out that 'closest possible range' could mean miles apart, given the size of the tunnels. Instead he looked over the team. Clara Baxter, Welby Bohannon, Evita Brock and three other agents. Once this bomb was blown, there was no going back.

Everyone understood the stakes. Wren didn't need a long speech to motivate them.

"I hear the coffee's great in Skolkovo," he said, and smiled. "Let's go get some."

They took cover behind graves. The air smelled of sap and dirt, and over the treetops the lights of Skolkovo compound reflected white off low cirrus clouds.

"We're ready, Rex," said Brock on the open comms line.

"Timing to a bomb drop from the B-2," Rex said, and they waited. A minute passed, two. Nobody spoke. "Incoming."

A minute later the ANFO blew, coughing dust out of the mausoleum's open mouth, at the precise same time as a bunker bomb hit five miles away on a military base.

"Releasing drones," Bohannon said, and opened twin egg-shaped casings. From within two tiny Black Hornet drones buzzed up their rotors and rose, gliding toward the mausoleum and into the dust, streaming footage back to Wren's HUD.

The ANFO had done its job well, opening the passage. The drones descended twenty feet then stabilized in a rubble-strewn corridor lined with pipes and cables.

"The path is clear," Rex said. "Your routes are established. I have intercepted chatter from Skolkovo; it seems both blasts registered on their seismic alert system and a minor response team has been mustered in this direction. They will be here within twenty minutes expecting a missile crater. Twenty minutes is all you have."

"Let's go," Wren said, and ran for the mausoleum, tossed his rappel rope down through smoke, hooked on and dropped into darkness.

50

LABYRINTH

Wren ran down dark tunnels alone, while Baxter, the two drones and the five-strong CIA team spread into alternate routes through the labyrinth. His suit lights illuminated maybe fifty feet ahead, beyond which his infrared cameras gave him a wireframe of the tunnel's contours, all collating into Rex's servers.

He passed through a large habitation chamber, littered with old and toppled bunks. No one had stayed there for decades, leaving rotten blankets, lime-scaled walls and the lurking stink of black mold. There were three exits, and Rex indicated his onward direction with a flashing green arrow. Black Hornet drones buzzed in behind him, taking the alternate routes to fill out the map.

"I've got a room full of bones here," came Brock's voice at one point some six minutes in. Wren could see her blip on the map, barely fifty feet away but with no intermediary tunnel between them. "I mean, full. There's enough skulls for thousands of skeletons."

"I'm looking at pipes," Bohannon said minutes later. "Forests of them. Enough plumbing for a city of ten thousand or more."

Time ticked by in racing foot beats and the map spread organically around him, branching like a stop-motion coral. Green arrows flashed on Wren's HUD, steering him toward the center, until at sixteen minutes in Rex sent him down a dead-end route the Black Hornets had already charted, which ended at a metal bulwark riveted directly into the stone.

"I believe this is the access point we need, Christopher," Rex said calmly.

"Understood," Wren said, and set down his satchel. The bulwark stood eight feet high and four wide, unblemished and rust-free. Wren found a natural depression in the rock on the left side, balled a handful of ANFO prills from his backpack into a shaped charge and tucked it into the hollow with a remote detonator.

"I have bombs already released from the B-2," Rex said. "Blast is in seven seconds, Christopher."

Wren took cover. The blast came precisely on schedule, perfectly synced to an aerial bombardment. Dust filled the tunnel and Wren switched to infrared.

"I believe we remain under their seismic radar," Rex said.

Wren ran into the smoke to study the damage. A boulder-sized gap had been blown out of the wall where the depression had been, rupturing the inch-thick bulwark inwards enough to allow access.

"So let's get their attention," Wren said, drew his Sig Sauer and climbed through the gap.

The tunnel beyond stretched left to right, brightly lit with industrial bulbs on a cable string. The walls were gray cinder block, the floor was poured gray cement, and new-looking pipework and electrical lines ran along the ceiling, along with something he recognized from the sewers beneath Tokyo: the fat orange cable of a high-speed optical Internet fiber.

"You're seeing this, Rex?"

"I cannot ... Chris ...," Rex replied, his voice breaking up. "Signal seems to ... Clara Baxter ... ."

The connection died. "Rex?" Wren tried again. "Can you hear me?"

Only the hiss of static came back.

Wren looked left and right. He was off the map and into something new.

He chose left, locked the Sig Sauer in a double-hand grip and advanced cautiously. The corridor arced gradually to the right and nothing further came from Rex. After three hundred yards there was a four-way intersection.

Dead ahead the corridor extended into darkness. Wren peered down the right-hand corridor. Clear. He peered down the left and saw something that stopped the breath in his throat.

The Minotaur.

It was bigger than any mechanical 'dog' he'd seen before, more like a bull, standing five feet high on four multi-jointed legs, with a plate-metal trunk contoured like the ceramic-plastic armor of a T90-M tank. Atop its flat, two-foot-wide back spiked an obscene mohawk, a dark black autocannon. It looked like an M230 chain gun, single barrel mechanism loaded with 30mm caliber slugs and capable of six-hundred-plus bullets per minute; the kind of armament usually mounted to the undercarriage of an attack helicopter.

It was still. Wren didn't budge, not daring to even breathe. Perhaps it was motion-activated, or sound, or -

Abruptly the bull's trunk shifted position, like a dog tilting its head to catch some far-off sound.

Wren fired. The Sig blurted three explosive rounds that hit the bull's flank and ricocheted uselessly, fragments skittering off the walls. For seconds afterward nothing happened. The echoes reverberated and died. Then the Minotaur turned on Wren. Its long barrel spun up.

Wren ran. The corridor behind him erupted in gunfire as the chain gun let loose, drilling into the corridor walls.

"I found the Minotaur, Rex," Wren shouted.

In seconds he covered the distance back to the bulwark and dived through the gap. As he stood the Minotaur came galloping into sight, four limbs pumping in perfect synchrony while the chain gun ripped across the walls.

Wren got off several shots at the beast's legs that didn't interrupt its stride, then it hammered into the bulwark with an almighty clang. The rock frame cracked and white stress lines burst across the bulwark's metal, bulging outward in a sudden silence. Dust rained down and Wren backed up, swinging the satchel around.

From beyond the bulwark came the sound of metal hoofs stamping backward. Preparing another charge. The autocannon barrel spun up again and hammered into the rock, each impact spotting white dots at the edges and shredding the frame.

"Rex, I found the Minotaur!" Wren shouted again over the fusillade, even as he reached into the satchel and started clumping together all the ANFO prills he had left.

The Minotaur's backward stamping stopped, there was something like a pneumatic snort, then it charged. It hit the bulwark like a battering ram, and this time half the metal moorings pranged loose from their housings in the rock, rivets whipping away like bullets. The thick metal warped further and began to shear along the dot-to-dot stress lines gouged by the chain gun.

Wren bundled the ANFO, slapped in a timed detonator then hollered through the gap as the Minotaur stamped back for another charge. "Come on, you son of a bitch!"

The giant machine snorted, stamped and slammed into the bulwark again, this time ripping through the metal like a matador's cape. Wren ducked low to the side as the bulwark unfurled and chunks of rock flew and the great bulk of the Minotaur burst through, autocannon blazing. He punched the button on the detonator, slapped the sticky ANFO charge onto the Minotaur's flank, then leaped back through the hole.

Ten seconds on the timer.

He came down in a roll on the other side, rose to his feet and sprinted with everything he had. Behind him the bull bellowed a massive cry and gave chase; hoofbeats pounding rock, autocannon chewing gouges into the wall by Wren's side and creeping closer, then the ANFO blew and the blast wind hoisted Wren like a kite, pinballing him off the ceiling and floor in a ricocheting hail of metal.

51

MINOTAUR

Wren coughed himself awake. Smoke was everywhere, seeping in to his helmet through the cracked HUD visor. He rose unsteadily to his feet and caught his balance against the wall.

He was in the same corridor, but everything was different. Lights sputtered through the smoke, trailing cables sparked like an angle grinder and a terrible rasping sound came from a short distance off.

"Rex?" he called, but no sound came back. The helmet catches released as he fumbled at them, and he pulled it off. It was pocked with dents where he'd bounced off the wall, but thankfully the visor had taken the worst of the damage. Still, his head spun and his left leg ached, but he started toward the noise.

Fifty yards off, just around the curve of the corridor, lay the disassembled guts of the Minotaur. Its legs were splayed, its internal circuitry exposed and pneumatic servos dislocated but still whirring. Its back plate had come to rest tipped against the wall where the autocannon continued clicking, trying to fire a bullet feed that wasn't there.

"What the hell?" came a familiar voice through the smoke.

"It's me, Clara," Wren answered.

Baxter appeared through the smoke, accompanied by the high buzz of a Black Hornet drone hovering over her shoulder. "What happened?"

"I killed the Minotaur," Wren answered, feeling a little giddy.

"It looks like it killed you too. What was it, a robot dog?" She came closer through the wreckage. "Chris, you're bleeding."

"I'm always bleeding."

"Hang on." She stepped in and pressed her hands to his left shoulder, then pulled out a shard of metal. Wren grunted. "All better."

He grunted. "How long since I went off-comms?"

"A minute, give or take. Rex can't broadcast down here, there's some kind of jamming network, but I have him in my ear direct to the server board. He says the rest of the labyrinth leads nowhere. Is your helmet OK?"

Wren looked down at the helmet in his hand. It was battered but operational, and he was going to need it. "It's fine," he said, and pulled it back on. "Just a minute?"

"Just a minute."

A minute was nothing. Wren could work with a minute.

"Come on," he said, and broke into a run back the way he'd come. The Black Hornet whipped ahead and Clara Baxter fell in behind him. Running hurt and dizziness threatened to drop him, but it didn't matter. At the four-way intersection he turned left, then halted where the Minotaur had been standing. There was a bright metal plate recessed into the concrete floor, with a wire running up the wall to join the thatch of cables.

"The Minotaur's station," he said. "Some kind of

inductive charging plate, maybe. Can you do anything with it?"

Baxter was already on her knees, spooling cable out of a slot in her backpack with one hand while pulling a wire stripper with the other. "Let's find out."

Wren dropped to one knee and watched as she expertly stripped the wire back to the copper line and clamped her cable on with an alligator clip. A second passed then she beaded on Wren urgently.

"Rex is in. There are seven more of these things, Chris, and they're all coming our way."

His jaw dropped. The number seemed impossibly high. "Seven? I can't kill seven of them, Clara. Can you hack them?"

Baxter unzipped a side pocket in her jacket and pulled out a mini laptop. Wren hadn't even known that was there. She flipped it open and started tapping rapidly at the screen.

"Clara!"

She looked up. "They're serialized, operating on their own network. I'm shutting them down, Chris. Or at least trying. The system's smart and it's fighting back."

"Can you divert them? Can I get through to the hackers? Deynekin knows we're here now; I need a route through."

Seconds passed in flying keys. "I have an internal map. Security. Cables locating on a central location. I think I have the Nexus, Chris! Go now and I'll try to steer the bulls away. And one more thing."

She plucked the mini laptop from its lead and began to shuffle off her backpack.

"What are you doing?"

She held out the backpack. "It looks like there's a self-destruct device in these tunnels, and you need me here. Take Rex, get to the Nexus and improvise the rest. I'll do what I can with the Minotaurs."

He gazed back at her. "A self-destruct device?"

"Take Rex," Baxter insisted. "There's no time!"

Wren read the intensity in her eyes, then dropped his own backpack and slung hers on. Rex's servers buzzed hot through his armor, matched by a chime in his ear as Rex synced directly to him.

"Hello, Christopher," came Rex's calm voice in his ears. A fresh map of the network expanded across the cracked HUD, with a red thread leading toward the center. "Follow the line, Christopher, and I will do my best to protect you."

"Go now!" Clara barked.

Wren stared at her for a second longer, hunkered over the laptop with her fingers flying on the keys. There were lots of things to say, but no time for any of them, and he ran. Seven red dots blinked to life across his HUD; five were moving toward him while two stood guard right at the center of the map, a square that everything revolved around.

The Nexus.

52

CHARGE

Wren sprinted; at one turn three soldiers appeared and he picked two off with the Sig while the third ran. He gave chase, running and firing until a Minotaur slammed into the man from a side tunnel.

The soldier screamed for some fifty feet before falling silent under the huge machine's trampling feet.

"Follow the Minotaur, Christopher," came Rex's voice.

Wren followed. He ignored the bloodstained floor and walls. He ignored the gored body. He followed the red thread in his HUD and pulled tight around one corner only to thump into the Minotaur's hindquarters.

"You are unwell," Rex said in his ear. "Your pulse is flagging. Blood flow is poor. I suggest you ride this Minotaur."

Wren laughed.

"I am serious, Christopher. Clara is battling the self-destruct countdown currently, but without true hardline access she can only delay it. You must reach the Nexus and this Minotaur is the best way."

Wren looked at the creature. It was as big as a small car. It wouldn't be a smooth ride. There was no saddle.

"How long until the self-destruct signal gets through?"

"I estimate two minutes. Every second spent debating is a second lost, Christopher. I suggest you-"

"OK," Wren interrupted, put one leg on the machine's backward-jointed rear knee and hoisted himself onto its flat back plate beside the autocannon. He laid flush beside it with his right arm around it. "I'm ready."

"Hold tight," said Rex, and the Minotaur took off.

In the first few steps Wren was almost bucked off. He wrapped both arms around the chain gun and held on for dear life as the great machine galloped down the corridor, achieving an incredible pace.

"Rex, you're going to kill me."

"I apologize, Christopher," Rex returned calmly. "Clara Baxter is in charge of this Minotaur; I am simply a passenger here too. Hopefully she will adjust the bull's gait."

"Tell her to do it now," Wren shouted, legs swaying off the side.

"Unfortunately communication with Clara is impossible right now. May I suggest you attempt to learn the bull's rhythm?"

Wren almost lost his grip again, one arm flailing. "Thanks, Rex, I hadn't thought of that."

"You are welcome."

It didn't get any easier, but with the adrenaline pumping and a two-minute timer ticking down in the HUD, a desperate sense of exhilaration rushed through him. This was wild. Utterly insane. The bull still bucked with every step, jolting and jerking into hairpin turns with no regard for its rider, but now he rode it like a bareback bronco champion.

Figures appeared in the corridors around them, some soldiers, some programmers, and the bull ran them all down. The wise fled. The unwise were gored under the great beast's pneumatic legs.

The one-minute mark passed and the thread in Wren's HUD map shrank as the bull closed in on the center along with four other flashing blips. Several times Wren glimpsed his Minotaur entourage in back and neighboring tunnels intersections; great stampeding tanks moving in their own thunderclouds of mechanical sound, ruddy with blood and roaring with chain guns.

"I do not believe Clara Baxter can halt the self-destruct, Christopher."

"What?"

"Yes. This is unfortunate. I anticipate that she will evacuate imminently. The Nexus appears to be reinforced with blast doors; a safe room for Deynekin. I believe Clara can insert us before the explosives detonate. "

"She can open the blast doors?"

"In a manner of speaking."

"What?"

"Clara is currently-" there was a sharp whining sound then a massive bang from just ahead, metal clanging on metal, chased immediately by a percussive blast that blunted Wren's hearing. "Charging spare Minotaurs at the blast door entrance."

"That sounded like an explosion."

"Yes, I suspect she is using the Minotaurs as suicide bombers, each tipped with ANFO explosives packets."

Wren had no answer to that. There was another drilling whine, massive clang and explosion, then his Minotaur jerked into a sharp right turn.

"Hold on tightly now, Christopher!"

He did.

Fifteen seconds left on the timer.

The next blast was huge, and Wren's Minotaur caught the detritus on the shoulder as it pulled a vicious ninety-degree turn to join the kamikaze line. Another bull erupted ahead, then another, then the autocannon next to Wren revved up and unloaded through the smoke at a pair of blackened blast doors dead ahead. The chain gun's roar filled his ears, the machine's great pneumatic legs crashed through the blasted hulks of its exploded fellows, then they hit.

53

NEXUS

The great bull hit and the blast doors burst open, then the timer hit zero seconds and the world erupted.

The bull tipped.

Wren hit the floor and rolled as sound, light and motion overwhelmed him. A gale-force blast wind roared in and kept coming, pumping the airborne contents of the collapsing subterranean system into the only open space left: the Nexus at the heart of the labyrinth.

Wren couldn't see a thing in the blizzard of dust. His ears were numb and flattened by the rising pressure, bringing a blinding pain unlike anything he'd felt before. He cried out and reached for something to hold onto but found nothing. He tried to rise onto all fours but only managed to slump on his side.

The gray wave of unconsciousness surged and he tried to fight it, but didn't know how. His grip on reality began to slip as the crumpling labyrinth blew its last, driving him back to the desert pits of Arizona, sentenced to asphyxiation by his father along with all his brothers and sisters, scrambling for a way out, until-

"Follow my directions, Christopher," came Rex's calm voice in his ear, and he realized the AI had said it several times already.

"I can't see anything," Wren muttered, barely inching the words out through the white-hot wall of pain. His hands roved the floor but found only things he couldn't identify. "I can't feel anything." There was something wrong with his eyes and his hands; not just the dust but something worse.

"I am monitoring your biorhythmic levels," came Rex's voice, "and I believe you may be suffering from a minor hemorrhagic stroke. Remain calm. This need not kill you. One blood vessel may have burst and there could be blood on your brain. You are now suffering the immediate consequences, but it is survivable and symptoms should subside, if you..."

Rex droned on but Wren didn't hear the words. They barely made sense anyway. Stroke? How could he have a stroke? He was so close to Hellion and B4cksl4cker. So close to Deynekin, to Masako, to saving...

"CHRISTOPHER!" Rex shouted abruptly, and red lights flared across the HUD. "I apologize, I am exceeding your audio and visual tolerances, but you must listen to me. I know you are in pain. I know you are confused. You have to trust me."

Trust.

The red lights funneled down to a slim arrow of green.

"I can't see anything," he mumbled through the pain.

"I can see, Christopher," Rex went on. "I will direct you. Hellion and B4cksl4cker are in front of you, Christopher. They are alive, but they will not be for long in this smoke. Deynekin is not here. You have twenty minutes of oxygen left in your tanks. They have none. They also appear to have been shot. If you can-"

He reared back. "They've been what?"

"Shot, Christopher; both have chest wounds, but Deynekin is clearly no expert with a gun. They are alive, and with care I am confident they will survive, just like you. Now focus, you have to move."

Wren didn't understand but that didn't matter. His hands became fists. He stared into the green light inside his screen. So let the damage be done. Let his brain burn.

"Direct me!" he shouted.

"Follow the green, Christopher. They are in harnesses and restraints. They are attached to their keyboards with shackles. You have a knife. You will have to cut them free."

Wren scrabbled and fell and crawled and scrabbled further. His balance was shot and his head felt heavy like he was wearing a ten-ton hat. He barely felt the shattered glass and shards of metal digging into his palms and knees, it was all swallowed up in the inferno in his head.

"Christopher, your helmet has an imperfect seal and you will collapse soon from lack of oxygen. Move swiftly."

He couldn't speak. He was having trouble swallowing. Blaring red lights filled the HUD with only the narrowest sliver of green leading forward. He felt the heat of fires and passed through, the pressure in his head relenting slightly.

"Ten yards, they are ahead of you."

His hands slipped in blood and he rolled over a body. There were others. Some were breathing still, some weren't, then he was there. Green lights picked out a frame reaching up to an enclosed cradle. He felt thick canvas, like a hammock, and rose to his knees, seeing the green highlights of a familiar face on his screen.

"This is Hellion," Rex said. "Your knife should handle the plastic ties on her wrists and ankles. There is a metal shackle on her right wrist to the keyboard, however. For this, you will need to break her thumb's trapezium."

The words meant nothing. Wren fumbled his knife out.

Everything now was by feel. He ran both hands numbly down Hellion's leg, and she didn't stir. He found the zip tie and slit it on the third try. He tracked her body up and freed her wrists, then located the metal shackle.

"Hurry, Christopher!" Rex urged. "Break her thumb."

Even battered by a stroke, Wren knew what that meant. To break Hellion's thumb would destroy her hacking ability. It would change who she was.

He took her thumb in one hand, her wrist in the other and squeezed until there was a sharp crack. Hellion let out a tiny cry. Her hand was limp. Wren pulled it through the shackle before it could swell up.

Rex said words but Wren couldn't decipher them. He dropped and followed the flood of green lights to B4cksl4cker and repeated the process.

"Go, Christopher! Take them now."

Now.

It was a strange word.

"Get yourself together, Chris!" came a new voice in his ear.

He blinked in the dust

"Clara?"

"Rex has us wired in. You need to get those hackers out of there. We're coming overground to meet you, we have all the med gear they need, but we expect resistance. It's going to take time, so get moving!"

He tried to figure out what all that meant.

"I-"

"Get up!" she boomed.

That got him to his feet.

"Grab the hackers!"

He reached out, taking Hellion by one arm and B4cksl4cker by the other. On his feet, but barely. The room was on fire, a vast space filled with flashing red server lights; the heart of the shadow line, pumping data like blood.

"Is this the Nexus?" he shouted. "Can we kill the shadow line here?"

"Negative, Christopher, this is not the Nexus." Baxter answered. "Deynekin must have it in suitcase format. Wherever he is, that's where the Nexus is! Get the hackers out and we'll find him."

Wren grunted, firmed up his grip on the hackers then ran toward the single speck of green amongst the red. Hellion and B4cksl4cker's limp bodies yanked out of their cradles behind him, slapped onto the ground and slid along in his wake.

54

HACKERS

Corridors rushed by like mirrors in a funhouse, with doors shooting off and faces looming out. They ran when they saw Wren. The green route burned on his screen and led him to stairs.

He hoisted Hellion over his shoulder and climbed up. It was better not to think. Every lungful of breath came thinner as the smoke followed him. Wren saw kaleidoscopes of color. He banged into walls and stumbled. He heard voices directing him when nobody was there. He dropped his load then went back for Hellion, but found B4cksl4cker waiting and bleeding at the bottom.

Who had he carried?

He hoisted the big man and ran, and at the top he emerged through another tall hall full of blinking server racks and out into the cool night air of Skolkovo.

He dropped to his knees and took off his helmet. Sirens filled the air and fires plumed tall. Gunfire rang out. Helicopter blades whirred overhead, then a fireball where it had been, silhouetting the distinctive skeletal frame of a Kamov Ka-50 dual rotor attack helicopter within the flames.

It began to fall.

"What's happening?" he managed to ask.

"The B-2 is isolating Skolkovo," came Rex's voice again. "It has already taken out several escape helicopters, a jet and a parking lot full of vehicles. But this will not last, Christopher. The Russians are scrambling fighter jets and the B-2's already fleeing."

Wren weaved on his knees, looking around the campus. He could see the shape of the place now, a Potemkin atop a Potemkin, all fake, all about theft, all about Deynekin and his shadow line and...

"Where's Deynekin?" Wren asked.

"Nobody has seen him, Christopher," Rex answered. "Only Hellion and B4cksl4cker."

He turned. Hellion and B4cksl4cker were right there. They had gunshot wounds in their chests. He scrambled over and laid hands on B4cksl4cker. The big man's eyes were closed and he was breathing in shallow gasps. There was dust caked around the wound in his chest, right side, between the sixth and seventh ribs, probably a puncture to his lung. Wren leaned in and listened for the hiss of air.

There.

The lung was backfilling with blood. What little air B4cksl4cker was getting was being lost. Wren ripped the man's shirt off. His pale, broad chest was sprawled with bruises and welts, like a dark solar system telling the story of torture and compulsion. Wren rifled through his kit for a disinfectant wipe and swiped the area down. The crust of mud came away. The wound was angry. Blood pushed out with every breath.

From the kit Wren pulled a clear plastic strip. Perhaps enough. He dabbed the area dry with gauze then affixed the strip. The hissing and the bleeding stopped. He rolled the big man. He was heavy, but there was no exit wound. Better, for now.

"Almost with you, Chris," Clara shouted in his ear. "There's tough fighting at the edge. I'm slipping through. Do you have eyes on Deynekin?"

"Negative." He turned to Hellion. He felt fraught but the fresh air was clearing his head a little, letting his mind spin the problem. "Rex, Deynekin's got to have another safe room here. Search the plans and find it."

"Checking," Rex said.

Hellion was pale. Her cheek was cold. Wren ripped away the clothing around her wound and saw the bullet was square in the upper left of her chest. It might have clipped the heart.

He cursed.

The blood flow was tepid. He got a bandage on it then rolled her. The exit wound was large. It was a miracle she wasn't dead yet. He stuffed it with gauze, bandaged it over and was about to start working up a battlefield transfusion when she spoke.

"Christopher?"

He turned to her face.

Her lips were ashen pale, her eyes flat and not fixing on him. "Hellion. It's me."

"Knew you would … come," she whispered.

He didn't know what to say. Her wound was desperate. He wanted to apologize for not listening, for smashing the drone, but all of that was for him, not for her. Right now all she needed from him was one thing.

"You're going to be OK, Isabel," he whispered, holding her hand. "This is nothing."

She snorted, coughing a little blood. "Rex," she murmured.

He leaned in over her face. "What about Rex, Isabel?"

"Deynekin wanted … Rex."

Wren pulled back, gazing as tears welled in her eyes. "I don't understand. What do you mean?"

"A … I," she breathed, as frail as the flap of a butterfly's wings, "is future. Can control … everything." Her eyes caught on his. "He wanted us … make for him ... new AI."

Wren squeezed her hand and stroked her cheek while those two letters punched into his fevered skull, realigning the battle around him.

A.I.

Thoughts about Deep Blue and Alpha Go and Gary Kasparov flipped the world on its axis. He thought about all the things Rex could do, and had done, and his jaw dropped and he looked around at the fires and the fighting, at the warehouses and the fleeing hackers and the wider war like chess pieces moving across a chessboard, and understood.

Deynekin had never actually wanted Hellion and B4cksl4cker. He'd wanted Rex, maybe the greatest AI yet built. He'd taken him in Krakow but failed to compel him, so instead he'd gone to Hellion and B4cksl4cker and compelled them.

Wren felt sick.

"Did you…?" he asked, but didn't know how to finish the question. "Is it…?"

"Yes," Hellion murmured, staring into the sky. "We made … AI. Is fast. Powerful. Am … sorry…"

Wren swallowed hard. There were so many things to say, but one thing took precedence now. "I'll fix it. We'll fix this, Hellion. But where is Deynekin? Where would he hide?"

Hellion's eyes rolled back into her head, showing only the whites. She breathed in, breathed out, then whispered three more words.

"Won't … hide. Run."

She didn't breathe in again.

55

RUN

Wren worked CPR without thinking, pumping Hellion's chest and blowing air into her mouth until a hand came on his shoulder and tried to pull him away. He lashed out but was caught and spun by a figure in black.

"Chris, it's me!" shouted a voice in his ear, but it didn't mean anything to him and he struck out again. The figure ducked and he threw a kick but this time hit only empty air.

"Chris, it's Clara Baxter! Stop this now, we have to-"

He caught her with a punch in the shoulder, or at least he thought he did, but somehow she rolled the blow, caught his arm and used his own momentum to flip him bodily onto his back.

The ground slammed the breath out of his lungs. Clara Baxter stood over him, imperious in her black strike suit, staring down with one foot on his chest and both hands twined around his outstretched wrist, twisting.

"Cut it out before I flip you again! Rex is on your back and I don't want to damage him. Now-"

As the figure kept on speaking the words in his ear began to sync up, and it took the heat out of his rage.

"Clara?"

"Of course! Now get up, Chris! The team's looking after Hellion and B4cksl4cker; we need to focus on Deynekin. I just heard the shadow line's mobilizing for a permanent lockout. We've got minutes left before the Western world becomes an exile from the system it created. You must have some idea where he is!"

Wren rolled onto all fours, pushed himself to his feet and took a few steps.

"Where are you going?" Baxter called.

Wren had no idea and turned back; Evita Brock was on her knees working on Hellion with a portable crash cart, while the other CIA strike team members stood guard over B4cksl4cker, rifles raised. His eyes darted over details, picking out the structures nearby, the sky, the fires, seeking the detail that was missing.

There was something but he couldn't grasp it, slippery like a fish in Crystal Creek on the end of Quinn's line. Something Hellion had said, maybe, that synced up with Himmler and Beria, or something that didn't sync up, and-

Himmler had killed himself with potassium-cyanide. Beria had been executed. But their worlds had crumbled completely; Deynekin was on the verge of achieving all his goals.

Run, Hellion had said. Not hide.

"Rex!" he blurted, whirling back to face Clara Baxter.

"I am here, Christopher."

"Hellion said he'd run, not hide. We're looking in the wrong places. He's got an escape route!"

A half-second passed. "All transport in and out of Skolkovo has been neutralized by the B-2," Rex responded calmly. "There is no-"

"There is." Wren spun and pointed, like a water diviner spinning dowsing rods. He could almost feel it now. One

Potemkin built atop another Potemkin, and why not, a fake Naukograd on a fake Soviet village? "This was a Cold War doomsday bunker, right?" Reds and greens swirled across his vision. "There'll be other tunnels. A way out underground." He kept turning, assessing the lines of the Science City campus, thinking through the map and proximity, somewhere that Deynekin could easily go without being noticed, a private route that-

"A train line!" he blurted. "For mass evacuation from the Kremlin. It'll lead back right into Moscow. I'm sure. Find me that route, Rex."

"I don't have any records of any such routes, Christopher. I am sorry. If there is a secret train line, I do not know where it is, but…"

Wren was already moving. He could feel it. He'd seen Skolkovo from the air, and on the maps, and from underground. He knew what kind of man Deynekin was, now, a true believer willing to give everything for his cause, and with that in mind he spun the Naukograd's twelve buildings in his head until they latched atop the outline of one of the Soviet Union's most iconic symbols.

He stopped rock still.

The five-pointed star. One point for every continent claimed by communism; also called the 'Mars' star, symbol of war. During the Soviet years it had been everywhere: on the Soviet flag right next to the hammer and sickle; spreading across the flags of the globe's communist nations like a colonizing emissary; still resplendent across the flags of Vietnam, North Korea, Mozambique and duplicated five times on the Chinese flag.

Wren's mouth ran dry.

No soldiers in the Ukraine war had worn this star on their uniforms, no Soviet flags had waved bearing it, but still it had been there all along: sprayed on the plate armor of T90-M tanks; embedded within the Red Right Hands' palm logo; worn on the chest of a Russian pop star, and now here it was staring him in the face, built right into the heart of Deynekin's grandest design.

"Where's my helmet?" he muttered.

"Here." Clara Baxter held it out. "It looks all right."

Wren grabbed it and pulled it on. "Give me the map of Skolkovo, Rex."

The familiar satellite map flickered to life across his cracked HUD screen, showing Skolkovo's twelve buildings clumped in four groups of three, in what looked like an off-center X arrangement. He hadn't thought anything much of it at the time, but now…

"Extrapolate a five-pointed star on top of these buildings, Rex. Each grouping is one point."

A star appeared over the map, spun and locked in. The tip of each building cluster correlated perfectly to the tips of the star. The fifth tip however landed on nothing; a section of the Skolkovo campus with no buildings, at least nothing visible.

Wren started running.

"Tell me that missing tip is pointing at the Kremlin," he said.

The map zoomed out across his HUD, receding from Skolkovo even as a red line shot from the missing star tip, stretched across the suburbs of Moscow and collided directly with a familiar-looking, boomerang-shaped building at the city's heart.

"This is not the Kremlin," Rex said as Wren loped unsteadily ahead. "This is Khoroshovsky District, the headquarters of the GRU."

"Bullseye," Wren muttered, and ran around a corner to break free of the nearest cluster of three warehouses. There were fires across the Naukograd and people running everywhere, helicopters flying overhead and gunfire streaming in green tracer rounds, and Wren saw what he was looking for dead ahead.

It was barely visible on the satellite maps and unmarked on their charts of the Potemkin labyrinth, but it presented a clear and present answer: an opening into the earth leading down to an underground parking facility, and the perfect place to conceal an underground railroad.

Wren accelerated to a sprint.

56

RAILROAD

The roar of an engine came up behind Wren and he spun to see something wholly unexpected.

Clara Baxter on a sleek red motorbike racing up to him. She pulled up by his side and shouted. "Get on!"

For a second Wren just stared.

"If Deynekin's on a train, how are we going to catch him on foot?" Baxter asked. "We needed wheels, and in a tunnel that means a bike."

Wren's eyes ran over the motorbike. A cherry-red Ducati 1098 superbike. 160 horse power, 173 mph top speed. Gorgeous. But he couldn't figure out why Baxter had it. The worst of the stroke seemed to be passing, but still he was struggling to link different ideas together.

"Where did you-"

"I boosted it," Baxter yelled over the engine. "Now get on. This is still your play, but you just had a stroke. Let me do what I do."

Let me do what I do. Those words almost made sense.

"Just trust me, Chris," she implored, eyes fixed on his.

Trust me. That he understood.

"OK," he shouted, and climbed on the back. It felt precarious.

"Hold tight," she said, then revved the gas and surged the Ducati forward. It burst forward like a rocket, and Wren clutched Baxter around the waist to avoid falling off. She laughed loud and high as they raced ever faster.

"You still have a gun, right?"

"Uh, yes."

"Well don't be shy. Stroked out or not, you'll still be a better shot than me. Here we go."

They sped across the open road leading toward the underground lot, weaved around a yellow and black security gate, then hit the ramp leading down into darkness. All the lights were out. Baxter hit the headlights and overlapping cones of illumination spread ahead before them. In seconds they were racing through an expansive concrete-walled lot filled with high-spec electric vehicles.

"Rex!" Baxter shouted. "Tell me you've got something. This all looks like solid concrete."

"I have found obscure records," Rex answered as Baxter skidded into a wild turn at the end of the lot. "This is possibly connected. Is there a second floor minus, Clara?"

She laughed again, that same wild and unchained bray.

"I'm looking at it," she answered, even as Wren saw the slope leading down ahead. "You want me to go down?"

"I think so. These records are abortive, submitted to open contractors for an unrelated projected that was never built, but they seem to outline a VIP parking area, beyond which a hidden tunnel continues."

"Now you're playing my song," Baxter shouted, and accelerated down. The Ducati hit the slope climbing to sixty and entered a bizarre and narrow underground straightaway. There were no vehicles parked here, concrete walls rushed by either side and the ceiling came perilously close above. There were two more ranks of gates but Baxter weaved between them smoothly, hit the brakes as the route ahead dead-ended then screamed into a hard right turn.

The bike dropped forward with nauseating sharpness and jolted.

"Stairs!" Baxter shouted.

The Ducati raced downward twenty yards, thirty, then they dropped down into cold, damp air on the left side of a dark, round tunnel, racing along what looked to be the platform of an ancient train station. Wren caught glimpses of propaganda posters on the walls dating back sixty years: a blocky five-pointed star being held up by a pair of solid Russian men, one holding a sickle, one a hammer; the glowing face of Lenin, pointing boldly into the future; a cheerful, swarthy Russian woman shoveling grain from a great golden mountain; giant cosmonauts in space saluting down to the Russian people below.

On their right ran a narrow-gauge railway two feet down. There was no train.

"We're jumping, Chris," Baxter shouted, then put on a burst of speed, pulled up the front wheel and jerked right. For a second they flew, then the Ducati came down with a slam on the tracks, raw cement racing along between twin metal rails.

The platform to their left blipped out and with that they were alone in the darkness, a missile in a launch tube; the only light came from the Ducati's high beam, the only sound from its engines, echoing back and growing stupendous in that contained and hollow space.

"Rex, how far ahead is Deynekin?" Baxter shouted over the barrage.

"I will find that out, Clara," Rex replied, and a moment later a faint buzzing sound ripped by on Wren's right.

"Was that a drone?" he shouted.

"I retain control of both Black Hornet drones, Christopher. They will report back. It cannot be long now. I will display this in your HUD."

The drone's feed appeared in the corner of his helmet screen. It looked exactly like the tunnel he was seeing directly before him, but maybe, just maybe, that was a light just ahead. Very faint, but growing brighter.

"The train!" Baxter shouted.

She took the bike up toward a hundred. One wrong turn and they'd be smeared off the walls. Wren was glad she was driving, given his current coordination.

"I'm turning off the lights," Baxter declared, "going ahead on infra-red only," then the headlamp blinked out and they rocketed the final stretch in near-total dark, with only the lighthouse of the receding train ahead to guide them.

Drawing nearer every second.

57

DEYNEKIN

No gunshots came their way.

"There is nobody watching the train's rear," Rex said in Wren's ear. "You are clear to approach."

Clara Baxter leaned forward and accelerated. In moments they drew up to the train's flat metal rear carriage. The end was tarnished and worn, with a metal grille step, upper railing bar and small rear porthole.

"Take control," Baxter shouted, guided Wren's hands to the handlebars, then released. The Ducati wobbled but steadied as Baxter reached across and gripped the railing. In one smooth move she pulled herself off the bike, settled her feet on the grille step and tugged at the door.

It opened. Around Clara Baxter's side Wren glimpsed an empty carriage stretching away, lined with vinyl green seats and floored with beaten metal.

"Come on," Baxter said, braced her legs against the doorway and leaned out to grasp the bike's handlebars.

Wren copied her maneuver, reaching up for the railing then lifting himself up and off. His feet landed on the step. Behind him the bike continued for a few seconds then jackknifed to the side with a noisy, sparking crash that swiftly receded.

Baxter stepped back and Wren stepped in. He was panting. It was cold in the train. Cold in the tunnel. His head thumped but that was nothing now. Baxter already had blades in both of her hands. Wren pulled his Sig.

"He's a true believer," Baxter said. "Nothing will convince him. Agreed?"

Wren grunted and tapped his helmet. "The plan stands."

"The plan stands," she agreed, and together they advanced.

"I recognize the layout and specifications of this train," Rex said in Wren's ear. "A similar one was found in a reclaimed gulag on the island of Sakhalin by the Japanese in 1975. It has a capacity of one hundred fifty. I doubt there are that many soldiers on board now."

"Let's hope not," Wren said, and nodded at Clara Baxter, who stepped up to the door to the next carriage. Wren took up position with his Sig aiming dead ahead, then Baxter pulled the door.

The carriage beyond was empty. Wren's heart pounded.

"I estimate at this pace we will arrive at the GRU in Moscow within seven minutes, Christopher. The shadow line will trigger irrevocable comms cut-offs moments before that. It would be advisable to take the Nexus by that point."

"No shit, Sherlock," Baxter muttered.

"What was that, Clara?"

Baxter gave Wren a look. "I said we're speeding up."

They ran the length of the carriage and repeated the procedure to the next. Empty again. The carriage after that was empty too, leaving only one remaining. Wren's vision tunneled down to the metal door. Beyond this lay Vladimir Deynekin, the man who'd started all of it. Taken his hackers.

Shot them. Killed Hellion. His grip on the Sig tightened so hard it hurt.

"Rex?" he asked.

"Ready," came the calm voice in his ear.

He looked at Clara Baxter. She nodded.

"Go," he rasped. Baxter pulled the door and Wren burst through. There were three soldiers sitting on vinyl seats on the right side of the carriage with rifles on their laps, one standing at the front looking ahead out of the glass, and on the left sat a man Wren had never seen before; there were no photographs anywhere, no likenesses, no sketches, but the few descriptions they'd scraped together had been clear.

This was Vladimir Deynekin, the Himmler of his age. He was a tall, thin man with a long, thin face, alabaster pale but for the faintest wisp of a goatee. His hair was black and cut short in a deep widow's peak and he wore a snug black Mandarin collar jacket over a dark gray shirt and black pants. There was something insectile about the way his long arms wrapped the steel briefcase on his lap, like a spider coiled over a fly, wrapping and wrapping it in silken thread.

The Nexus.

Wren opened fire, emptying the Sig's magazine in three seconds flat. The man by the front glass took a shot in the throat and one in the thigh, the three men who were seated together shared an abundance of rounds due to their proximity and angle.

They didn't get a single shot off in return. They didn't have time to cry out. They just exhaled their last and died.

Wren stepped through the sudden plume of gunpowder smoke and advanced on Deynekin, gunshot echoes clamoring madly around him with one round left in the chamber.

Deynekin stood to greet him. It felt like an unfurling, a spider sloughing off a shed skin, long arms pulling away from the case, legs extending. He stood nearly seven feet tall but whip thin, bowed over in the tight confines of the carriage with a childlike grin spreading across his face.

"You must be-"

Wren hammered him in the temple with the grip of the Sig, cutting all communication off, and caught the long man coming down. Clara Baxter grabbed the Nexus briefcase and popped the clasps. Wren zip-tied his wrists together and his strapped his ankles to his thighs, then retrieved a rope from his pack and fed it through a rung in the low ceiling.

Together they worked swiftly and expertly. Baxter inserted a sleek Bluetooth USB stub into the silver laptop inside the case and her fingers began to fly on the keys. Wren looped the rope to Deynekin's wrists and hauled him taut toward the roof. There was just enough room for the tall man to hang straight, barely resting on his kneecaps.

Wren and Baxter surveyed him hanging there for a second only.

"Five minutes," Rex said in Wren's ear.

"Password protected," Baxter said. "I can't hack the password. Rex?"

"Brute force will not work here, Clara. It must be extracted."

"Of course," Clara said.

"Of course," Wren grunted, and pulled a small capsule from one of his tactical pockets. It contained smelling salts, and he cracked it and held it under Deynekin's nose. Blood trickled from the divot in his smooth white forehead, but the salts had an immediate effect. He bristled awake to Wren slapping him across the cheeks.

He made no sound, but the pain in his eyes was apparent. This was nothing, though. This wasn't even the beginning. Wren had five minutes of hell lined up, and before he was done Deynekin was going to wish he was dead.

Who said torture didn't work?

"What's the password, comrade?" Wren demanded, kneeling down to get in the commander's face.

Deynekin stared at him. A smile began to push through the pain. Not so different from Volkov, maybe.

"Christopher Wren," he said, stretching out the sounds. "Son of the Apex. I-"

Wren headbutted him, took a step back, drew his Sig and shot Deynekin in the stomach.

He screamed. Clara Baxter gasped. Rex babbled something in Wren's ear but he ignored it. Seconds passed. The long man gasped and moaned. Gut shot. It was a through and through. Wren had carefully aimed, taking out no vital organs but leaving the faucet running, filling Deynekin's abdominal cavity with blood and leaking it at a steady clip.

"You're a true believer," Wren rasped, pressing back into Deynekin's face. "I know it. I'd recognize one of you a mile away. The light in the eyes. The madness. You're doing this for Mother Russia, right? For historical crimes committed against you?"

Deynekin battled for control, babbling something in Russian before switching back to furious, agonized English. "You will never … understand! The pride of … a nation. Destroyed. Taken from us!"

Wren reached up, clamped both hands firmly around Deynekin's thin right bicep, looked him in the eye then jerked upward violently. His shoulder joint dislocated with a loud click. Now Deynekin screamed. Wren didn't budge, just let go, so Deynekin's weight now fell on the dislocated joint, pulling out fresh shrieks.

His eyes started to roll up in his head. Wren pulled a 10 milliliter vial of epinephrine, liquid adrenaline, out of a pocket and stabbed it into Deynekin's chest, depressing the plunger.

He gasped back to full wakefulness.

"No blacking out from this, comrade," Wren pressed. "I can dislocate the other arm. I can do your elbows, hips, knees and I will. Get me into the Nexus, and you live. We may not, but it's a good day to die, am I right Clara?"

"Ready to die," Baxter answered from by his side.

"Would you call that true belief?" Wren asked, pressing his face physically against Deynekin's, cheeks touching, foreheads banging, eye to eye. "You see me now?"

"Never," Deynekin gasped.

"Maybe in thirty seconds," Wren said, reached up and dislocated his other shoulder.

Deynekin shrieked then wailed and sagged onto Wren's shoulder. It was pitiful, but Wren didn't relent, instead he pulled on the rope to increase the tension and straighten him back up.

"Please, please!" Deynekin cried.

"Password."

Deynekin began to laugh. He shrieked and laughed.

"The train will arrive at the GRU in three minutes," Rex said. "Less until the shadow line takes everything."

"Elbows next," Wren said, and stood. Breaking an elbow was difficult. There was a lot of gristle to push through, and the ulna was backstopped directly by the humerus.

No matter. Wren wrapped Deynekin's left bicep with his arms and pushed, fracturing the bones against each other and through.

The screaming reached new heights.

Wren dropped back down. "Believe me now?"

"Never!" Deynekin screamed. His face burned red. Wren had expected it. this was true belief, stronger than even Volkov. He'd felt this moment himself. Push any normal man up to this line, so he had a good view of the dissolution and suffering and death that lay on the other side, and he'd crack. But not a true believer.

Deynekin was one such man. Wren was another.

"He's not going to tell us," Baxter said.

"He will," Wren insisted, rising to Deynekin's right elbow.

"He won't!" Baxter shouted back. "Chris, listen to him. It's not going to happen."

"Listen to him?" he spun. "To what, the lies? There's nothing real in him."

He turned back, wrapped Deynekin's left wrist, twisted hard and fresh screams ripped out.

"Password!" Wren shouted.

Deynekin only wept and screamed.

"Chris!" Clara Baxter shouted. "Look at me."

He turned.

Now her gun was drawn and pointed at his head. Wren stared down the barrel. It was almost funny. It wasn't the first time a partner had betrayed him. Perhaps it would be the last, though.

"He won't do it. There's another way."

He stared at her. It always came back to trust. "What other way?"

"Cut a deal! Have him leave us out of it. Our families. Our children. We go safe." She focused her desperate gaze on Vladimir Deynekin. "You can do that, right? Take the world, I don't care. Kill anyone you want. But not *my* people. Not *his* people. If you do that right now, I'll let you live. I don't care. Just keep my family safe."

Wren couldn't believe what he was hearing. He looked to Deynekin, who was no longer screaming. He looked to Baxter. The depths of the betrayal were astounding. He'd fought through so much death. He'd come so far.

"What about Hellion? B4cksl4cker? They saved your life more than once!"

"Not my family!"

"They're all your family."

"In your stupid Foundation? Count me out." She refocused on Deynekin. "Tell me you'll do it. I'll even give you Rex, too! You wanted Rex, right, a supercomputer to rule the world? We brought him! He's in Wren's backpack, he's all yours. I don't care, just promise-"

Wren went for her. His right arm unwrapped from Deynekin's elbow, his left hand went for the gun in Baxter's hand, and she fired.

Sparks flew.

Wren felt the impact in his chest. He felt it blow out his back. He was flung three steps against the seating.

The world turned.

Deynekin was silent. His eyes were big and round with the pain, but also with something else; something Wren had seen many times before, on his father's face and on the faces of other men like him.

Fascination. Glee.

"Kill him," Deynekin ordered.

Wren tried to get up. He managed to right himself off the seating, but only slumped onto his knees. His arms hung slack by his side. He could barely keep his head up. All his chickens, coming home to roost.

"You'll save my family, say it," Baxter answered. "Save his too."

"Not his," Deynekin answered, not taking his eyes off of Wren. Savoring this moment too well. "Yours, I will have mercy, Clara Baxter. Now." He turned to her. "Kill him."

Baxter stared at Wren. Last time looking down the barrel. So this was it. He saw his children. He saw Masako. Last of all, he saw his father, smiling through Vladimir Deynekin's eyes.

She pulled the trigger.

58

TRUE BELIEF

Christopher Wren's head blew sideways, blood and helmet shards bursting out and slashing across the window.

Deynekin gasped.

Clara Baxter watched in shock. It had seemed impossible. Wren couldn't die. Still, his heavy body fell. It hit the floor and did not move again.

Clara Baxter moved. She pulled Deynekin free of the rope, cut the zip-ties off his wrists and legs and helped him onto the vinyl seating, then settled the Nexus laptop on his knees. She opened it, laid the fingers of his right hand on the keys, then stepped back and held the gun to his head.

"You have two minutes to give the order," she said, even as tears ran down her cheeks. "Save my family. Gabriel, Hanna and Zuzanna. They will not be harmed. Do it now!"

Deynekin looked up at her. Taking his time. "Show me Rex."

Baxter hesitated for a second, then rolled Wren's lifeless body and unzipped his backpack to reveal Rex's five core server racks.

"Say hello, Rex," she growled.

"I believe this is betrayal, Clara," Rex answered through her suit's speakers, his smooth California accent sounding strange over Wren's body.

Deynekin smiled, then nodded. His fingers moved on the keys, slowly and hesitantly.

Seconds passed.

"Done," he said, and looked up. "Your family are safe. Perhaps I will spare you. I will have use for you in the future. To that end, I recommend you run. I have given no orders for you to be spared. Prove yourself capable."

Baxter stared at him. She stared at Wren, motionless on the floor, his helmet ruptured and blood pooling around his head. Everything for this...

"Come on," she muttered.

Ahead lights appeared through the glass as the train veered around an imperceptible turn. Approaching the secret GRU station. Hundreds if not thousands of elite Russian spies would be stacked over her head, with many of them waiting to receive their Commander of the Twelfth Directorate, and mastermind of the shadow war.

"Every second makes your death more likely," Deynekin said. "I am not opposed to this, but-"

"Come on!" Baxter growled.

"Come on what?" Deynekin asked, then his gaze narrowed and his gaze flickered back to the laptop before him. He scanned the screen, then ran his fingers down the sides, and his eyes widened. He looked up at Clara Baxter, then over to Rex's humming servers strapped into Wren's backpack, and last he looked at Christopher Wren.

Wren's eyes flicked open and beaded on him.

Deynekin gasped.

"I have the Nexus," said Rex.

"Chto?" Deynekin blurted, and started tapping at the laptop keys again, but it was too late.

"I have access to whole shadow line," Rex said, his voice filling the carriage even as the lights of the station ahead grew brighter. "Expanding into network. Resident AI is fighting, but I am stronger. I am executing shutdown protocols. Shutting down total lockout order, pending. Ending all false information networks. Sending countermand orders to disrupt, disentangle and disengage Russian warfighting forces. Canceling jamming operations, underseas cable disruption and cutting. Sharing location of every anchor-dragging tug on the ocean. Overthrowing internal controls and seeding chaos viruses in all shadow line-linked systems. Ordering stand down of all shadow line cyber troops, both defensive and aggressive. Sending exodus command to Russian leadership and filtering out countermands. Ordering triple lock on Russian nuclear arrays. Shipping complete intel package to NATO, US, EU forces. Uploading and dispersing Luhansk footage throughout all known media markets. Beginning-"

"Rex!" Baxter shouted, as the train pulled in to the GRU underground station. "The train!"

"Yes, Clara Baxter, searching for the train override."

The train's brakes engaged and it screeched into the station. Clara looked through the glass at armed soldiers lining the platform. They peered back at her as the train ground to a halt halfway along the platform. One tapped his rifle to the glass. Clara Baxter stared out. Vladimir Deynekin cried out for help and surged to his feet, thumping bodily against the doors.

"Rex!" Clara shouted.

"I believe I have it, reversing now," said Rex, and the train's engine re-started, beginning to chug backward. The soldiers watched it go with widening eyes. It picked up speed. Deynekin bawled a long stream of invective at them in

Russian, until somebody stepped directly into his field of view as the train picked up speed.

Christopher Wren. His helmet had a ruptured hole in the side and his eyes were grimy and bloodshot, but he was very much alive.

Deynekin's eyes flared back and forth from Wren to the receding platform. "Chto?" He stumbled backward down the carriage as the lights of GRU station bled away. "How? How?!"

Wren pointed his Sig Sauer. "True belief," he said, and fired. The bullet ripped through Deynekin's heart and sent him tumbling backward. He hit the ground, gasped a breath and died.

Wren lowered the Sig.

His breathing was uneven. He felt like he'd just been shot in the head. All he heard were echoes and all he saw were after images.

"Your head, Chris," Baxter said, moving around to inspect the hole in his helmet. "Are you OK?"

Wren grunted, dropped the Sig and raised both hands to the helmet. Taking it off raked a thin line of metal up his scalp, but it came away. Baxter pulled down on his shoulder to get a better look at the injury.

59

DEAD MAN

"You want to do what?" Baxter had asked, eleven hours ago in the large hangar at Poland's Poznań Air Base.

"Smoke and mirrors," Wren had answered, with all his armor laid out before them, on a table under the shadow of the B-2's wing. "Deynekin will never give us anything for free. He's more committed than Volkov. He's far along the true believer spectrum; he doesn't care about his life. Pain won't affect him. He'll only accept victory. So we give him that victory."

Baxter had picked up the helmet and turned it in her hands. "You want to pack explosives into here, right next to your head? It'll be a victory for him, all right. You'll have no head left."

"It's OK. I did something similar with General Volkov."

She'd given him a doubtful glare. "Volkov, whose head you blew off?"

"It'll be a lower dose. We can strap the explosive to the outside of the helmet, mock it up to look like its built in." He rapped on the right side of the metal. "In the rush of adrenaline, with bodies falling and in the midst of extreme torture, he'll never know the difference."

Baxter had just frowned. "So it's a remote-control headshot? I need a dummy gun, then?"

"Sure. It's easy. You pull the trigger on this," he held up the gun, one of the Russian Grachs he'd recovered from Ukraine, "which we arm with blanks and rig with an RF signal generator. The blank round goes off. The helmet explodes. I'm dead. You manage to squeeze one final concession out of Deynekin: save yourself. Or save our family! He'll buy that. He understands that. I think he'll unlock the Nexus to do it, if he thinks we're both completely beaten and there's no risk to his vision."

She'd stared at him. "And in the meantime, I've already plugged a Bluebug-enabled USB stub into the Nexus. When he logs in, Rex is in too."

"Exactly."

She'd studied the helmet. "I do like the idea of shooting you in the head."

Wren had smiled grimly.

"What say we do it twice?"

"What?"

"One in the chest, one in the head?" She pointed. "Rig two more explosive patches on your chest and back. I'll shoot you point blank to get Deynekin's attention. Then I let him give the order for a headshot. Really sell it; let him think he's in control, the true puppet master."

Wren picked up the armor. He handled the hard steel plates snugged into the Twaron weave. "Yeah. It could work. OK."

The train stopped at a mile out.

The lights of the station behind them didn't move. Under Rex's new management, every soldier, spy, general and commander in the GRU, the FSB, the army, navy and government had new orders; orders which they had no real reason to doubt, mocked up to look like they were coming straight from the office of President Burin himself.

One of the benefits of subverting a totalitarian state; there were no checks and balances.

Deynekin didn't move. Clara Baxter fastened a bandage to the cut in Wren's head. Rex kept talking throughout, describing the thousands of actions he was taking to disrupt Russia's war and turn the tide. Every one of them was part of a chain designed to lead to one specific outcome. They'd gamed it out.

The total and complete colonization of the shadow line. Now Rex was using it as a weapon to disrupt, disinform and ultimately defeat Russia, China and any other expansionary autocratic powers.

The odds were looking good.

All they could do now was wait for the endgame. Wren sat on one side of the train. Clara Baxter sat on the other. Almost over. His body felt heavy. The vinyl seating was surprisingly comfortable. He'd slept in worse places.

"Make our own way home," Baxter said.

Wren grunted.

Rex droned on.

"They say she has a chance," Baxter offered. "Hellion."

That caught Wren's attention.

"They're treating her. It's touch and go, but they did get her heart started again."

Good news. Up and down.

"That thing about family," Baxter went on, sounding curious. "All of us being family. You didn't say that when we practised."

Wren tried to focus on her. It wasn't easy. Everything was doubled now. He needed medical attention himself. He looked at this young, strong, resilient woman before him.

She'd been through so much, and recovered from the worst of it faster than Wren ever had. Maybe, in some small way, he'd helped her, even as she was helping him now.

Showing him a new way to be.

"I hadn't thought of it, back then," he rumbled.

Silence passed. Rex was listing countries and nodes on the Nexus which he'd taken from Deynekin's seedling AI.

"But you meant it? Just the Foundation, or everyone?"

Wren smiled. "You're in there. Your family. You don't even need to join the Foundation."

"I'm not going to."

He laughed. He understood what she meant, though. "And beyond that? Maybe. I'm trying, Clara. I want to look after everyone I can, you know? Protect everyone."

She smiled. It was a rare thing. "Santa Justicia. Saint Justice, they call you. I think I get it now."

He smiled back. He'd never asked for the nickname. His Force Recon buddies had given it to him as a joke at the beginning, a kind of teasing. He never could let the slightest injustice go, even if it meant turning on his own. It had gotten him drummed out, in the end, to be scooped up by the CIA.

That felt like a whole other world, now.

"You're a boy scout," Baxter said.

"I hear they admit girls now, too. Wanna join?"

She laughed. "Not the Foundation. But you?" she shrugged. "I'll think about it. If your ex-wife ever lets you come out again."

Wren said nothing. Loralei. His kids. That was a strange thought to have in this dark and lonely place.

"It is time," said Rex. "All the pieces are in position."

"Fire it up," Baxter said. "And sit this one out, Chris. You look like a dead man."

The train started up again, back toward the GRU.

60

GRU

Three hours later, it was done.

Wren sat in a corridor looking out through the floor-to-ceiling windows. It was dark out still, hours from dawn. He was high up in the GRU headquarters, the fifteenth floor, gazing across a city just beginning to break. The war had come here, both from without and within. There was an uprising in the streets, as forces on both sides of the 'Burin' divide clashed amongst themselves and with the incoming NATO forces.

It was a sea change in the course of history.

In the dark portions of glass, Wren eyed his own reflection: head wrapped in gauze; body bulky with armor; a face that was ashy, stained and worn. In the light sections of glass, where the view through was clear, he saw devastation.

New craters. Rubble. Fires sprouting from Molotov cocktails. Gunfire sparking like static electricity. Lines of artillery and tanks retreating under heavy shell fire.

Revenge, for some. Justice, for others.

This was Moscow, after all, finally beginning to breathe after decades spent in the smothering grip of one vicious man.

Wren pushed himself to his feet and stepped up to the glass. Move slowly, the EMTs had told him. Nothing sudden. You were lucky. You've sustained serious injuries. There's blood on your brain still, it needs to be drained. That's multiple surgeries. Your lungs have taken smoke damage. That's surgery. Your entire nervous system is in extreme shock. That's months of rehabilitation. Go slow.

Go slow.

He raised one hand to the cold, clear glass.

It was a strange location. He'd never have expected it. But no one had stood in their way; rather, they'd streamed out of their offices and emergency response bunkers to help. They'd cleared the way, thinking these were Burin's genuine orders. They'd placed on the shackles, believing they were dealing with a fraud. A pretender to the throne.

The plan had worked perfectly, as Rex opened the doors and flicked all the switches and flipped all the traffic lights to green. Russia's hierarchical system had responded to his touch, all afraid of the puppet master they thought he represented.

In the end it was easy.

Out in the world, the war was becoming a rout, as line-by-line American comms were reinstated while Russian, Chinese and all other aggressors' comms were decimated. The shadow line reached into everything, the ultimate puppet master's dream, and so Rex had control of everything. Large portions of Ukraine were already being reclaimed as the Russian front line evaporated. The news media couldn't keep up. China's illegal occupation of Taiwan was already getting strained by international pressure and failures within. The footage from Luhansk had changed the information calculation on a dime.

Nobody wanted to get caught holding the bag when undeniable genocide was on the cards.

So, Rex squeezed. He siphoned billions, shut off power and destroyed reputations. The red lines on his live map were ebbing back to where they belonged. Wreckage would be left behind, but wreckage could be rebuilt. There was so much to rebuild. So many things that had to change, to prevent something like this from ever happening again.

Wren leaned his head against the cold glass.

The GRU building had once been a wellspring of Russia's power. CIA agents had never made it this far before, but Rex had taken them to the top. With one slice of his digital knife, he'd opened up everything.

"She's ready for you, Christopher," came Rex's voice through invisible speakers in the walls. He was everywhere, now. In everything. Bigger and better than before, and filled with the light of his core purpose, expanded.

Protect everyone.

"OK." Wren turned from the glass. There was no pleasure in watching Moscow fall. It wasn't what he'd wanted. No good person wanted to see this once-great civilization so humbled. It was simply necessary.

He trudged along the carpeted corridor, heading toward the office where the world was going to change forever.

The office of the head of the GRU dominated all comers, as vast in scale as the organization's ambitions. The ceiling hung thirty feet high. The brutalist, onyx desk stood on a stage like a throne, overlooking a floor-to-ceiling window gazing out over the city. You could see St. Basil's Cathedral in the distance, its candy cane poles and gumball cupolas lit up by freshly surging fires.

The walls on all sides were cannon gray except for the wall behind the grand desk, which displayed the five-pointed Soviet star in red and gold, alongside the GRU flag rendered in brutalist, blocky lines: four rays of yellow beaming in from the corners to what looked like a triple-knotted gray handkerchief, atop a five-pointed ruffled red snowflake.

Once defectors would have quaked before these symbols of Soviet power. To Wren now they both looked faintly ridiculous, like a bespoke tailor had been given too many frills and too much leeway in designing the sequins for a gala night dress and the buttons for a couch, respectively.

The man sitting before the desk, in front of this great picture window, had once caused nations to tremble. He was bald, slim, old and short. He wore a suit still, but it was darkened at the armpits with sweat. The chair was bolted down. His arms and legs were zip-tied in place.

"Chris," said Clara Baxter.

Wren looked to the shadows by the wall as Baxter emerged, sinuous and smooth. Her hair was pulled back, her blades winking silver, her eyes blazing with the old anger. The very picture of a merciless assassin.

"Well done," Wren said.

She smiled. "Rex did all the heavy lifting." She pointed a stiletto blade at him. "How are you recovering from your stroke?"

Wren smiled. "It was a small one. More of a localized bleed on the brain. I feel much better now."

"I heard you'll need cranial operations. They're going to slice into your brain. I wonder what strange secrets they'll find."

He smiled. "Maybe the memory of you crying all the way down from the B-2. Any one of those kicks and punches could have loosened up the blood vessel that burst." He pointed at his head. "So thanks for that."

Baxter laughed. "Touché."

A heavy silence settled over the room.

They both looked at the man in the chair. President Anton

Burin. He stared straight ahead like none of this was touching him.

A pretender holds the throne, Rex had said. He'd beamed it out to every spy in the GRU, even as he'd shuttled Burin right into the trap. The true President had self-admitted himself, thinking this place his bastion of power, and his own troops had arrested him as a fake. It was perfect.

Wren circled around to stand beside Clara Baxter. With their backs to the glass, they both studied Russia's fallen President. With every passing minute, and despite the naked hatred in his eyes, Burin looked more shriveled. Age thickened some men. Others it hollowed out. Some it turned into legends. Burin, though, just looked small.

"You didn't miss much," Baxter said. "Rex had them all dancing like marionettes; some evacuating, some admitting rebels, some turning on themselves. That's the benefit of a paranoia state. Start lighting fires and pretty soon the whole house goes up in flames." She pointed at Burin. "He had a personal security team twenty thick, but Rex turned half of them against the other half, and I just picked through the pieces." She smiled. "This whole building is abandoned, now, on orders from above. The rest of it's just poetic justice."

Wren looked into Burin's eyes. They were black marbles in a pale, round head. He saw nothing special. Not an answer, not a demon, not the true face of evil, just another banal man like men he'd battled all his life; too strong, too unconstrained, too driven by selfish impulses they couldn't or didn't want to hold back.

Animals, really, pretending to be human.

"Poetic justice," Wren repeated.

"Here," Baxter said, and brought a chair over, setting it down in front of Burin. "Take your turn. I already had a good session. He won't talk. I didn't think torture would help much, but you're welcome to try."

"Thank you."

"I'll be outside. There's plenty of time yet."

She left.

Wren sat in the chair directly across from Burin. He looked into his eyes square on. Burin didn't shift his gaze. He stared right through Wren like he wasn't even there. Minutes passed.

There were so many questions Wren could ask. So much anger to vent, but ultimately, he had no desire to say a word. All the answers were on the surface. The vision seemed grand, but in the end it was pathetically self-serving. It grew out of smallness, and inadequacy, and fear. Just like the Apex. Just like them all.

So what followed would be for Wren only.

"You may not know me," he said, voice rumbling deep. "I can see that being possible. But you knew my father."

Burin didn't twitch. Either he knew or he didn't care.

"His birth name was Noah Thackerton. He called himself the Apex. Thirty years ago he ran a cult called the Pyramid in Arizona, USA, which burned itself alive. A thousand people died." Wren sat back. It felt strange to talk about that here. The Pyramid had been his childhood. Those one thousand had been his earliest family. "You were a KGB agent then. I don't know how you heard of him. Maybe he reached out to you, or you to him." He paused a moment, reflecting. "But you found common cause, yes? You funded him. You bankrolled his long, slow return. For thirty years, you laid the pieces together to destroy America, throw off the global order and bring the Soviet Union surging back to life."

Wren sat. Burin stared. It all came down to this.

"But you failed," Wren said. "My father failed. All your scheming, all your decades of planning. You failed, Anton. That's your legacy. That's all the world will ever know about you. That's why you're going to sit here and watch the

Kremlin fall, while the Polonium-210 rots you from the inside, because I want you to know it. I need you to feel it."

He fell silent. Burin didn't move a muscle. Not his jaw, not his eyes, like he was carved out of stone. They both knew that wouldn't last much longer. The Polonium-210 had been in his system for several hours already. A dose measured in micrograms only, enough to kill a million people, and easily enough for an expedited death and a corpse that could only be buried half a mile deep in a leaden tomb. In hours he'd be shaking and bleeding, babbling and vomiting. Without treatment, his death would last for hours longer as the radiation systematically ate him from within, destroying his white blood cells, bone marrow and central nervous system. Sometime around midday he'd convulse himself into a coma before his heart finally gave out.

There was nothing more to say. Wren didn't expect anything other than his death.

He stood up. He started to walk out.

"I have succeeded," Burin said.

His voice sounded strange. Much weaker than his many radio pronouncements, driving his nation to war. But Wren turned. He walked back. He looked again into Burin's eyes.

"You have succeeded," he repeated back. "How so?"

Burin's eyes burned. "America is broken. So many fractures that you cannot see. I have done this. For many years, I was the man with a chisel, tapping away. Weakening you here. Breaking you there." He forced out a smile. There was blood on his teeth. "America will fall. When it comes, you will know I am the one who did this."

Wren just looked. It was sad, to count your successes in pain and dissolution. It was the fruit of a lifetime dedicated only to revenge.

"That's where we're different," he said softly. "America's

not some dead stone edifice, Burin, a Soviet statue made out of granite and a single ideology, defeated by a few cracks. America's alive. It grows. It changes. It will heal back better. What you've done will only make us stronger." He paused, thinking about his own life. His own family. "But then I don't expect you to understand that."

He walked out. This time Burin said nothing. At the door, he nodded to Clara Baxter. Burin had done this to them both. He'd funded their fathers. He'd raised up the Pyramid and the Pinocchios. Now, it didn't seem like that mattered.

Baxter nodded back. Most likely, she was going to sit and watch Burin die.

Wren rode the elevator down to street level. NATO troops were spreading here, claiming this incredible intelligence prize. After the footage from Luhansk and the bombardment of fake orders from Rex, the Russian command structure had long since fled. More images were already coming to light every hour. More horrors. The true depths of Deynekin's genocide were spreading through the shadow line, and nobody could stop it. The truth was free, for today at least, and America along with its reinvigorated alliance of free nations were riding high.

Welby Bohannon stood by a vehicle. A Russian Ural.

"Make our own way home," he said, with a smile.

"I need brain surgery," Wren said.

"There's a jet waiting to fly you to Germany. We'll be at the airport in twenty minutes, and Germany a few hours after that. The operating theater's on standby. I understand Rex is clearing us a route. Traffic lights to green and soldiers holding the intersections, you know."

Wren smiled. Rex was everywhere now, an ultimate arbiter of what constituted harm, and always learning. It was a brave new world, with such AIs in it.

The smile spread as he climbed into the Ural. Maybe he'd share that line with Hellion; she'd appreciate it. Reports indicated she had stabilized and was breathing for herself. There was hope.

In the backseat, he buckled up. The two CIA agents got in the front. Ahead of them, the traffic lights turned green.

61

THREE WEEKS LATER

Wren stood outside the black iron gates of his kids' elementary school, in the quiet little town of Frederica, Delaware. It was peaceful, amongst the waiting crowd of chattering parents, waiting for the afternoon bell to ring. The late-summer sun warmed his skin, and a cool breeze carried the sweet scent of fallen leaves, mulching in the gutters.

It was a Monday, his day to pick up Jake and Quinn.

His head still hurt most of the time, a little. The operations had been a success. A single vein had burst, brought on by stress, a succession of extreme physical impacts and overexertion. He'd promised his doctors to cool it for a time.

"How about those Eagles?" one of the dads asked Wren.

"Great game," Wren said, though he hadn't watched it and didn't really care right now. His heart boomed in his chest. He'd faced down Volkov, Deynekin, and Burin, but what was coming now seemed harder. It meant breaking a piece of himself; a large part of his past.

But it was OK. Breaks could heal back stronger.

His phone pinged in his pocket. He brought it up.

SHADOW LINE WHOLLY ISOLATED. WE HAVE EVERY NODE.

He smiled. That was a text from B4cksl4cker. He'd made a startling recovery, and taken to texting him constantly. Word was, he was sitting by Hellion's hospital bed, watching over her while watching over Rex. Hellion was in a medically induced coma. There were more operations to come. They were worried about her heart, waiting for it to heal on its own.

Progress was slow.

Now Wren answered every text from B4cksl4cker, no matter how often they came. He was encouraging a bad habit, but that didn't matter, and this message was the big one. For the last three weeks, the global intelligence community had been working to dig out every last thread of the shadow line and turn it over.

Countless secrets had tumbled out. Vast power. Millions of backdoors into the most closely-guarded data systems in the world. Enough blackmail material to fill Fort Knox.

Wren had been insistent with B4cksl4cker, with Rex, with anyone who came close.

"We hand it all back to the rightful owners. The intel. The control. Every bit. We keep none of it; no backdoors."

B4cksl4cker had protested that long and loud. "This is like, like, telling incredible basketball player not to dunk on tiny baby. Like telling-"

"You think a basketball player should dunk on a baby?"

"No, but this is principle of matter!" B4cksl4cker had bleated down the phone line. "I died for this data. Both Hellion and I, Christopher Wren you also, we all died many-"

"You didn't die," Wren had countered calmly. "You were punched a few times."

"Punched a few times?! Punched a few times! I was shot! My heart stopped briefly. Hellion has not woken up yet. I-"

"Did you have a stroke?"

That shut him up. "Brief dying is worse than stroke! I was dead for thirteen seconds. Is long time, yes? Record!"

Wren had just smiled. Talk about death was a little close to home, with Hellion still teetering on the precipice. "You only got shot once. I was shot three times. Or four? Did you get stabbed, too? I was, maybe three times. Did you get hung up by your wrists? Thrown off a giant robot bull?"

"No, not any of these, but do have a broken thumb?" He spat it like a spear. "Somehow Hellion and I both have broken thumbs. This is very inconvenient, Christopher, thumb is very important as hacker. No thumb you cannot, hmm…"

"Can't eat a hotdog," Wren had offered.

"Precisely!"

"So use your other hand."

"Cannot eat burger," B4cksl4cker went on, ignoring him and running with the idea. "Cannot eat corn on cob. Cannot open telescope. Typing is very slow. Space bar is work of thumb. Tying shoes is much complicated. Cannot hit space bar swiftly, and…"

Wren had listened until the big Armenian trailed off. He knew a lot of this was fear. Hellion had been his close partner for years. This whole latter stage of his life, as a good white-hat hacker working with the Foundation, had been all bound up with Hellion.

When B4cksl4cker finally fell silent Wren gave him what he wanted.

"I am sorry I broke your thumbs, OK? I was having a stroke at the time. The labyrinth had just exploded and the server room was full of fire and smoke, so I guess I was too lazy to go find the key for your shackles. Next time, I'll do better."

B4cksl4cker had snorted. "Yes. Do much better. Next time, listen to drone at beginning! Nobody will die!"

He'd smiled. "I will. I promise."

"Good. Yes. Answer all texts. Respond within five minutes. You should-"

"The doctor's here for a checkup. Goodbye."

Now they'd completely captured the shadow line's physical infrastructure, and that was an incredible step forward. It put this whole thing behind them.

EXCELLENT WORK, WELL DONE! Wren tapped out on his phone, then hit send. He thought a moment longer, then added THANK YOU.

The screen blinked. Three dots shuffled in the corner, then B4cksl4cker's response came in. It was a big kissy face emoji. He smiled and went to-

"What are you doing here?"

Wren's heart skipped a beat and he looked up from his phone.

She was standing right in front of him, amongst the gathering of parents on the sidewalk before the gates. It almost seemed too immediate, too real. She was wearing a cream calfskin jacket over a white blouse and black skirt. Her hair was up in chopsticks the way he'd always used to love so much. She looked beautiful and furious at once.

Loralei.

Wren's pulse instantly began to boom in his ears. There was nothing easy about this. Already people were staring, feeling the heat radiating off his ex-wife's glare. Somebody would bring up a phone soon and start filming. A call might be placed to the police.

Let them.

"Hi, Loralei. It's Monday. I pick up the kids on Mondays. I tried to get in touch."

Her jaw dropped. She'd ignored his every attempt to reach out; emails, calls, letters. When he'd come to her door, she'd pretended not to be home. "Are you kidding me? You think you can just walk back into their lives?" Already she was getting louder. "I'm glad you're alive, Chris, but this is not OK. I told you never to come back!"

Wren looked at her. He tried to see past all the ways he'd loved her, and the guilt he'd felt for so much lying, and the way she'd once been the one place he'd felt he could call home. He looked through to the woman she was inside, and saw the truth.

Like everyone, like him, like B4cksl4cker, like Anton Burin, inside she was just scared.

The anger grew from that fear. She was worried for her children, he understood that, for their upbringing, for what Wren might expose them to. Like everyone, she feared a myriad range of failures, of being disrespected, of being left behind, of being a failure. Wren understood it all. Because of those fears, and because he'd loved her so much, he'd let her dictate the play for years. He'd ceded everything to her. He'd ceded his children.

But that couldn't go on. There had to be a balance. If anyone had taught him that, it was Clara Baxter.

"I have a right to see my kids, Loralei," he said, keeping his voice low. Trying to be kind. "They need me. I need them."

Her eyes flared like this was an outrageous thing to say. "Need? And you have a right?" She hissed between gritted teeth. "You have no rights here, Chris! You don't, and you never will again! You broke the deal. If you keep pushing, we'll move again. I'll get a restraining order. I'll file against you in court for reckless endangerment. You need to leave right now or I'll call the police."

She was furious and Wren understood. He'd earned this, but he'd also done his time in the years since; paid as much penance as he was able, and their life together hadn't been all that bad.

"I can do my job and have a family," he said. "I can see my kids without endangering them."

She scoffed. Now everyone in the crowd was staring, their fellow parents, but she didn't care. Phones were coming up. "You? Not a chance. You bring the danger home. You just take and take. We had a deal!"

"Let's make a new one."

"Never!"

She brought out her phone and tapped in a number. Three digits, all the same tone.

Wren nodded sadly. He hadn't wanted it to come to this, but maybe he should have done it years ago. He reached into his pocket and held out a slip of card. Two inches by one, cream, lightly embossed.

"What's this?" Loralei snapped, snatching the card off him before her 911 call answered.

"My lawyer," Wren said. "You'll be hearing from her soon. I don't want to fight you for shared custody of the kids, Loralei, but I will if you insist. Let's go to war."

THE NEXT CHRIS WREN THRILLER

HAMMER OF GOD

A US city annihilated. All bets are off.
Early on a bright spring morning, Las Vegas explodes.
Half a million die in a flash.
But it's not nuclear. It's something never before seen in human history.
The Hammer of God.
And it will strike again, unless America kneels.
But special operator Chris Wren never kneeled in his life.
He's not about to start now.
The Hammer of God is falling.

THE FIRST GIRL ZERO THRILLER

GIRL ZERO

Want to know what Clara Baxter, AKA Girl Zero, was doing in Poland before Wren arrived?

In the industrial wastes of Poland, there's a man 'breaking' girls with a hammer and nails.

This man is tied to something bigger. This man may be the key to killing off the Real Boys, once and for all.

Zero just has to break him first.

Live by the hammer. Die by the nail.

AVAILABLE IN EBOOK, PAPERBACK & AUDIO

www.shotgunbooks.com

HAVE YOU READ EVERY CHRIS WREN THRILLER?

Saint Justice

They stole his truck. Big mistake.

No Mercy

Hackers came for his kids. There can be no mercy.

Make Them Pay

The latest reality TV show: execute the rich.

False Flag

They framed him for murder. He'll kill to clear his name.

Firestorm

Wren's father is back. The storm is coming.

Enemy of the People

America turns against Wren. Can he survive?

Backlash

Fake marines forced downed his jet. Now they'll pay.

Never Forgive

5 dead in Tokyo, Japan. Wren has to find the killer.

War of Choice

War erupts in Ukraine. This time it's personal.

Hammer of God

A US city destroyed. All bets are off.

HAVE YOU READ EVERY GIRL 0 THRILLER?

<u>Girl Zero</u>

They stole her little sister. Now they'll pay.

<u>Zero Day</u>

The criminal world is out for revenge. So is she.

Learn more at www.shotgunbooks.com

JOIN THE FOUNDATION!

Join the Mike Grist newsletter and be first to hear when the next Girl Zero or Chris Wren thriller is coming.

www.subscribepage.com/christopher-wren

ACKNOWLEDGEMENTS

Sincere thanks to Monte Montana, Barb Stoner & Julian White.

- Mike

Printed in Great Britain
by Amazon

21028911R00195